Craig Cormick is a multi-award-winning science communicator and author. He has published over 30 works of fiction and non-fiction, and has been a writer in residence in Malaysia and in Antarctica. He enjoys messing with history just about as much as history enjoys messing with him.

Years of the Wolf

By Craig Cormick

Years of the Wolf

All Rights Reserved

ISBN-13: 978-1-925759-70-9

Copyright ©2018 Craig Cormick
V1.0

Printed in Garamond and Goudy Old Style typefaces.

Cover photograph: photographer unknown; source: Migration Heritage Centre; not subject to copyright.

IFWG Publishing International
Melbourne

www.ifwgpublishing.com

To all those who have ever endured
the madness of internment.

Trial Bay Gaol (Photo: Photo Australian War Memorial)

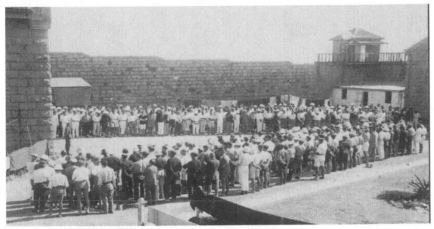

Roll call at Trial Bay (Photo: Karl Lehmann. National
Library of Australia)

Trial Bay Guards, c1917 (permission: Trial Bay Gaol Visitor Centre)

German internee in woman's costume (photo: Paul Dubotzki, Australian War Memorial)

German internee in woman's costume (photo: Paul Dubotzki, Australian War Memorial)

German internees dressed for a performance
(photographer unknown; source: Migration Heritage Centre)

This story is true.

Except for the bits that aren't.

They are a different kind of truth.

German internees changing into women's costume
(photo: Paul Dubotzki, Australian War Memorial)

"The wolf lifted the latch, the door sprang open, and without saying a word he went straight to the grandmother's bed, and devoured her. Then he put on her clothes, dressed himself in her cap, laid himself in bed and drew the curtains."

Little Red Riding Hood – by the Brothers Grimm

1
A New Day
1917

In the two years he has been interned in the old stone prison, Arno Friedrich has shared many of the feelings of those men who live in close confinement about him—boredom, fear, anger, desperation—but he had never felt terror until the night Hans Eckert was murdered.

And he alone had seen the killing.

Arno had stirred in the night and seen the dark shadow moving along the stone wall of their prison. It paused at each cell and peered in, then moved on, dragging its feet like a half-human, half-beast might. A tall furry man-thing come for blood.

It found it in Herr Eckert's cell.

The elderly man was tossing restlessly in his sleep, fighting off some dark nightmare of his own, as the beast stepped through the open doorway into his cell and stood over him. It paused there, taking in the scent of him. Smelled fear in the sweat on his skin. The beast then reached down one hand and clasped it over Herr Eckert's mouth. Saw his eyes open. Saw him stare in terror. Then it slashed at his throat. Its talons as sharp as a trench dagger—ripping the life out of him.

The man-beast stood there until the blood stopped flowing, and then moved back from the bed, stepped outside and merged into the shadows and was gone.

And Arno Friedrich sat up in bed in his own cell, his heart beating madly in fear—recalling the terror of that night they came for him in his sleep. The night he first felt the violent touch of a world gone mad.

They had also come for him in the night, during the hours of deepest

1

sleep, so that he always had trouble afterwards remembering what was a dream and what was not. They knocked upon the door once and then kicked it in. Heavy boots marched into the small room and they shone a bright light upon him. Dazzling him. Then they kicked the bed. It rocked beneath him while he struggled to open his eyes properly.

There were six of them. Tall. Darkly dressed. Helmets tilted low. Pale faces scowling. No emotion showing in their deep-set eyes. Like six dark angels, he would later recall them.

Then an officer stepped forward, motioned to the soldiers to stop, and he threw back the bedclothes. Arno Friedrich was nearly naked and he tried desperately to cover himself with his hands. Tried to hide his erection from them. The officer stared at him a long moment, as if he could read the intoxicatingly sweet dreams that he had been embracing. Then he stepped back. The six soldiers lowered their rifles at Arno. Long sharp bayonets pointing closely at his skin. So close he could feel the chill from the steel. More menacing and effective than the blank empty rifle barrels, they knew.

Arno blinked up at the six men. He shook his head a little, like trying to shake away a bad dream. Like trying to swim up through warm water and trying to reach the surface. He blinked again. The six men didn't move. But they seemed suddenly closer. The bayonets pressing into him.

Then the officer spoke, "Up!"

Two of the soldiers moved their rifles, leaving a space for him to rise from the bed. But he lay there, still not fully awake. Still flailing as if in deep water. Still trying to reach the surface.

"Up!" said the officer again. Louder. The soldiers took it as a command and two of them reached forward, grabbing him by the arms. They lifted him quickly to a sitting position, almost dragging him onto the floor. The officer turned to a chair by the wash stand and lifted Arno's clothes up with a short stick he held. He flicked them at him in a quick whipping motion.

"Get dressed!" he said. Softer now. But still a command.

Arno had trouble sorting out the clothes. He struggled to turn them the right way around, to line up the buttons and button holes, to get his legs cleanly into his trousers. The soldiers kept their bayonets close as he fought to dress himself.

Then the officer said, "Go!" and turned and walked out of the room.

One soldier now grinned—just enough to show a glimpse of white teeth—and he grasped Arno firmly by the arm. "Up!" he said in a vicious imitation of the officer, and hauled Arno to his feet. Then he whispered, "You filthy Hun!"

Arno looked back at him, as if not understanding the words. The soldier gave him a rough shove. "Out!" he said. Arno fell to the floor boards. The soldiers' bayonets followed him down. He turned on his back and stared up at the soldiers. He looked into the faces and slowly reached up one arm. Pointed to the crutches leaning on the wall by the head of his bed. One by one the soldiers turned to look at them until one seemed to get his meaning. He was harmless. He was a cripple. They could have no use for him, surely. And Arno, still young enough to think that his wit could save him from petty authority, said, "So if I close my eyes you cease to exist, yes?"

Nobody laughed. One soldier took the crutches and threw them to him. "Up!" he commanded. Arno struggled to rise with them until two of the soldiers grasped him by the arms again and hauled him up. They let him fit the crutches to his armpits and then led him out of the room.

The truck stood way out the middle of the yard. Its engine was idling softly. It sounded to Arno like distant thunder at the coast. Soldiers stood by the tailgate, looking across at him. Arno could see other men sitting in the truck. Half-dressed. Heads bowed.

Then he heard a quick knock and the kicking in of a door to his left somewhere. He tried to turn his head and see whose place they were entering now. Tried to see who else they were after. But he stumbled. Landed heavily in the dirt.

The soldiers were quick and had him by the arms again. Hauled him up and dragged him to the truck, leaving his crutches on the ground. Arno tried to turn his head and protest. Tried to call out. Tried to tell somebody what had happened. But they grabbed him by the hair. Tilted his head back. Hissed, "Quiet! No noise!" Then lifted him into the truck and levelled another bayoneted rifle at his face and waited for him to bow his head. And sit there silently.

Presently the truck was full of silent men. And with a sudden lurch it moved off into the darkness.

In the morning, those who had not been taken peered cautiously out of the doors of their small migrants' huts, and saw Arno Friedrich's crutches lying in the yard—as if he had limped out his open door and suddenly cast them aside and either walked away or perhaps even flown up into the sky.

It is an early June morning today, and Arno Friedrich is standing up against a chill rock wall of the prison courtyard, searching for traces of Herr Eckert's death. For two years he has risen in the darkness and made his way out into the prison yard, past the many unlocked doors, to await the light of the new day in the imprisoning walled courtyard. For two years he has stood there to ensure that the many dreams of his fellow German internees that fill his mind each night return to the rock and do not escape into the light of day.

He does not know how it happens, but the most fervent and fevered of the men's dreams come to him. Their fears. Their passions. Their longing. Their troubles. And he finds it increasingly hard to tell what is real and what is dreamt, in this prison where every day is so like the one before it, unless he stands at the rock wall at the start and end of each day, and feels the dreams retreat into the hard granite each morning. This prison where 400 or so men have been interred for no other crime than having been born German. Or Austrian. Or having been born in Australia, but to German parents—as was Arno's case.

His parents died when he was young, and German is a language he speaks imperfectly. So to the camp internees he is not German enough, but to the authorities he is too German. Officially he is an enemy alien. He, himself, is no longer sure what he is. A protector of them all, he would like to think. The one who keeps the nightmares contained.

As the youngest of the civilian internees by many years most of the elder men think of him as a boy, and treat him with something akin to fatherly affection. Others tend to ignore his presence altogether.

Arno is happy to be ignored and to be left alone to observe, for he knows the darkest secrets of them all, and what hides behind the smiles or aloofness of the men. He knows who dreams of dressing in women's clothing. Who dreams of going to school with no pants on. And who dreams of wetting the bed. And he knows who has the worst nightmares of creatures that come into their rooms at night and drag them from their family beds and cart them off into the darkness.

He is the keeper of those dreams and nightmares and knows that he has the task of keeping those two different worlds—of light and darkness—apart.

Herr Eckert's nightmare is still fresh in his mind and he needs to ensure that it has fully returned to the dark rock and does not seep into their prison. He stands by the wall for some time, feeling its re-assuring hardness. Then he turns and begins making his slow way around the prison walls. He limps along in the shadows, clasping his crutches close to his body so they won't creak. But this morning he moves too close to the stone wall and feels the knuckles of his hand scrape against the rock. A sudden sharp point tears the skin. He stops and looks at his hand. Feels the wound. Feels the thin trickle of blood. That could be thought of as a bad omen, he thinks, but sometimes, things are just things.

He looks at the blood on his knuckles and thinks that he will write that word later in his diary—*Blut*—to remind himself that it has happened on this day. He only writes single short words or phrases—the language of confinement. Just enough to mark it from all the other days of sameness.

He grasps his crutches again and continues on his way. He stays close to the wall, keeping to the darkness. He stops again under the southwest watchtower and looks at his wrist-watch, straining to see the hands. 6.45am precisely.

He tilts his head back and looks up over the grey walls, his neck bent far back, peering beyond the cold granite that encircles him. Waiting for the light to come to the sky. Waiting for some colour to fill the day.

He can hear the guard moving in the watchtower above him, and he steps in closer against the wall. Standing silently in the shadows. Waiting. There is something different in the way the man up there moves, he thinks, as if he is not peering out towards the ocean today, as is his custom, but looking into the prison yard.

Any change in a life of sameness unsettles him.

Then he hears a low warning rumble of faraway thunder. Arno tilts his head a little to listen to it. Then he inhales, searching for the scent of rain. But there is none. He waits, but he does not hear it again. He stares at the sky. It is still too early to see if there are clouds today, so he continues on.

He makes his way along the southern wall, clinging to the shadows, and stops at the corner of the cells there. There are two large cell blocks for all the internees, both running out from the main hall, which lies in the very centre of the prison, like the shape of a large V. The internees are two to a cell. There are 50 cells on the lower level of each wing. Another 50 on the upper levels. Over 400 men interned together.

Arno stands by the wall and listens for the sound of Herr Schröder singing softly within. He can hear the deep bass voice echoing lightly, as if it is coming from the stone itself. It is Wagner. Herr Schröder's favourite. Herr Schröder has a recurrent dream of flying. Or floating. In his dream he is able to lift off the ground and float graciously over the prison walls, and then above the long rocky peninsular by the Macleay River. And from there he drifts along the coast back to his family in Sydney. Arno enjoys his dreams the most, even if they fade before he has ever gone too far southwards. One day, he likes to think, he will make that long journey all the way back home, and Arno will be there with him. He wonders what he would do when he reaches home? Sit down with his family to a formal dinner, or take his wife upstairs to their bedroom—to ravage her or to just curl up in her arms and cry?

Arno looks up towards the sky again. Like he is watching the words of the song float up into the slow growing blueness. He looks at his watch once more. 6.55 exactly. In the next cell Herr Schultz and Herr Schmidt will still be sound asleep, worn out from another night of arguing philosophy. Both men have nightmares of being lost in dark forests. They are the only two cell mates who share similar dreams. In the cell next to them, Herr Voigt will be awake, softly muttering his morning rosary. His dreams are more fearful. He dreams of dark angels come to punish him for a life-time's accumulation of petty sins.

Arno knows that if he were to press his ear close to the stone there, he could just about make out the words. Like he knows the early morning routines of most of the 400 inhabitants of the prison. He has stood outside their cells in the dark of morning and in the shadows of night. Has listened to their private lives seeping out between the bars, escaping into the darkness. As he has shared the dreams and nightmares of so many of them. Memories of children. Lustful imaginings of wives, girlfriends or unknown women. Dark creatures in dark places. And so many dreams of confinement. Being buried alive and unable to escape. Drowning. Trying to run from pursuers and unable to make any progress. Being surrounded by fierce creatures. Or attacked by wild beasts.

He knows the prison and the internees like none of them know it. As none of them know he is their protector.

He grasps his crutches tightly and limps on, pausing every few steps to reach out and lightly touch the walls. The stone is dark and cold beneath his fingers, but by mid-day it will be warm as the sun's bright light brings colour and texture to it.

Arno Friedrich makes one lap of the prison walls every morning, before the full light of day arrives. Before the other internees are awake. And he makes one lap the last thing at night. Before the light has faded. Ensuring the world is safe for them all. Knowing that it is only through his vigilance that the dreams and nightmares are kept in their proper places to only emerge at night time. He runs his hands over the dull granite walls as the sky turns dark above him and the light goes out of the world. And then he goes back to his own cell, closes the barred door and lies down on his bunk, confident that he has protected everybody one more day. And perhaps writing some key words of events that have happened in his diary. Trying to remember particular details or words spoken to him. Trying to make that day different from every other day of the two years he has spent inside the old prison as an internee.

Each day trying just a little harder to distinguish the memories from the dreams.

Arno moves past the kitchen now and can hear the rattle and clatter of the kitchen staff preparing the morning's meal. He pauses and inhales deeply. Bread and porridge again. He stays there awhile tasting the fragrance of the warm bread in the air. It has an aroma that makes him think of comforting dreams and warm clouds.

The kitchen staff arise each day at 6.00am and make their way in the darkness out to the old kitchen. There they begin cutting vegetables, rolling dough, heating up the ovens and boiling water. They prepare enough food to feed the 400 men, and for what gain? Some of the internees shake their heads at the kitchen staff who toil long hours for no pay. They are prisoners of the kitchen, they joke, calling them the washing up warriors

But Arno has seen them often enough in the early mornings, busy at their labours, and with sleeves rolled up high while the other internees sleep. He sees they are happy in the fulfilment of the work. These are men who have been bakers and butchers and restaurant owners. They had once been a part of a community. They had greeted their customers each day and showed them their best produce. Prided themselves in its quality. Chatted with them about their domestic lives. Talked about families and sick children and the next holidays. And then one day they arrived at work to find they were declared enemy aliens. The Hun! The customers kept away from their shops. Their incomes fell. Their pride fell lower.

And then the soldiers came for them. Sullen men with guns. Took them away from their families and their communities and their businesses. They were interned and all they had left was their work.

Arno moves on. He makes his way around to the eastern wall and suddenly stops. His way ahead is blocked. There is a truck parked up ahead in the thin space between the small infirmary building and the wall. That is rare. Most deliveries from the nearby township are brought by horse and cart. Trucks are for something altogether more serious. The truck's headlights face him like two eyes. Arno feels a moment of panic. This is the truck from his dreams. His memories have come for him again. He stares at the dark metal body of the truck, and then takes a few steps closer and reaches out and touches it. It is cold and hard. It is real.

He looks around for any soldiers who might be around this early—knowing only the guard towers are manned at this time of day.

Trucks rarely come inside the prison. Food and building materials are delivered to the front gate and carried inside by the internees. Something is new today. Something has happened. He shakes off the unsettling feeling that thought brings, and smells the faint bitter tang of exhaust fumes around the vehicle. It has not been there long, he thinks. He looks around once more, then he squeezes up between the truck and the wall and slides down the length of the truck—feeling the chill of the metal and the chill of the stones pressing him between them. It is an uncomfortable feeling. The truck is parked slightly askew and as he reaches the khaki-painted rear of the truck it squeezes him very tightly into the wall. He turns his body sideways and pushes a little. Feels himself jammed—unable to move. He feels his heart starting to beat faster. It sounds to him like rapidly approaching footsteps. Soldiers will come and find him, he thinks. Will point their bayonets at him. Will throw him to the ground. Then cast him into the truck.

He closes his eye and lets the feeling fade from him—being absorbed into the stone. He then leans heavily on his foremost crutch. Pushes back on it. Until he feels himself breaking free of the grip of the metal and granite. He takes two steps backwards. Then looks down at the ground. He carefully lowers himself to his knees. Then onto his stomach. He is beside the rear wheels and peers under the truck. It is very dark and a little muddy and smells of oil and petrol. He bites his lip a moment, and begins dragging himself forward into the darkness. Keeping his head low. Careful of the sharp gravel under him. Cautious of the hot metal above him. Wary of touching any part of the truck.

When he emerges again he sees the sky is much lighter now. The rock walls and the truck are a new colour. Like arriving into another world somehow, he thinks. He looks around carefully then gathers up his crutches and slowly stands up. The tailgate of the truck is down and he can see it is empty inside. Wooden benches run down each side—ready for somebody.

Arno looks from the truck to the small infirmary building. He listens carefully and can now hear murmured voices from inside. He looks at his watch. 7.05. Doctor Hertz, the camp's doctor, would not normally be in the infirmary until 7.30, checking on any patients that might be there before breakfast.

Arno considers the truck for a moment and hauls himself up onto the tailgate. From there he can peer into the infirmary window. Like all the prison buildings it has small windows, set up high. But from the height of the truck it is like looking down into some underground bunker. He can see a soldier standing inside the dim room and he can see the tall thin shape of Doctor Hertz. The two men are standing very close together, as if they are discussing something of great intimacy. Arno peers around for Nurse Rosa, but she is not there. She won't normally arrive from the nearby town of Kempsey to start her day's work at the infirmary until after 10.00, he knows.

Then the soldier turns his head closer to Doctor Hertz and Arno can clearly see it is the camp Commandant, Captain Eaton. He is equally tall and thin as Doctor Hertz, but with brown hair that is not as dark as the doctor's, and with a thin moustache, where the doctor is always clean shaven. They look like brothers, sometimes, Arno thinks. One the good brother and one the evil brother. The Commandant puts his hand on Doctor Hertz's elbow and draws him a little closer. Talking into his ear. Arno can't hear the words, but sees Doctor Hertz nod his head as they talk.

Then suddenly they step apart as Jacob Meyer, the doctor's intern, walks into the room. He holds out a small silver tray and Doctor Hertz places something on it. He nods to Meyer who turns and leaves them. The Commandant leans closer to Doctor Hertz again and continues talking softly. Doctor Hertz looks back and nods once more. And Arno wants to press his ear up against the window and hear those soft words. Wants to know why the doctor looks so terribly sad.

He leans out from the truck a little, hoping to see the two men more clearly, and as he does he can now see there is a man on the infirmary bed. He tries to see who it is but cannot make out the face. He tries to remember if the infirmary had any patients yesterday. He thinks it has been empty, and they have not had any patients since last week.

He raises one crutch against the wall and leans forward from the truck's tailboard onto it, to peer even a little closer into the room. He leans out until he can reach out one hand and touch the stone wall of the infirmary. And just as he feels the cold hardness under his hand he sees Meyer walk back into the room, holding Doctor Harts small camera. Meyer has used it to take pictures of his misshapen legs for Doctor Hertz, for his medical records. Doctor Hertz has examined him often. Told him that if he had his surgical instruments he could operate on him. Could help him to walk. But as an enemy alien in internment, all he could offer were therapeutic massages to the feet, applied each day by himself or Nurse Rosa.

And then Arno feels his feet wobble a little. He tries to readjust his stance and realises he is perched too precariously high above the ground to be thinking of the firm fingers of Nurse Rosa running over his legs and feet. Pressing into the flesh as if shaping the muscles and tendons to her liking. The slightest of smiles on her face. Perhaps. Arno tries to concentrate on the men in the infirmary, but can feel the nurse's fingers against his skin. Can feel his knees are starting to give way.

Meyer raises the camera, aims and the flash bursts. And Arno Friedrich sees a quick image of the distorted face of Hans Eckert lying on the bed, as if revealed in the dark by a single lightning bolt. His mouth is wide open. Red blood trickling from it. A look of horror on his face, with his eyes empty and dead. His throat ripped out in a bloody mess.

Arno falls from the tailgate of the truck and lands heavily on the ground. He lies there a moment looking for the khaki legs of soldiers. Waiting for them to surround him. Then lift him to his feet. Press bayonets into his skin. Cast him into the truck again. Take him away somewhere.

But nobody comes.

He quickly lifts himself up and steps back into the shadows. Presses himself hard up against the dark granite wall until he is certain no one has heard him. Knows no one is coming for him. Then he crawls back under the truck and then makes his way back around the walls. All the way back around to his wing of the prison and then on to the safety of his own cell.

He swings open the door and limps in. Lies down heavily on his bunk. Feels sweat all over his body. The taste of fear in his mouth. The memory of Herr Eckert's face in his mind.

He looks across at his cell-mate, Horst Herschell. He is awake and is watching him. His face as drawn as an unfed dog. Arno wants to say something. Tell him that Hans Eckert has died and that his nightmare death has become a reality. That it really happened. That the dream world of the night has entered the day. But Horst sniffs and turns over on his bunk, his face to the wall.

Arno sometimes thinks of Horst as living, breathing, farting pile of blankets that just happens to occupy space in his cell. He looks at his watch. 7.15. The internees will be waking for breakfast soon, he thinks. Ready to begin the day—thinking of course that it will be just like any other.

Then he thinks of the dark figure that detached itself from the shadow of the wall in the dream. It must have been Herr Eckert's dream at the moment of his death, he thinks. Which means he was murdered. By one of his fellow internees!

The Commandant of the camp, Captain Eaton, sits behind the heavy wooden desk in his office, regarding the death certificate before him, and pondering the report he will have to write. The death will of course be explained as natural causes. The murderer in the prison will need to be found or he will have to hand over the prison to military police. And he knows how they will treat the men from his visits to Holsworthy intern-ment camp near Sydney—where the 5,000 or so men interned there are treated little better than cattle.

He has over 400 men under his command who have been gathered from their homes and businesses and offices from all over Australia, and even as far as Singapore and Ceylon and Hong Kong and India. There are teachers and merchants and scholars and self-made men. They have been handpicked as the elite and privileged, and sent to this old gaol at Trial Bay, at the mouth of the Macleay River, in northern New South Wales.

Captain Eaton has repeatedly told the men under his charge that they are the lucky ones. Told them they were chosen because they were well-educated, or were businessmen or professionals, but as such they were expected to behave better than common internees in other camps. They were also given more freedom within the internment camp. Freedom to organised a newspaper and an orchestra and a theatre company. Freedom to run their own small businesses. And freedom to know they are still prisoners, living in an abandoned gaol on a remote peninsula some 300 miles north of the nearest large city—often further from their wives and children.

The Commandant has a photograph of the internees arriving at the prison in 1915. The men look stunned. Weary. Peering around themselves in disbelief. They were assembled in front of the old prison in their best suits, holding suitcases they had probably brought from Germany many years before, as the guards herded them towards the gates.

Captain Eaton sometimes wonders what the convicts of the last century had felt when they had been brought to the prison when it was first built? What might a photograph of them have captured? He turns his attention back to the death certificate and thinks of the dead man's face. The horror on it. Who could have done that, and for what reason?

Doctor Hertz knows what is at stake here, and will do as he is advised, for the Australian Government has little tolerance of, nor interest in, his internees, and would welcome the opportunity to shut down this remote camp of privilege and send all the enemy aliens to Holsworthy. There was a memo recently about a gang operating in Holsworthy known as the Black Hand. A group of Serbian thugs were running an extortion racket inside the camp. There had been one death there already and the MPs had been sent in. Could it be something similar here, he wonders? Whatever the motive, it seemed that one of the internees, of good breeding and education, was actually a savage murderer? It seemed unbelievable, but what other possibility was there? He would be held accountable regardless.

He knows the Department of Defence would not be happy with the way he runs the camp, and the way he has ignored the many memos sent to him outlining new censorship requirements, tougher disciplinary measures and more vigilance against sedition. No visitors are allowed that are not sanctioned by the Department of Defence, and almost none ever are. He must ensure no journalists are allowed into the camp under any circumstances. He must ensure that the local population not be allowed near the camp except for essential services. He must ensure discipline and order are maintained amongst his internees.

His internees! That is how he thinks of them. Though he knows his wife bridles at the expression. She will make a fuss when the news of Herr Eckert's death reaches her though rumours. She will say it is one less Hun to be worried about. One less potential murderer and child rapist threatening the nearby towns of South West Rocks and Kempsey. Then she will talk of her brother Matthew again. Remind him what a fine man he was, and what a he would have made of his life had he not been killed by the Germans in France.

Then she will ask him again why he did not feel the urge to request a transfer to France to avenge her brother's death? Will wait for an answer that she knows he will not give her. But he has never told her of his diagnosis of a weak heart. He knows she would consider it further evidence of his general weakness. As he knows she will retire to bed early with a headache and lock the door of her bedchamber.

He wonders though if most of the men and women of the nation spent a day inside the prison observing the daily habits of routines of them men under his care whether it would soften the national obsession with demonising them as brutal Huns? He knows they are officially classified as Enemy Aliens, but he finds them neither the enemy nor alien. He also wonders, not for the first time, if it is his own wife's growing prejudice and hatred towards them that mitigates his own feelings to them?

His own father had been a mean-spirited man of a thousand petty prejudices and hatreds, and the Captain had resolved as a young man that he would never follow his path, and whenever confronted with bigotry and prejudice he would attempt to look beyond it. Ironic then in that striving so hard not to turn out like his father he had married a woman so much like him in temperament.

He considers the death certificate again. Natural causes. As if there was some world where a man having had his throat ripped out roughly could be considered natural. What nightmare world exactly might that be, he wonders, and would it ultimately be any crueller than the world he was living in?

Arno Friedrich looks at his watch. 7.22 am. He can hear the noise of men leaving their cells above and around him. He looks over to Horst Herschel's bunk. He is looking at him again with that sad look that seemed deep-etched into his face. Neither man says anything. Most days they lie on their bunks, staring across the vast distance between them, occasionally sniping at each other. Horst Herschell tells him that his poor German makes his ears hurt. Arno responds with more badly pronounced words.

Herr Herschell dreams of a farm he lived on in Germany as a child. But in his dreams the farm is in ruins and the cattle are all dead, and Horst Herschell walks amongst the carnage looking for a young boy that might be himself.

They have long ago run out of conversation with each other. But if you cannot talk without conflict, then it is better not to talk at all. That is one of the camp's mottos. They've dozens of them, all created by the camp committee—elected internees who ensure there is a motto for everything. A healthy body and healthy mind make for a healthy person. The devil makes friends of idle hands. Camaraderie makes for good comrades.

Arno Friedrich would prefer: Let each man live in peace and stop inflicting endless mottos on the others. But peace is not a word that is spoken inside the internment camp, for the whole world outside is at War. That is the word that obsesses everybody. But it is another word that nobody will speak.

Krieg—he whispers it to himself sometimes. Just so he can hear himself saying it. But only ever a whisper, so he doesn't let in loose inside the prison. For he also fights a daily war with many of those around him, who do not accept him, but who he has taken to protecting from the horrors that dwell in the walls and come out at times to haunt their nightmares. He has this gift for some purpose, he reasons, but he finds balance in being able to torment and tease his fellow internees in small ways.

Unlike most of the cells in the prison, theirs is rather sparse of furnishing and mementos. Most of the internees have hung pictures of loved ones on the walls of their cells, or scenic pictures cut from magazines, and have built shelves for books and knick-knacks. Others have built small desks and chairs, that might have a vase or a carving on it, or an embroidered cloth. Things that have some texture that is soft and a scent that is not of stone and iron. Anything to make each cell look a little more like a room rather than what it actually is. But Arno and Horst Herschell either lack the interest or the mementos to surround themselves with. They have one small bookshelf each mounted directly onto the stone walls and a cracked and flaking small mirror that they share, though Arno finds the world looks less grim in the larger ones in the communal bathrooms.

Arno looks at his wrist-watch again. 7.25. Almost time for breakfast. He says it aloud to Horst, *"Frühstück."* One of the few words the elderly man responds to. Then Arno stands up and swings open the cell door. All down the corridor men are emerging from their cells, making their way to and from the washrooms, getting dressed and cleaned for the day ahead. Whatever it may bring.

"Schinkenspeck mit Eiern," says Arno to some of the men walking past him. Bacon and eggs. But they pay him no heed. They know it will be *Bröt und Haferschleim*—bread and porridge. It is rarely anything different than the solid Australian country diet that the men have so long grown sick of.

Arno grips his crutches and joins the long line of men shuffling slowly down the corridor towards the kitchen. He listens to the mumbling small talk and attempts of the men to hide their despair of another day in prison. And one of them is a murderer, he thinks.

Then he wonders who will be the first to tell the internees of the death of Herr Eckert? Doctor Hertz? The Commandant? Will an announcement be made at breakfast? Arno looks back to the men either side of him, watching them shaking sleep and dreams out of their heads. There will be no gentle way to tell it.

When he reaches the front of the breakfast line he is given a plate of porridge and several slices of bread. He knows that it will smell better than it will actually taste, as if the bakers have somehow kneaded the sour disappointment of internment into it. He makes his way back to the large dining hall and stands under the entrance archway, looking around at all the men that he knows so well—and also so little. He wonders how they will react? He takes a seat by himself, as is his habit, on the end of one of the long benches and starts eating his porridge. Slowly. Looking around every few mouthfuls, waiting for Doctor Hertz or the Commandant to enter the room. Waiting for somebody to make the announcement. To say the words. To change this day.

He has a spoonful of porridge poised before his mouth when Herr Herausgeber joins him at the bench. *"Guten Morgen,"* he says brightly. Arno shoves the porridge into his mouth and nods to the elder man.

Herr Herausgeber had been a rubber plantation manager in Malaysia. Lonely, middle-aged, balding and divorced. But still a manager! He walks and gesticulates with a nervous energy that makes his limbs look as if they half-turned to rubber themselves. In internment he has turned his frantic energies to editing the camp newspaper, *Welt am Montag*—the World on Monday. He is a man driven by a fear of failure, Arno knows, and he has a belief that Arno overhears much of the camp gossip from the guards in English and can pass it to him.

He leans forward a little and tells Arno in a confidential whisper, "I am writing an article on how close the final great advance is, describing how the German army will push the British right back to England soon. Will push them right across the ocean to Australia."

He winks as he talks, as if they are confidants in a conspiracy, and his fingers wobble about in the air like toy soldiers. "The German victors will liberate us all," he says. "They will throw the guards into this prison in our places."

Arno has heard all this before. As have most of the men in the prison. But it is Herr Herausgeber's way of swapping information. He tells you a secret and then demands one of you in return. Arno shrugs, not giving up anything easily, and Herr Herausgeber changes track. "I envy you your youth, do you know?" he asks. Then says, "I know how frustrating it must feel to be denied the opportunity to wear the uniform of the Kaiser, and fight for the Empire. To hasten the defeat of the British."

Still Arno says nothing. Herr Herausgeber shows his teeth and scowls. His aggressive side starting to emerge. The one that desperately want to believe that Germany will send troops to this distant part of the Pacific Ocean just to free them. To free him. And how easily they will defeat the men who guard them here.

"My boy, they are fools," Herr Herausgeber tells Arno. "Just look at them." He is always disparaging of the several dozen guards who look over them to anyone who will listen. Badly dressed. Ill-disciplined. Lazy. "A small squad of German troops would over-run these farm boys in fifteen minutes," he says.

And he despairs that his precious rubber plantation has been left in the hands of men like these. "They do not have the discipline to run these things properly," he says. "The British will never win the war if they rely on colonial troops like these."

"Peasants!" he says, as if insulted that he is not being guarded by elite British troops. "They are worse than peasants. They are convicts!" he says.

Arno Friedrich listens patiently to Herr Herausgeber's tirade, for he is wondering what he will write about Herr Eckert's death in his newspaper? More to the point, he thinks, what might he be permitted to write about the death? And the whole prison will know the news already, but will undoubtedly devour whatever he writes eagerly. They will point to the words and read them aloud to their cell-mates or comrades, and say, "Listen to what it says here…" And they will all listen, as if it is somehow actual news to them. The power of their own printed words in their own language is another peculiarity of confinement.

Arno Friedrich looks at his watch. It is 7.45. Doctor Hertz still hasn't arrived for breakfast and the quickest eaters have already finished. Those with things to do. Jobs in the yard. Clubs to organise. Rehearsals to attend. Many of the elderly men will drag their meal on for as long as is possible though, with nothing else to look forward to but lunch and then dinner.

"Have you seen Doctor Hertz this morning?" Arno suddenly asks Herr Herausgeber.

"No. Why? Has something happened?" Herr Herausgeber leans forward over the table, his eyebrows raised way up high on his head.

Arno just shrugs. Doesn't want to say yes. Doesn't want to say no.

"Is somebody seriously ill perhaps?" asks Herr Herausgeber, sniffing for a story. Prepared to wrangle the information out of Arno. He looks around the hall, trying to see if somebody is not there. "Have you heard something?" he asks Arno.

Arno makes as if he is squirming a little on the bench. As if he is privy to information that he shouldn't really be sharing. "Well…" he says, and looks around. And just then Doctor Hertz strides into the hall. A bowl of porridge in one hand and a plate of bread in the other. He sits at a table and the men look up and smile and greet him warmly. He is joined by intern Meyer and Arno sees that some of the men look away, their faces reddening a little, remembering the lust with which they had watched him enter the hall the previous evening.

Herr Herausgeber turns and watches him. Smiles. Turns back to Arno. "He was brilliant last night, wasn't he?"

Arno nods. Jacob Meyer had been Brünnhilde the queen of the Walküries. It was one of his best roles. Dressed in long flowing robes and wig and padded battle armour, he looked ready to carry off those who had died fighting for her. And every man in the hall, for the duration of the play, had wanted to be the one who would die for her. Longed to be carried away in her strong arms, and pressed closely to her breastplate.

Men dress the parts of Isolde and Salome and other women of mythology, but their favourite is Brünnhilde—warrior princess and Walküre, who selected those who died valiantly in battle to be carried to Valhalla, the hall of the gods. Arno knows that many of the men go to sleep with dreams of her firm fingers on their bodies and wake to the briny smell of guilt and self-pleasure.

There is a very popular photograph that many of the men possess. It shows a beautiful Fraulein standing by an open window. No bars on it. She is wearing a thin white dress. It can only be a woman at home in Germany, dreaming of her love who is away at the front, or incarcerated in some enemy prison perhaps. They have all dreamed of her at some time. Dreamed of the soft touch of her lips and the firm press of her breasts against them. Dreamed it was not one of their comrades in a woman's dress.

During the nights Doctor Hertz uses his skills to transform men into many different roles in their theatre productions—soldiers and warriors—and women—their features well-hidden by the soft lights and make-up. Another transformation between light and day.

Arno Friedrich watches the doctor begin an animated conversation with the men around him and looks around to see if the Commandant is going to enter the hall now. Then turns back to watch Doctor Hertz as he talks and eats.

Herr Herausgeber is watching him too, and Arno bites his lip and then changes the subject, "I have heard the Australian guards share your belief that the German troops will come as far as Australia."

Herr Herausgeber eyes focus like a bull staring at a taunting cape. "Yes! Did not Australian troops over-run the Bismarck Archipelago? So, it is a matter of pride to take it back from them! Once Paris and London have been taken the Kaiser will send an invasion force and they will chase the Australian troops right back to Sydney and Melbourne. They will land on the beach here to liberate us. We will wake up one morning and see the smoke of a dozen German troopships on the horizon. The Australian guards will flee into the bush, of course, and we will welcome our liberators with the gates flung wide open."

"That is exactly what I have heard them say," Arno says, and settles in for the fantasy telling, nodding as if he has never heard any of it before. Thus he doesn't see Doctor Hertz finishes his meal, make a parting comment to the men around him and then rise to leave, excusing himself with pressing business in the infirmary perhaps. He walks past their table and has almost stepped beyond them when Herr Herausgeber sees him and quickly raises his hand, like a small pupil in school might. "Doctor Hertz," he says.

"Yes?" says the doctor, turning to him.

"Is somebody quite ill?" he asks.

Doctor Hertz gives a short quick smile and says, "Why yes. Herr Eckert came down with a sudden case of heart disease late last night. He has been taken away to Kempsey already. They will take him onto a hospital in Sydney to treat him."

"Heart disease?" asks Herr Herausgeber.

"Yes," says the doctor.

"Is it serious?"

"It can often be," says the doctor. Then he asks, "How did you know to ask about him?"

"Young Arno here told me," he says.

"Did he?" asks the doctor, turning to regard Arno carefully. "Did he indeed?" Then he smiles again, briefly, and with little of his characteristic warmth, he turns and quickly strides out of the hall.

Sergeant Gore holds the small circle of soldiers away from him at arm's length, pointing his bayonet at them. He moves rapidly from one man to the next, holding it level at their throats.

"Do you think you can take me?" he asks. "Come and try it!"

Although he is smaller and older than any of the young privates who stand around him, he has the body of a bull, and none is eager to be the first one to try and take him. The Sergeant's eyes dart from one soldier to the next, sharper and more menacing than the long metal blade. "Who's going to be the first then?"

The soldiers around him move uneasily from foot to foot, perhaps getting ready to spring, perhaps getting ready to step away. Six of them. Tall. Darkly dressed. Like six khaki brothers, whose names didn't matter anymore. He can see their pale faces scowling in the morning's first light, and it made Sergeant Gore grin. But he can also see the caution in their eyes. And can see how hard they are trying not to show it.

"Never had a real fight before, have you?" he says softly. "Not with a real fighter." One of the soldiers licks his lips a little. Another swallows twice. Sergeant Gore fixes that one with a quick glance, then thrusts the bayonet in the direction of another man, leaving an opening.

And Private Gunn, a stocky young red-headed local boy, takes it. He jumps quickly. Both hands trying to catch the bayonet hand before it swings back. His is fast for a large youth. Not long in uniform, but he has spent years wresting angry bulls in the stockyards. He knows he can take the Sergeant if he can get in close and catch him around the arm. The Sergeant is much shorter and older. Probably slower too.

But the Sergeant is faster. One moment Private Gunn has his hands on the arm with the bayonet, the next the Sergeant has him around the throat. Has turned him around. Has forced him down at the knees. Has the bayonet held tightly against the pale soft skin under his chin.

Private Gunn can feel the strength in the short stocky arms. Can smell the scent of wild victory coming off the Sergeant's skin. He blinks once. Twice. Sees the startled looks on his mates' faces. Can hear the Sergeant hissing in his ear, "You're dead, Gunn!" Then he feels the chill of the steel as it is dragged slowly across his throat. Then feels the force of the Sergeant kicking him to the dirt.

"That's how it's done," Sergeant Gore says. "You want to be real soldiers? You want to learn how to kill Germans? Well you have to learn a lot more than drilling on a parade ground and shooting at targets on a rifle range." Then he reaches down and lifts Private Gunn to his feet. Gives his neck only the briefest of glimpses. Knows he isn't seriously hurt. But knows the younger man will think a little bit harder about trying something so stupid next time.

"I'm only one man," says the Sergeant, looking beyond the six men, as if looking thousands of miles away. "If you'd have rushed me all at once I wouldn't have stood a chance. I would've only been able to kill one or two of you at most—and you'd have me. Overwhelmed me by sheer strength of numerical supremacy. Remember that!"

He looks back at the men. Watches their lips moving as they repeat the words. "That's what wins battles," he says.

The men nod, twitching uncomfortably in their coarse woollen khaki uniforms. Knowing what he is going to ask them next is, are they really willing to fight for the King and Empire? Really willing to fight to protect their loved ones? Really willing to kill the enemy in hand-to-hand combat if they have to?

But he asks, "What wins battles?"

"Numerical supremacy," they say as one.

"Yes, that's right," he says. "And one other thing."

The men have to wait for him to tell them.

"Occasional rat cunning."

Barely half an hour after breakfast the whole prison knows that Hans Eckert has been taken to Sydney. Some claim to have heard the truck departing shortly before they awoke. Others claim that Herr Eckert had personally told them that he had not been feeling well, and that his heart was acting up. Others, more elderly, return to their cells and lie down, with their hands over their own hearts, thinking of how active Herr Eckert had been, and wondering if the sudden twinge they feel in their own chests might also be heart disease?

Only Arno is wondering why the doctor has lied, as he makes his way around the main courtyard after breakfast. Perhaps, he reasons, the doctor does not understand that a nightmare has reached out and killed a man, refusing to be incarcerated in the stone walls around them. Perhaps he believes that someone within the prison has committed murder and he feels that needs to be kept a secret?

Arno is unsure if he should tell the doctor what he knows. As a man of science, he would most likely not believe him and suspect him of having something to do with the death. Arno doesn't like that idea at all and so keeps pacing the yard, waiting for the gates to open to the outer world. Like most of the men he has no wish to return to his cell for the day and he goes to join most of the men at the main gates.

Arno looks at his watch. 9.05 am. The guards are late again. The internees press up close to the gates and mumble loudly. They stare out across the dirt road that leads towards the tree line. Just beyond the prison is thick bushland, with a single thin road running through it. The internees call it, *"Der dunkel Wald"*—the dark woods. As if it is the place where all things disturbing lurk. They are forbidden to go towards the bushland and there are armed guard posts there. They are told there are poisonous snakes and spiders and wild animals there too. They are told it is dark and unknowable. Arno, being Australian-born, has a different sensibility, and often misses the scent of eucalypts close by. Or the crunch of leaf litter underfoot. The whirrs and clicks of bush insects.

The internees stand at the gates with their hands on the bars—their fingers on the other side of freedom. And Arno wonders how these men might react if they knew that the walls that inter them held their nightmares, and that they might now somehow reach out and attack them? Then Arno sees one of the soldiers step from the guardhouse and, ignoring the internees, slowly make his way over and unlock the large barred gates. He looks just like any other of the guards—khaki uniform and belting. The guards are more alike than the internees here.

The men shove against the gates like unruly children, pushing them open, and they flood outside like they are going to a carnival. Arno steps out with them, and pauses. He looks around at the wide expanse of ocean all around them, shading his eyes carefully. There is not a single point inside the prison walls from where he can see the bright blue of the ocean, and every morning, as he steps outside, it seems to him to be brighter. It stretches around the peninsula and is so wide that it seems to go forever. It fills him with a feeling of calm and a sense of place that is unachievable inside the prison walls.

Herr Herausgeber had once told him that you could not photograph the ocean properly here because it was impossible to take it all in. Arno has to turn his head slowly when looking at it all, so that the wider world will not suddenly overwhelm him. He cannot see the smoke of any troop ships out there today. Not even a solitary fishing boat.

The other internees push past him and advance down the small path away from the prison, down towards the small village of wooden shacks they have constructed around the lower walls. They have built summerhouses and cafes and taverns out of scrap wood and packing cases. Painted backdrops of Alpine mountains and forests hang behind some of them, left over from plays or operas performed in the prison. The small buildings have Germanic names over their doors, saying in Gothic script, Beer Garden or White Horse Inn.

This is where many of the men spend their days. From 9.00 to 5.00 the gates of the prison are opened and the men are allowed to escape its grey shadows and enter the world of imagining in their small cafes and taverns. They have reconstructed buildings from their youth, from a Germany of the last century that they can distantly remember. Arno has no way of knowing if they have been faithful to their memories or not. He suspects not, but most everything he knows about Germany he has learned from them. The poetry of Goethe that they recite. The music of Wagner and Beethoven that is played in concerts. The look of the Alps and the forests as painted on the canvas sheets behind the small shacks they have built. For all he knows it is just another dream fantasy of the men.

Arno makes his way slowly past the painted German village down to the beach on the inside of the peninsula. The long white crescent of sand runs away around to the distant entrance to the Macleay River. He stands a long time looking across the wide bay. He looks for any changes in the water. He looks for any boats. Any activity across at the settlement of South West Rocks at the river's mouth—some 20 miles away.

They are also told that the locals at the township are hostile. If anybody was able to make their way through the forest or across the bay the townspeople would be waiting for them. There is no need to say anything else. They are people whose sons and fathers and brothers and uncles are fighting in the trenches. Being shot by German artillery. Being bombed by German airplanes. Being killed by German soldiers. They have no reason to be sympathetic to any German they meet. "The Hun!" the people from South West Rocks call the internees. "A threat to the war effort." "The enemy!" And Arno knows that no matter where he was born and how well he speaks English, he will always be one of the Hun to them.

Arno turns his head the other way, towards the end of the peninsula, where the prison walls stop just short of the breakwater. It cuts out across the bay and provides safe shelter for them on the beach. The waves here are gentle and slow. But out in the bay, they are told, the current is strong and dangerous. Many boats have been lost to it, they are told. It will drag a man right out to sea. It will even drag granite boulders out to sea.

Herr Herausgeber has an old photograph of the prison from the last century, in the tiny cell that is his newspaper office. It shows the convicts labouring on the breakwater. Breaking heavy rocks, dragging them to the ocean's edge and tipping them into the sea. He has told Arno that the prison had been built as a public works prison, and that it was believed that the convicts would be rehabilitated by hard work. They were to construct a breakwater that would run almost half a mile across the bay, making it safer for shipping.

At the turn of the century, he has told Arno, just before the prison had been abandoned, the breakwater had only extended 900 feet out— less than half its planned length. But now, only 15 years later, it is only about 400 feet long. For over 20 years the convicts toiled to cast thousands and thousands of tons of granite rock into the ocean, working like an army, advancing forward slowly each day—but it was a futile battle, for the powerful currents of the ocean kept dragging it all away.

Arno has often wondered if they will still be interned here when the breakwater is finally worn away altogether, like one of those stories of purgatory where a bird flies to a mountain and pecks at it once every hundred years until it is all gone. For life in internment seems like a version of purgatory.

He leans forward on his crutches now, and watches several bronzed and athletic men on the beach before him, warming up for their morning's exercise. Some walk briskly on the sands, admiring each other. On some rare days it is possible to see a few of the men completely naked, lounging on the sand with their hairy naked penises flopping on their thighs, as if it were the most natural thing in the world. But not today. Today a dozen or so men, the camp's official athletics club, assemble in a group for a photograph. Herr Dubotzki, the camp photographer, is quite skilled at his art. He had run a studio in Adelaide, it was said. Has even held exhibitions. He now instructs the men to move closer together. They hold their stomachs in tightly and stand in close military rows, mimicking the soldiers' stance that they have never known.

Arno Friedrich makes his way down to the sand, skirting the men, keeping well away from the aim of the camera. He mocks the athletics club, as he knows they would never ask him to join them. Big men who play at children's games and dream of being bullies in the schoolyard, he thinks them. At the water's edge he slowly takes off his clothes, including his watch and his regulation white canvas hat, and places them all by his crutches. Then he limps awkwardly into the water on misshapen legs. It is warm for this time of year, he thinks. Like the North Sea, some of the men tell him.

"But isn't the water warmer here?" Arno has asked them.

"No. The German water is just as warm as the water here!" they state. More fantasies, he thinks.

He makes his way out to where the water is above his knees and then, exhaling suddenly, lowers himself up to his neck. He feels his testicles shrink a little and press in close to his body. Feels all his muscles tighten. He moves his arms about and lets the water take his weight. Lets his legs float up behind him. He kicks and feels them propel him along. His feet no longer useless. He lets go a fart that sends bubbles up around him. "Photograph that," he mumbles.

Then he turns and begins swimming. Strong slow strokes that carry him out past the other bathers who are splashing each other like people on holidays. He puts his head down and swims. Way out into the bay. Swimming in a straight line. Towards the small island that lies to the north of the river's mouth. Freedom Island, it is called. A small green island, far, far away, with no buildings, no dark woods and no granite walls. He keeps swimming until he reaches a point level with the end of the breakwater. Then he stops and treads water. He can feel the strong grip of the ocean current around him, tugging at him, trying to coax him out to sea.

He turns around in the water and looks back to the prison. The low dark walls make it appear like an old castle on the rocky headland. He can see the guard in the southwest watchtower, but he can't tell if he is watching him or not. He imagines you could stand in the tower there and could look out to sea all day long and never need to see even one stone of the prison.

He treads water for a few minutes more, as if trying to decide something. Then he swims back to shore.

Perhaps another day, he thinks.

Private Gunn stands in front of the small mirror in the guards' barracks' washroom. He tilts his head back to examine the red welt that runs across his neck. He admires the precision of it. It never broke the skin until just that little point at the end where a small blood clot has now formed.

It will be easy enough to pass off as a shaving accident to the other guards, he thinks. They'll never suspect a thing. And to the other members of the Dark Knights, it will be a mark of pride. Something to show them how he had dared, and stepped close to death.

He takes up his shaver now and runs it slowly across the welt line. Tries to imagine what it felt like for the Sergeant to have his life in his hands. To know how easy it would be to cut his throat. And he wonders if he could ever do it? Could he grab a German by the throat and plunge his bayonet into the neck? Draw it right across so that the blood spurted out?

Not that it would be the first throat he'd ever cut. He'd slaughtered dozens of lambs and calves. Pigs too. Had seen the fear in their eyes as he approached them with the large knife. Listened to the squealing as he grasped them by the throat. Felt the sudden kicking as he plunged the knife in. Then slit. Long and hard. Let them fall to the ground to struggle helplessly in their own blood.

But they were animals. They weren't men.

Private Gunn holds his shaver against this throat. Moves it softly across that red welt line once more.

At 11.05 Arno Friedrich is lying on an old and chipped white-painted iron bed in the small infirmary, looking down between his legs at Nurse Rosa. Every day should be so pleasant as this, he thinks. Her face, as ever, shows little emotion. Arno wonders what secrets she hides. Wonders what she might dream of. She is no longer young, but with dark hair and fine-angled features she is considered by all the internees to be quite beautiful—particularly so for men who only otherwise see pretend women.

She only ever hints at her past when talking to Arno and makes references to China and India and the mountains of Europe. She has a French accent, but speaks German well.

"How does this feel?" she asks, as she carefully works the muscles of Arno's misshapen legs.

"Good," says Arno. Although he wants to say, "Wonderful." Her experienced fingers massage the pain out of his legs as if it was a physical thing she was able to draw out of him. She gives a mere hint of a smile, and puts his foot down and lifts up the other one. She holds it tightly against the starched white cloth of her uniform—against her lifted thigh—and begins massaging it. Arno closes his eyes. He does not want Nurse Rosa to see the things he knows in them.

So many internees have dreamed of her, using brief glimpses to assemble her naked body, filling in the gaps of what they have seen with their imaginings. The shape of her upper arms. The freckles on her back. The shape of her clavicle. The way her neck slopes into her shoulders. The curve of her breasts. The alabaster slopes of her thighs. The dark forest between her legs.

For one half hour each day he is the luckiest man in the camp, some of the men have told him. Or they joke that they have a deformity in their penis, and wish that Nurse Rosa would massage it straighter for them.

He, in turn, tells them how he feels when she takes hold of his feet, presses them tight against her thigh and begins massaging them. Watches the agony grow on their faces. But today he feels more strongly the memory of Herr Eckert's dead body, lying on the bed where he himself now lies. The thought makes him shiver and makes goose bumps appear on his skin.

He keeps his eyes closed and tries to concentrate on the sensation of Nurse Rosa's fingers. Sometimes strong and hard. Sometimes soft and gentle. And a momentary dream image reaches him, of a man roughly taking her in the darkness, her face twisted in protest and pain. Another of the inmate's dreams threatening to escape into the reality of daylight, he thinks.

He opens his eyes suddenly and looks at her. She smiles, a little quizzical, and asks, "What have you been up to today?" In German. As she asks it every day. They talk a lot, but always the same questions and answers.

"Swimming. Sitting in the sun." The usual answers.

"You should get involved in camp activities more," she says. "I hear your drama troupe is very good."

"Yes. But I prefer to watch," he says. She nods and turns her attention back to his feet. She turns one foot as she works, slipping it just a little further up her thigh.

"I prefer to dance," she says.

This is new. "What type of dancing?" he asks.

"All kinds of dancing. As long as there is music and a partner to dance with."

"Where do you dance? At South West Rocks? Kempsey?" He's never known exactly where she lives.

"No. Not here," she says.

And then Arno asks a new question. "You are not happy here?"

She regards him and says, "Here is a place that feels eternal, but is really only ever temporary."

"Why are you here then?"

But she shakes her head. "That is too long a story."

"Your German is very good," he says. "Better than mine." An old line. Safer ground.

"Yes. Much better than yours." The safe answer.

He wonders if she has a German ancestor that she has hidden from the authorities. One French grandmother and one German perhaps? He imagines her as a young girl, wearing her red nurse's cape, visiting her grandmother and listening to her telling her folk stories in German. He smiles at the thought of it. But he is also a little saddened by the thought of it, for he wishes he had similar memories.

Instead he asks, "Have you been a nurse long?"

"Long enough," she says.

"Have you ever seen a dead person?"

She stops. Puts his foot down. Puts her hands to her hips. "What a question!" she says. "What makes you ask that?" He can see from her eyes that she has though. Another part of her secret life.

He opens his mouth to answer and Doctor Hertz walks into the room. "How are you feeling?" he asks Arno. As he asks every day.

Arno looks up at him and says, "Good enough." As he answers every day.

The doctor motions for the Nurse to stand back and he takes up one of Arno's feet himself. He looks at it carefully, as if studying it for any miraculous changes. He turns it a little to the left, then turns it a little more to the right. "Hmm," he says, and then bends the toes backwards. Arno gasps.

"Does that hurt?" the doctor asks.

"A little," says Arno.

The doctor bends the toes the other way. Arno says nothing through the pain. The doctor is smiling to himself, as he often does. He is a handsome man, Arno supposes. High cheekbones and fair hair. Well adaptable to the many heroic stage roles he plays.

The doctor picks up his other foot. He holds the two together, and sighs heavily. "It would be such a simple operation you know," he says. "I could cut some tendons from behind your knee and attach them here." He stabs at the foot with his fingernail. "And you would be walking like normal people."

Arno thinks that he does not know any normal people, least of all the doctor. Though he has told Arno about the operation so often that Arno feels he could perhaps do it himself one day. An incision behind the knee. Cut loose some of the tendons there to loosen the tightness in his legs. Another incision in the foot. Long and narrow. Attach the tendons. Encase the feet in plaster. Let them grow. And then, perhaps a month or two later, break open the plaster, and like a butterfly emerging from a cocoon, his bent and broken feet would be beautiful and wholly formed and strong enough to hold up his thin and weakened legs. And the first thing he would do, he thinks, would be to dance around the infirmary with Nurse Rosa.

"I think you are walking too much on your feet," Doctor Hertz suddenly says.

Arno lifts his head and looks down between his legs again. The doctor does not meet his eyes, but keeps working on his feet. "I think it best if you keep off them for a while. Not too much exercise, hmmm?"

"What about swimming?" asks Arno.

"Swimming is fine," says the doctor. "But not too much wandering around the yard at all hours. It might not be good for you." He places Arno's foot back on the bed. Leaves one hand on top of it. Pats it once, and then, still without looking at Arno, turns and leaves the room.

Lunch in the main hall is mutton and potatoes. Arno Friedrich sits by himself and eats and listens to some of the older men in one corner singing a song together. Some tune from their youth that takes them back over the oceans and the years to a country where Bismarck was a saint and German expansion their right. Arno Friedrich, with no such memories, watches the men as they finish their meals and wonder back out the yard again.

There are only a few men left still sitting at the tables now, chatting and slowly finishing their lunch. He sees two in particular, sitting alone at a far table. Not eating. Saying little. Staring around the hall. One is a tall man, Herr von Krupp, an aristocrat, with a long slightly-greying moustache, waxed in full flight. Arno's nickname for him is the Eagle, as he has constant dreams of flying. And falling. Terrifying spirals to earth from great heights. The other, Herr Schwarz, is of less noble birth, but has a position of authority in the camp, running the athletics club. He is much shorter, his skin almost swarthy and his hair jet black. He dreams of marching along with a troop of young men in lederhosen, and suddenly discovering he has no pants on. His strong fingers are running back and forward on the table now, betraying his nervousness.

As they sit there, like two Prussian Lords, a pair of younger men come past. They are in high spirits and are slapping and elbowing each other, in a mock fight. One suddenly grabs the other in a headlock and wrestles him to the ground. His friend screams a little and flails his arms around trying to grab his assailant's head and break his grip.

Herr von Krupp says nothing, but turns his head quickly towards them. And glares. The man applying the headlock releases his friend and stands up straight. As if snapping to attention. The other man looks up and then also jumps to his feet. Herr von Krupp says nothing. Still just glares. Both young men then bow their heads a little, looking at the ground around them. Herr von Krupp makes a small dismissive noise and the young men turn and walk quickly away.

The power of the high born, thinks Arno. But the higher the birth, the further the fall.

He watches the pair until they have left the hall and then looks around like he is surveying his domain. Then he looks back to his comrade at the table. Herr Schwarz blinks nervously. Finally he nods, just a little, and slides one hand across the table until he touches the taller man's fingers. He draws his hand back quickly with a fold of money in it. Then, quickly, glancing around, he slides a single photograph back across the table.

The tall man places his hand upon it and draws it to himself. Then turns it over and carefully examines it. It shows a woman, standing by a pier. There is a ship in the background, sailing towards her. He examines the woman carefully. She is a little plump, and has a hat drawn down over the top of her face. But he can clearly see her eyes. Smouldering. And her lips are puckered towards him. Inviting. One strap of her dress hangs off her shoulder, and one hand draws up her skirts a little, showing a pale plump leg, the other is cupped under her breast. Her short stubby fingers, pressing into her flesh.

The tall man's fingers shake a little as he looks at her and his eyes narrow. The small man looks away for a moment. Then glances back. The tall man has put the photo away. Now he smiles briefly, like the momentary glimpse of gold in a man's purse. Then he stands.

"*Ist es gut Herr von Krupp?*" asks the small man.

"It is as good as you promised," says the tall man, and marches out of the hall.

Captain Eaton has been working with his men to try and collect intelligence all day—though his troops and intelligence are not words he would normally consider in the same sentence. The bulk of them are rural lads, denied service for physical or other ailments that has deemed them as unfit to run headlong into the enemy's machine guns in Europe. Asthma, weak eyesight, poor co-ordination, donkey-brained stupid. But they made up for each with brutishness, ignorance and racism. Those solid traits that made Australian troops such valued soldiers of Empire.

The Commandant sits in his office, in front of the twin flags of Great Britain and Australia, with a portrait of the King between them. Watching him. Unsettling him. He knows that men like Sergeant Gore salute that picture more readily than they ever salute him. He has Sergeant Gore on the task of trying to find out if Hans Eckert had any enemies. He was one of the few internees who had had his own cell, even though that had only been a temporary measure. He had been a businessman in Melbourne before the war, though not an exceedingly wealthy one, so there were many more likely victims of extortion than him. He was an active member of a few of the internees' societies, and frequented one of the Alpine cafes outside the walls often.

The Commandant decided he would have the cafe monitored for any indications of trouble there—but he doubted that would result in anything. There was nothing like being watched to evoke good behaviour, he knew. Also, the camp committee were generally quick to report any problems within the camp—and how they'd solved it—before he was ever aware of it.

But he doesn't wish to go to the camp committee with this. That left the possibility of unnatural sexual acts, that Herr Eckert may have been either involved in, or caught up in. He was aware that the sins of self-abuse were rampart in the prison—though no one would ever admit to it—and he knew that several men had been caught in Holsworthy Camp performing unnatural acts on other men. There were even reported cases there of men working in small groups, holding a victim down and sexually assaulting him in turn. But if you treated men like beasts, they would surely act like beasts.

Could such a thing happen here though? And if so, how could it have led to such a brutal murder? The man's throat had been ripped out as if giant claws had done it. There had been no other marks on him. No sign of being held down by a group of men. No damage to his clothing. Or was it simpler? A warning to others that this too would be their fate? If so, he thought, he had rendered it ineffective by removing Herr Eckert's body. And if that was indeed the motive, what might he have driven the attacker or attackers to do next to make their point?

And that thought, he finds, is more unsettling than the stern gaze of the king behind him.

The day passes slowly and by early evening Arno is once again making his way around the walls of the prison. He has thought carefully about Doctor Hart's words, and has decided that he must keep all the men safe from whatever other nightmares might emerge from the walls, and to do that he cannot let anything interfere with his routines.

He stands at the southwest watchtower where he had been standing that morning, looking up at the guard in the watchtower above him, waiting for the daylight to come. But now he is waiting for the light to fade. Already it is growing late and he can see the sky dimming and can see the colour going out of the granite stones about him.

He looks up to the watchtower above him. The guard is silent there now. Obviously looking out across the bay. Watching the sun set. Staring at the blooms of colour spreading across the horizon and the water—that Arno will never see. Paying no attention to life within the prison walls. Perhaps blotting it out altogether.

Arno knows the guards often drink in the evenings. Several have been caught and disciplined for it. But they continue to do it. It is in their brutish nature, Herr Herausgeber claims. But Arno knows that the German internees also have their own hidden stills. He looks up and wonders if the guards in their watchtowers ever consider that they are prisoners too, confined to their small wooden boxes up on the prison walls.

He reaches out and touches the stone wall now, trying to feel the stirring of anything in there. He holds his arms out wide, pressing his body flat against the cold rock. He stays there so long he feels the chill of the stone enter his body, as if he is slowly turning to stone himself.

He stays, pressed against the stone wall, until the dinner bell sounds and then he peels himself away, not having detected any danger, and makes his way to the hall to join his fellow internees. They will be safe this night, he thinks.

The Dark Knights are gathered on the small beach on the ocean side of the headland. They are wearing dark clothes with their faces darkened, just like a raiding party would dress. Metal trimmings have been removed from their uniforms, and Private Strap has even put his socks over the outside of his boots. Told the others he did it when he was a youngster. Said it really worked to soften your footsteps.

The others are not inclined to laugh at him until they see how Sergeant Gore reacts. Maybe there is some sense in his idea. But maybe not. The men stand together rubbing their hands briskly. It is a little chill tonight, though not as chill as it would be in France they know. It snowed there. Something they can only imagine.

"I'd kill for a smoke," says one private.

"And the Sergeant would kill you if you lit one," says another. "Every sniper for miles would see it."

"What snipers?" the first asks.

"The Sergeant'd be worry enough," says a third.

They all agree.

One of the men, peering at his watch in the darkness, unable to really see the time, says, "Okay, I think it's time." The men exhale and turn to face the small cliff before them. They remember the stories the Sergeant has told them of how he'd landed under the Turkish cliffs at night. How they'd struggled ashore with packs and animals and woke every Turk on the peninsula with the noise of it. And how, if only they'd sent a raiding party ashore to silence the sentries, the army would have strolled right across the peninsula the next morning.

That's what they were training for now. Night attacks. Learning how to sneak up on an enemy soldier and silence him quickly and quietly.

"In teams of two," says the private with the watch. "Who's going first?"

"We are," says Private Gunn, and indicates Private Strap. Thinks maybe the padded boots might give them some advantage. Thinks that even though he was always a bit of a dill at school at South West Rocks he might really be onto something.

"You first," he whispers, and sends his old school chum on ahead of him. The two men reach out to the cliff and begin slowly making their way up. It is hard going. The stones slide out from beneath their feet and they scrabble for hand holds on the few clumps of grass and small bushes. Trying to be quick. Trying to be quiet. Wishing they could shout out just how fucking hard this was to their mates behind them.

But they know the Sergeant is up there ahead of them somewhere, standing in the shadows. Waiting for them. By the time they reach the top of the small cliff they are panting heavily. "Shit, that's some work," says Private Strap. Private Gunn can only nod his head in agreement. He's done in. But he knows that was the easy bit. They've now got to crawl up the slope ahead, through the bushes, to reach the marker stick that the Sergeant has stuck in the ground there. And that is where Sergeant Gore will be waiting for them.

"You go that side and I'll go this side," whispers Gunn. "If we split up one of us might stand a better chance."

"What about numerical supremacy?" asks Strap.

"I think this one calls for rat cunning," says Gunn, and starts picking his way through the brush, bent double. It is too dark to see properly and he nearly trips over twice as he walks. He hears the sound of every branch and leaf he steps on and wishes he had put his socks over the outside of his boots too. He wonders how close to the marker stick he's gotten? Decides to risk lifting his head for a look. He stands up slowly and looks about. It takes him a moment to see where he is. Too far to the left. He wonders where Dougie Strap is? Wonders if he's closer to the marker stick than he is? Then he hears the soft footsteps behind him. The dill is following him!

But it isn't Dougie Strap. He's already been taken out of the game. It's Sergeant Gore and he has Private Gunn around the throat again. Pulls him up close to his body. Holds the bayonet against his throat. Then against his stomach.

"One—two!" he whispers. "You're dead. Now be a good boy and sit down and shut up and wait for your mates to come along."

Dinner in the old prison is mutton and potatoes. As it was the night before. And after the tables are cleared, the men begin getting the hall prepared for that night's concert. Benches are turned around. The floor is swept. Curtains are brought down over the small stage while men struggle with the backdrops and stage sets. The kerosene lamps are filled, then dimmed a little. When all is ready the men begin taking their seats. It will be another full house performance. Like it always is.

There is a chalkboard that announces tonight's performance will be a 'Surprise Item'. The men like that. They have probably seen the play performed already, but the thought of a surprise keeps them tense. They tap their feet eagerly on the floor, fidget and talk to each other, speculating on what the play will be. They wonder which women roles might be in it. Wonder what they will be wearing. Wonder how they will look.

Eventually the orchestra gathers on their seats in front of the stage. The men in the hall wait patiently for them to tune their instruments. They know the orchestra are good and certainly better than any they have heard in Brisbane or Adelaide or South East Asia. Herr Schröder, their conductor, has forged the many amateur players into a first-rate concert orchestra. They only have 23 players and lack some essential instruments, but he is a talented arranger, and a skilful conductor, and often has them playing as if they were the Berlin Philharmonic themselves.

The internees' favourites are Beethoven and Wagner, but tonight, when the orchestra strikes the first notes it is apparent this is a new piece. The men in the audience smile and some shake their heads a little in pleasure. As the first bars play some of the men mumble, "Mozart."

"Ah—Mozart," some of the others agree. It is a light and lively tune and several of the men dance their fingers to the music and then stand and clap heartily when it is done.

Herr Schröder then turns to the hall, bows low, stands up and announces, *"Eine Kleine Nachtmusik."* Then he turns back to the orchestra, lifts his baton, holds it there a moment and then flicks it down quickly. The orchestra comes in on the beat and the combined instruments surround the hall with a thick tapestry of music. All the internees are smiling now. Some are rocking their heads to the music. Others have their eyes shut tight, trying to evoke memories of previous evenings when they might have attended concerts, dressed in their finest suits, with a pretty woman or their wife on their arm.

When the piece is finished the men once more rise to their feet in applause. Some wipe tears from their eyes and look around at the men about them and see the same emotions on the faces there. They keep clapping. They have no need to say anything.

Herr Schröder then directs the orchestra's exit and then Doctor Hertz comes out onto the stage, wearing a familiar harem outfit, heavily-disguised by multiple veils. He is Scheherazade! This was one of the doctor's early ideas—and the men warmed instantly to the thought of the captive bride who has to tell stories for 1001 nights to win her freedom.

Some nights Doctor Hertz plays Scheherazade, and some nights, if he is in the play, another man takes her role. She is always heavily veiled so it doesn't matter. The men sometimes have to work hard to guess who it is under the veils and ample padding, and the following day's conversation at the breakfast table would often be conjecture, or small bets, as to who it had been—with the men having to wait for the doctor to arrive and tell them. Others choose not to know, preferring to believe it was a real woman there before them.

Scheherazade performs a short twirling dance for the men, her arms wind-milling around her gracefully. Then she stops and turns the other way. Then her arms freeze in a position, held out from her body. They remain motionless there for a few heartbeats, then the hands slowly bend at the wrists and glide back towards her body like small birds—and embrace her. Then she removes one single veil and drops it to the stage, and announces, "Tonight's story is one whose title I shall not reveal—but I am certain that it is a story well known to you all." Then she too bows and leaves the stage.

The men fidget in their chairs, eager for the curtain to rise.

Private Simpson, one of the few guards who is a war veteran, stands in the eastern watchtower looking out into the darkness over the prison and beyond. He can see the distant lights of the township of South West

Rocks and wonders if there is going to be another dance there at the Royal Hotel this Saturday? He is listening to the sounds of the orchestra floating out of the hall. It isn't too bad, tonight, he thinks, but he prefers the marching stuff. This music jumps around like a night insect or something. Not his taste at all. You couldn't even dance to it.

The last dance he had been to was a real ripper. The local sheilas weren't too bad. A bit big and beefy for his tastes—but friendly enough to a man in uniform. Those guards on leave would always come back with stories about who had gotten a root and who hadn't. Like they were returning from a raid and telling how many Huns they'd bayoneted. The Sergeant was always telling them not to stir up troubles with the locals by getting into the knickers of the sheilas, and warned them that if they did they'd have to be ready to marry them, or face up to their brothers and fathers. But Private Simpson was country-born and he knew that if a local sheila fancied you then you had a fair chance of getting her on her back. Especially if you'd served overseas. Even more so if you could get her to think you were just about to be sent over.

He leans against the wall and smiles a little. He's used that line a few times himself. Had some local farm girl pressed up against the wall of a dark barn, running his hands up and down her dress. All over her. Christ, he thinks, it's been a while though, and he could do with another root soon enough, regardless of what the sergeant reckoned.

It isn't natural for so many men to be without women for so long, he thinks. It has a way of bringing out the beast in you. But maybe that's what the top brass wanted, to encourage you to fight.

Still it wasn't natural. No wonder the internees carried on the way they did. Then he had a sudden thought—maybe the Sergeant was scared of women. He'd met a few blokes like that. Most of them were a little mad, and he was a mad bugger alright. War did that to some blokes, he knew, sent them right over the edge. Only a small handful of the guards had been over there and knew that though. Some had been at Gallipoli or in France, and then been deemed unfit for further service and had been sent home. Home to this. Like that crazy bugger Private Cutts-Smith. He had a dangerous streak to him, like that scar on his face was a warning to people that he was to be left alone. And who bloody knew what he might have been like before the war?

It was Simpson's lungs that had copped it. A gas attack in France. That was bloody something that didn't bear remembering. And he reckoned his ears had suffered a bit too. Or at least he tells the sergeant that every now and then when it appeared he hasn't responded to an order quick enough. The Sergeant was sometimes a bit softer on those who'd been over there. Sometimes.

He looks down at his watch. It is too dark to see. He lifts the cover off the lamp by his feet and peers at it again. 8.50. Over three hours still to go. He covers the lamp again. They aren't meant to have too much light in the towers. It makes you go night blind and then you couldn't see a thing out there. Not that he reckons there is ever going to be anything much to see.

But the Sergeant had given all the men a lecture this week about extra vigilance. Told them that military discipline has to be upheld. Told them they should never take things for granted. Told them to be ever alert.

Alert for what? Private Simpson wonders. He pulls out his tobacco pouch and rolls a small cigarette. Thin and bent. He lights it and draws it in slowly. Then holds it down below the rail where it won't be seen. That's what a fellah needs. A smoke now and then. He coughs and wheezes and has to wait a minute to get his breath back. He wonders if his lungs'll ever be right again. Takes a deep breath of the chill night air then takes another small pull on the cigarette.

This is better than the front, he thinks. A smoke and bit of music. The tune isn't to his taste, but it's alright. When he first got posted here he was determined to hate the internees. He imagines he could sit up in the tower and snipe at them down in the yard. They were the enemy. Huns! But it was hard to maintain that. None of them were soldiers. They'd never fired gas or bullets at him. And a lot of them seemed pretty lonely and miserable themselves.

He coughs again and then unbuttons his top pocket and pulls out a small flask. Takes a quick sip. Just a small one. The Sergeant has warned them about drinking on duty—threatened disciplinary action to anyone caught. But what kind of a guard would he be if he wasn't able to even see the Sergeant stomping around the prison yard? Then he takes another pull on the cigarette. He smiles to himself and looks out into the darkness of the headland. It is so dark out there in the bush that a hundred men could be sneaking up on them and they'd never know it until they'd reached the walls.

The thought makes him peer into the darkness. And for a moment he thinks he sees a dark shape moving there. A man running, bent low. Or maybe an animal. He stares harder. But there is no other movement.

He shakes his head and turns back to look beyond the prison, far off towards South West Rocks. Yeah, he could do with a dance this Saturday. A few cold beers. Maybe a few more. Some local sheila pressed up close. Getting his end in. He hears the music stop and the internees burst into applause.

Cripes, what a fuss, he thinks. And you couldn't even dance to it.

The men are staring into a forest. Heavily wooded and dark. There is a short bird-like trill in the air that rises and fades. Then a dark figure is seen moving behind the trees. Just a vague outline. Stooped and menacing. Then it is gone. They listen for the bird call again, but there is nothing. Just the dark stillness of the woods. It makes them uneasy. They look for movement.

Then they hear soft footsteps in the distance. They peer expectantly. It is a man and a woman. They stride into the forest dressed as if they are on their way to a ball. The man has on a dark tuxedo and top hat. And the woman, ah the woman is beautiful. She is young and thin and wears a long flowing gown. Her bust is not too big, nor small, and not too exposed, with a string of pearls hanging invitingly over it. She has blonde hair tied up above her head.

She hangs onto the gentleman's arm and looks about in alarm. Then, throwing one hand up to her forehead, she says, "Oh Hänsel, I fear we are lost."

"Be strong, dear Gretel," he says. "We shall overcome all adversity." She clasps his arm tighter and he smiles into her eyes. They stand there for a moment as if they might kiss—and then suddenly Hänsel looks up and points. "A house," he says. "We are saved!"

Now, through the trees they can see there is a house. Light is shining onto it, showing it in a clearing. It is brightly coloured and decorated as if it were made from gold and silver. The thatch on the roof is like thick wheat.

Hänsel and Gretel make their way over to the house. "Look at these riches," says Hänsel, and his eyes open wide. "It is beautiful," says Gretel.

"We should take just a small amount to sustain ourselves," says Hänsel. "Do you think we should?" asks Gretel. "But there is plenty for all," says Hänsel, "And we require so little." He steps up to the house and begins scrapping at the wall.

Then the door burst open and an ugly old woman steps out. *"Ein Hexe!"* says Gretel—A witch! The old woman is wearing a khaki-coloured dress with brass buttons up the front. She points a rifle at Hänsel and Gretel and says, "You are my prisoners!" And at gun point she forces them into the house.

It takes a while to see clearly on the inside. It is so dim. The walls are tall and dark. Granite blocks. The windows are barred. Hänsel is in a tiny cell and Gretel is slaving over a large pot. The witch is sitting on a chair, drinking and smoking. Gretel looks at her carefully as she works, watching her drink more and more.

"When will you let my brother free?" she asks her sweetly.

"When I am good and ready," says the witch, patting her belly. "Only when I am good and ready."

"But we have been prisoners here for over two years now. Surely you realise we can't do you any harm?"

"What has harm got to do with it?" asks the witch looking around. "I can keep you here because you are in my power. And anyway, I want to fatten up that brother of yours a little bit more."

"But the food you give him is so bland, how can you expect to fatten him up?"

"I'll keep him in his cell until he fattens up," she says. "But tell me, does he look any fatter to you? I can't see so well."

"No," says Gretel. "In fact, I think he's losing weight."

"You're not exercising in there are you?" the witch demands, standing up and pointing an accusing finger at Hänsel. Then she sits down heavily. Takes another long drink from her bottle. Belches loudly. Then leans back in her chair, her head nodding slowly.

Gretel, still stirring the pot, watches and waits. Soon the witch is snoring. Then Gretel lowers the spoon and tip-toes over to her brother's cell. She places her fingers upon her lips to let him know to be very quiet. Then she tip-toes back to the sleeping witch and pulls a large ring of keys from her pocket. She quickly opens Hänsel's cell door and the two of them move to the back of the room where they pull something out of a box. They are tall Prussian Guardsmen's hats. They put them on and Hänsel then snatches up the witch's rifle and shouts in English, "Up! Up!"

Gretel kicks the witch's chair and she falls to the floor. She looks up in surprise to see the two of them now both shouting at her. "Get dressed! Get up! Out! Now!"

She cowers beneath them and they reach down, grasping her by the arms and drag her into the empty cell. Hänsel slams the door and Gretel locks it tight. Then they embrace and look into each other's eyes—and then they kiss.

Private Simpson jumps up with a start and points his rifle into the darkness—ready to fire. Then he realises he has been dozing. The applause and laughter from the audience down in the prison hall has startled him. He thought—just for a moment—that it was that distant roar of an attacking enemy on the Western Front.

Private Gunn, a local boy, is sitting in the barracks snapping the newspaper in front of him. Over and over. As if crackling the paper might affect the words somehow. Might make them fly around the barracks and assault the other men the way they are attacking him. He had been reading the roll call of the dead and missing, and finds it overwhelms him. So many new names every day. You could cut them out and start sticking them up on the walls of the prison, he thinks, and you'd soon fill the whole prison walls in them. The idea of that many dead is more than he can take in, so he turns to things in the paper than he can better grasp.

"Listen to this," he says in a loud voice, his face reddening like his short-cropped red hair. "Just listen to this and see if your blood doesn't boil. It says here that the Hun have not only raped and murdered nuns in Belgium, but that they have chopped the hands off little children."

He looks up over the top of the newspaper to see that the men around him are listening. Are looking at him. Then he snaps the newspaper again. "It says here that there are dozens of children in Britain, refugees from France and Belgium, with no hands! Chopped off by the Hun!" His voice breaks a little. "'Struth! Dozens of 'em, it says."

He folds the newspaper and throws it the man next to him. "They're animals," he says. "I can't wait to get over there and teach them a lesson."

He looks around the barracks and his eyes catch those of another member of the Dark Knights. They nod at each other silently.

The man on the bed next to his though, Private Cutts-Smith, a wounded veteran of France with a large angry red scar across one whole side of his face, hands the newspaper back to him. And as he does, he turns his face so the normal side is facing Private Gunn.

"No," says Gunn. "Read it. Read what they're doing to women and children. It'd make you want to sign up again to go back over there—sure it would."

But Private Cutts-Smith shakes his head a little. "I don't reckon anything's make me want to go back over there again."

"But read what it says," says Gunn, still red in the face. "It says they're killing nuns and children."

"It says that in the paper, does it?" asks Private Cutts-Smith slowly. He holds Private Gunn's glance a moment, then turns his head the other way to stare at him from the burned and twisted side of his face. He lets the newspaper fall onto Private Gunn's bed and he lies down and looks up at the ceiling. Perhaps remembering all the stories about the front that he'd ever read in the papers before he got there.

Arno sees the dark figure making his way down the corridors of the old prison towards him. Sees the slow predatory gait and thinks it might be the man-beast returned. And he thinks in an instant that he has misunderstood the creature—it might not be Herr Eckert's own nightmare that had slain him, but the nightmare creation of one of the other men, who is knowingly or not, slaying his fellow internees through his nightmares.

But the figure, he now sees, is not walking down the corridors as he first thought; it is making its way through a dark forest. Dead branches reach down to pluck at the figure, but it expertly weaves its way through them. It is hunting something. Arno can feel the emotions in the figure. Lust and hunger. They mask the identity of the dreamer as effectively as the dark cloak it wears. He can only follow the dream and hope to identify which of his fellow internees it is at some point.

The figure slows and moves more cautiously now. It is close to its prey. It moves to a large tree and peers around it. Arno can hear soft children's voices on the other side. A young boy and girl. The figure watches them closely and sees they are lost. This fills the figure with glee. Then the boy and girl see a house through the woods and run towards it. The figure follows them and then the background changes and they are in the house. Or an office. Or a school room. And the young boy and girl are captive inside it.

The young boy is in a cage and the young girl is doing domestic chores. She sweeps and bends over to pick things up. The figure is not in the room with them though. He is in a nearby room peering in through a hole in the door. He watches the young girl closely. Watches the way she bends over, revealing a glimpse down her top, or the shape of her rump.

She is not a young child anymore. She is perhaps fifteen or sixteen. Not an adult either. Her low-cut blouse allows a view of her small breasts when she bends over, and her dress is short enough to see the shape of her legs.

The lust and hunger in the figure watching is frantic now, and Arno can feel the desire building as the figure frees his dick and starts violently rubbing himself. The girl perhaps knows he is there—but perhaps not, yet starts moving her hips a little, as to encourage him.

Arno can feel the figure's climax building. Can feel the lust possessing him as if turning him into a wild beast. He wants to reach out and grab the girl. Throw her to the ground and rip her clothes off. Press his body to hers. Taste her skin in his mouth. But he makes no move to come closer to the dream girl. He does not attack her. He just stands there watching. And rubbing himself furiously.

Until the climax comes. Like an earthquake shaking the dream apart.

And as the dream fades into feelings of relief and pleasure and shame, Arno knows the figure. Recognises the man as the transforming lust fades. It is Herr Herausgeber. He has had similar dreams before. The dreams of a man with a dark side to his passions, and Arno wonders if those passions might be strong enough to lead to another's death?

2
Another Day

Arno is making his way around the prison walls again in the pre-dawn darkness, running his hands across the cold stone walls, trying to find any trace of Herr Herausgeber's nightmare when he sees movement up ahead of him. He moves a little closer to the wall. Cautiously. Then sees it is a man being set upon by two or three others. Their outlines are dark and indistinct. Even the sounds they make are muffled, like they are coming from a long way away. Suddenly one of the figures glances up and sees him. It snarls, or something like it, and pulls the other figures away into the darkest shadows.

By the time Arno reaches the place they are gone. He looks around on the grass beneath his feet and there is no indication that anyone had ever been there. He touches the wall at that spot and is certain he can feel an angry growl vibrating softly through his hands.

He stands there for the longest of times, no longer certain that his understanding of the worlds of dark and light are correct. No longer so certain that he has any power to protect the other internees in the prison. Wondering if he is in a dream of his own or not.

The news is all around the dining hall the next day, before Herr Herausgeber has even arrived to hear it. Herr Eckert has died on the journey to Sydney. A doctor had declared him dead on arrival. Heart disease. It could kill anyone at any time. The news makes for a very quiet morning meal. Many men stare silently into their porridge, stirring lumps around in the bowls or stirring thoughts around in their minds. It is their first death in the camp. The first real reminder of their mortality. It makes them remember there is still a wider world out there—a world still at war. That unspoken word.

Arno sees Horst is particularly shaken by the death. His face looks pale and he goes back to their cell after having only a few nibbles at his bread. Arno imagines he will be lying back on his bunk now, turning into that living breathing pile of fetid blankets, wondering if he too is about to die suddenly? Wondering perhaps if he could at least get to Sydney before he dies? Wondering if that would be worth it?

Horst's wife and two small children are in Sydney. He doesn't talk about them much, but he writes incessantly—and he receives letters regularly. His wife prints in a tiny hand that is near indecipherable to anyone but Horst. It looks like some sort of a code to Arno. When Horst gets the letters he lies on his bunk and reads them and re-reads them all day long. Then he adds them to the cardboard box of letters he has on his shelf. Some days he will take them all out and sort through them, as if putting a jigsaw puzzle together.

Arno has been Horst's cell mate for two years now and he doesn't even know the names of his children. Doesn't even know their ages. Maybe he'd told him once, when they were still speaking, but it has long since faded from his memory. He often wonders why Horst doesn't display any pictures of them though. Most of the internees with family have pictures of their wives and children stuck up above their beds. They go to sleep looking at their wives, and cuddling the memories of their bodies with them, and wake up to the smiles of their children.

But the two of them have no reminders of family on display. Horst because he hides them and Arno because he doesn't have any. He wonders if it would be worse living in a cell where every day he would look up and see another man's family—wife and children, or parents and grandparents. Perhaps a photo of a child in Germany, standing by a parent, holding his father's hand. But would he wake up each morning and imagine that the photo was of himself? Was his own father?

And Arno suddenly resents Horst for not having pictures of a father on his wall and for hiding them from him. Like he hides so much from him. He's woken some nights and thought he could hear Horst sobbing quietly, and looked across to see him masturbating under his blanket. That is something else nobody talks about. Though some warm Saturday mornings, after one of the more erotic plays, the cells reek of the humid fug of semen.

Arno wonders how the convict men of the previous generation had fared. Whether the guards worked them to a point of fatigue to keep their callused hands from flogging themselves, or whether they engaged in more hidden activities? He knows there are some men in the prison who are more affectionate with each other than is talked about. He's heard the soft moans of cell mates on his early morning circuit of the walls. Heard the groans of passion and release escaping up through the bars and knows the dreams that some men have of finding love in another man's arms. But it is also never spoken of.

It is said that the French and English might engage in homosexuality—but the Germans, never! Yet Arno knows, like all the internees know sooner or later, that they are as human as each other. For so very few of them have ever looked at another man on the beach, and suddenly felt as giddy as if a wave had tipped them sideways. There are so many emotions and passions locked up inside the men, all locked up in the old prison.

And then Arno sees Herr Herausgeber arrive to breakfast. He watches him sit down at a distant table and sees him hear the news of Herr Eckert's death from those around him. He too shows shock and sadness. But Arno can see he is already planning how best to write the story. Should he talk to the dead man's friends, or write a long metaphorical obituary of him as a hero—the first amongst their comrades to fall?

Arno gathers his crutches and limps over to the editor's side. "I've just heard the news," he says to the older man. "It is tragic isn't it."

"Yes, my boy," says Herr Herausgeber, shaking his head. "I cannot understand how such a thing can happen so suddenly."

"Heart disease," says Arno, and also shakes his head.

"Terrible. Terrible," says Herr Herausgeber, stirring his breakfast around and around.

"I've heard," says Arno, lowering his voice, "that it is brought on by masturbating." He gathers his crutches and limps out of the hall, leaving Herr Herausgeber with a spoon full of porridge frozen half-way between his plate and his gawping mouth.

At 9.00 Arno is again standing at the prison gates, looking at his watch, waiting for the guards to come and open them. When the guard finally steps out of the guardhouse, he smiles to some of the men he knows by name and makes a big fuss of putting the key into the lock just so, as if it is some vastly complex task that needs great skill to perform. Finally, he stands back and the internees push the gates open and surge out.

Arno follows, shielding his eyes from the bright blueness of the ocean. It seems so much brighter than it had been the day before. So large. So calming. He breathes in the scent of the land and the sea. It is quite windy today and he knows the language of the wind through the trees and shrubs is an unknown language to many of the internees, while the language of the wind through the barred windows is one that they have learned.

He turns his head slowly, looking for the smoking stacks of ships. Looking for anything new. But like the day before there is nothing, so he follows the internees down past the little village of cafes and inns towards the beach. It is still windy even on the inside of the headland, and many of the men do not come all the way down to the sands. The athletics club is there on the beach, of course. They are always there. It is a matter of pride and principal for them. But few of them are going into the water.

Arno makes his way across the sand and then down the water's edge. He stops there and turns back to look at the prison walls behind him. No matter where you look on this beautiful headland those stark stone walls always draw your eyes back to them, he thinks. And Arno wishes that for just one day he was rid of them. Wishes he could sit somewhere and not have to see the prison. Wishes he could find a small cove somewhere sheltered from the wind where he could see only the ocean and the sky. No prison, no guards, no inmates—and no granite walls.

He turns and looks along the breakwater across the bay and he wonders how far he would have to go to find somewhere that was far enough to be free of the prison, but where the war hadn't yet reached? He looks towards the northern end of the bay, towards the low shape of Freedom Island—and he stares at it and wonders how it got that name—and wonders if it too might just be a fantasy?

Arno folds his clothes carefully and places them by his crutches. He turns and limps into the water, making his way out until it is above his thighs and then he drops quickly up to his armpits. He exhales sharply. Feels his testicles retreat. Squeezes his legs together a little. There is a chill current in the bay today. He flaps his arms back and forth under the water, getting the blood moving. Then he turns and begins swimming with a strong slow stroke that carries him steadily onwards.

The wind is raising waves about him today. They batter him in the face as he swims, slapping him as he tries to take a breath and pushing water into his mouth. He lowers his head and keeps swimming. It will be much rougher further out, he thinks.

Soon he stops and treads water. He feels the strength in his legs as they kick beneath him, holding him up. He feels the emptiness beneath his feet. The chill of the deeper current down there. The cold water makes him think of sharks. He has been told they like to follow cold currents. Several have been sighted in the bay and they have built a little watchtower on the sands where men take it in turns to watch for the dark menacing shadows in the water.

Arno turns and looks to the raised chair. It is empty today. He wonders whose turn it is to be on guard duty? Then he turns and looks to the prison. He can see a guard in the southwest watchtower there watching him. Perhaps. He wonders if he can see sharks from there. It is a much better height, but too far away to shout any warning though. But not too far away for the guard to shoot him if he needed. And he wonders if he could ever be driven to want to kill another man. He tries to feel deep within himself if he could. Then he suddenly feels the skin on his legs turning to goose bumps, as if something chill and dark had come very close to him. He turns and swims quickly back to the shore, leaving that knowledge that had touched him out in the chill currents of the bay.

Captain Eaton is sitting in his office, under the portrait of his King and the two crossed flags, and is staring at Sergeant Gore, who stands stiffly to attention in front of him. "So you are saying your investigation has achieved nothing?" he asks the Sergeant tersely. Though it was difficult to expect it to have really, he knows, considering the Sergeant does not know how Herr Eckert was murdered. He has only told him that he was found dead in his cell and that foul play was suspected.

The Sergeant has just reported to him that Herr Eckert had few friends, no known enemies, and did not appear to be involved in either gambling or illicit alcohol production or consumption.

The Sergeant does not meet his eyes. Staring fixed at the King. "But I am sure you have done your best," he tells the Sergeant, softening his tone.

The Captain had reported to his wife the previous evening that one of the internees had died, with even less information than he had given the Sergeant, and she had reacted as expected, cursing his Hun soul to damnation.

"The man was a businessman, not a soldier," he had protested.

"He was a Hun!" she had replied. "We should never have let them into the country. We should put them on leaky boats and sent them to prison camps on remote desert islands."

"There is hardly cause for that," he had said.

"If you don't see it you are a fool, or a coward," she had told him.

She would fit in well in the Department of Defence, he thought, and despite his promises to himself he had carried the pricks of her barbed words into work with him, making him short-tempered.

"Sergeant," he says, in what he hopes is more comradely tone than he is used to addressing the man with, "These are troubling times."

"Yes sir!" barks the Sergeant. Captain Eaton feels his shoulders sag just a little. He wonders if he could share his burden with this man? Wonders if he has a distant wife as well? Wonders if could just talk to him?

"Sergeant," he says again, realising he does not even recall his first name, "I am greatly troubled. Assaulted on all fronts, as it were. Our position is perilous."

The Sergeant says nothing. Remains at attention. Staring fixedly up at the portrait of the King, as if it might be addressing him personally.

Captain Eaton brings his hands together and knots his fingers tightly. Then he separates them. Then knots them again. "The death of Herr

Eckert is not good for us, you understand. Not good for us at all."

The Sergeant says nothing.

"And things are a bit awkward on the home front," the Captain adds, staring down at the desktop. "Not as good as I'd like them to be. Not getting the type of support I would like, don't you know?"

Still Sergeant Gore says nothing. Good, thinks Captain Eaton, the man is a listener. "I've been trying to determine how to improve the situation, but it's not easy, not easy at all. We're so isolated here, after all."

He looks up and sees the Sergeant's eyes glance at him briefly, clearly having no idea what he is talking about. "And news from the front is not good," he continues. "So many good lads dying, and we're stuck here unable to do anything about it." He shakes his head a little. Feels his shoulders sagging again. Lifts them.

"I don't quite know what to do, Sergeant." He stares at the man who nods his head and says, "Yes sir!" Then snaps his attention back up to the portrait of the King on the wall.

Captain Eaton stares at him for a while. He is a little envious of the man's war experiences. His control over the men. His respect from them. He knows how different that makes them, and knows he will never really be able to talk to him.

"That will be all," he says.

"Sir!" barks the Sergeant and spins on one foot. He stamps the other down hard and marches out of his office. Captain Eaton waits until he is gone before letting his shoulders sink heavily down around him once more.

It is 11.07 by Arno's watch and he is in the infirmary with Nurse Rosa. She has lifted one of his feet against her thighs as she massages it, turning it one way and then the other, working on the muscles within.

Arno has his eyes half closed and is looking down between his legs at her. Her brow is slightly knit, concentrating on her work. Then she suddenly looks up at him and smiles. "The other foot," she says in German.

"Ja," says Arno. Then he asks, "Where did you learn your German?"

"In school," she says. As she says whenever he asks.

But today he wants a different answer. "Do you know what I think?" he says.

"No. Tell me."

"I think you might have learned it from a family member."

She gives him a sharp look. "And why might you think that?"

He shrugs. "It is just something I imagine."

"Tell me what else you imagine," she says, still working on his leg.

"I imagine your mother or father was German," he says.

"*Nein,*" she says. "They were French."

"Your grandmother then?"

She does not answer.

"What was she like?" he asks.

"All I will tell you is that she was wise enough to tell me not to answer any dangerous questions like that," she says.

"Do you remember her well?" Arno asks.

"I remember many things about her. What do you remember of your grandparents?"

"Nothing," he says. They had never left Germany. A country he has never visited.

"Then your parents?" she asks.

He wants to tell her those few memories that he has of them. He has a distant misshapen memory of his father guiding him along some bush track, holding his hand to keep him from stumbling. Has another ill-formed memory of suckling his mother's breasts as an infant. And snuggling up between them both in bed—the softness of his mother and the tough firmness of his father. But he suspects they are as much imaginings as memories. His earliest solid memories are of being shunted between smiling but unspeaking aunts. One, small and fat and smelling of cabbages and vinegar, took his reluctant hand and led him to school, and another, thin and unsmiling, picked him up afterwards. None of them seemed to know what to do with the young crippled boy. Until he was old enough to go out to work. But who wanted a migrant worker who was unfit for any manual work? So, he had trained his brain. Learned English. Learned a little accounting. Learned to be useful in an office. But he also learned that no matter how much of the language he acquired he would never really be accepted here. He would always be a migrant—a boy without a country as much as he was a boy without a family.

"My family are not very interesting," he says. "Tell me more about yours."

But she will not be drawn any more. "Enough questions about me," she says. "Tell me some news from inside the camp instead."

The ways she says camp makes it sound as if it could be a fun place to live, like some kind of an adventure, rather than imprisonment.

"There is nothing much," he says. Nothing except Herr Eckert's death, he thinks.

She turns his foot a little to one side. "Well what are the men talking about this week then?"

He knows he is meant to say, "Just the usual." Though he knows that down in their cafes and clubs by the walls of the prison the men talk guardedly of two main things: the war and sex—which are both talked of in euphemisms. But Nurse Rose must suspect that the men talk of her, as they watch her like a wolf watches its prey whenever she walks through the yard wearing her little red cape and cap. She must know that some men circle around the infirmary building all day, longing for just a glimpse of her, and if not for Doctor Hertz, men would be wounding themselves just to be admitted to her care. Just to be near her. Arno knows they would cut themselves with knives or would bite their fingers off, or would scald their chests with hot water, if only she would be the one who would treat them.

But Doctor Hertz has made it very clear that he will not treat any cases that look slightly self-inflicted, and that Nurse Rosa is only there as his assistant. Which makes many men resent Arno. Most are too polite to say it, but some have told him he is a faker. Told him he could walk, except that then the Nurse wouldn't jerk him off every day. Some resent his treatments by her hands so much that they have told him that he should never have been allowed out of Holsworthy with them, for he is not really an elite like they are. Then they will tell him that his German accent is worse than a Frenchman's or a Pole's, and that he tortures the words of their mother tongue. But then they might calm down again and plead with him to describe in detail what she does to him each day.

He decides that the next time someone asks him, he will tell them, "She dances for me." But what he says to Nurse Rosa is, "They are concerned about Herr Eckert's death."

Nurse Rosa looks at him and he sees the sadness pass across her face. "Yes. I heard about his heart condition. It was very sudden I was told."

"Was he being treated here for it?" Arno asks.

"No. It was unknown until he fell sick."

"They lay him right here on this bed," says Arno.

She nods again, then thinks. "How did you know that?"

And Arno thinks of telling her then. Feels that she is one person he can trust in the prison, and he can tell her that he saw Herr Eckert there, and he knows he did not die of heart disease. He can tell her that he saw the blood and the look of terror on the dead man's face, and that intern Meyer took a photograph of his body. That they know he was murdered, even if they don't know it was by a nightmare creature, but are covering up. That she needs to know what type of man the doctor is.

He feels he could just say it. Just keep talking to her and say it. But then, as if summonsed by his thoughts, Doctor Hertz walks in.

"How are you feeling?" he asks Arno. As he asks every day. Arno looks up and says, "Good enough." As he answers every day. Then the doctor puts one hand on Nurse Rosa's shoulder and she turns to smile at him. A warm smile that Arno has never seen before.

"We have to discuss some patient photographs when you are finished," he says.

"Not long now," she says, and looks back to Arno's leg, but with that smile still on her face. Arno lies back and closes his eyes, thinking that he understands a little better now the jealous feelings the men have towards him.

Arno makes his way into the cell just in time to see the small bird fly up from Horst's bunk and speed out the window. He only catches a quick glimpse of its tiny pale body with a streak of red in it somewhere. It must have landed on the barred windowsill and for some reason decided to fly into the cell. It had settled on the bunk beside Horst there. Why had the small bird not feared Horst? He thinks all this in the time it takes for the bird to speed out the cell window. And then he sees Horst's hands fly up after it, as if attempting to follow it out of the bars and away.

Then he sees his own diary open on the bed in front of Horst. He looks at it. Looks at Horst. His cell mate closes it and throws it to Arno's bunk. Shrugs. Mutters, "Mad ramblings!" And he turns away from him.

In the afternoon Arno has time to fill and he wanders down to the small village the men have built outside the lower walls, deciding to treat himself to a meal. He is still trying to understand the danger he feels they are all in during the darkness. He goes into one of the huts there, grandiosely proclaiming itself the Cafe Alpine. A group of men are sitting inside, staring at pictures on the walls. Some are of Alpine scenes from Germany, or perhaps Switzerland. Tall peaks with snow on them. Some are shots of German towns, and some are of women, smiling at the camera.

Arno sits by himself and watches the way they stare with a deep need at the soft curves of those female bodies. These men without homes. Men without women. Men with nothing but their fantasies and memories. He has shared the dreams of all of them. The longing for a wife, a girl from one's youth and even the rotund man with the dark moustache, Herr Schmidt, who dreams unashamedly of his childhood teddy bear climbing into his bed and fondling him.

The cafe proprietor comes over and Arno orders beer and veal. *Bier und Kalbfleisch.* Then he sits and waits and thinks again of Herr Eckert, and Nurse Rosa, and the doctor, and he watches the men again watching the pictures on the walls. As if it is all a part of a big puzzle.

The men's conversation is about memories of home. What a town looked like in winter. What a particular dish tasted like. What an old girl-friend's smile was like. But their eyes never leave the pictures.

After a while his meal is brought to him. Arno eats slowly. *Bier und Kalbfleisch.* But he knows it is mutton dressed as veal. Knows it is ale dressed as beer. As he knows they are men dressed as women.

That evening's play is announced during dinner. It will be the story of Pandora's box. Many of the men wink at each other and laugh. It is a crude expression that most are familiar with. They haven't had a saucy play for some time and so they are settled into the audience extra early, tapping their feet and fidgeting. Waiting expectantly.

The orchestra plays briefly. Something sultry that few know the name of and most do not care. They are all awaiting the play. Waiting for Scheherazade to come on stage. Waiting to watch her move slowly from one side to another, her hands encircling her body like caresses, slow and fast and slow again.

When she finally comes they aren't disappointed. She is in good form this evening. As she removes one of her many veils, she says, "Tonight, the story of Pandora. The first woman on earth—given to man to prove his undoing." She dances again. "Fashioned by the gods of Olympus at the request of Zeus, father of the gods, to bring ruin to mankind." Again the hands encircling her body. "She was given life by Athena. Beauty by Aphrodite. And she was taught guile and treachery by Hermes—then she was sent to the realm of men."

She dances to the edge of the stage and then pauses. "Pandora was the most beautiful of women, but she had a casket that contained all the evils of the world, and had been bidden by Zeus never to open it. But could woman be trusted? That is the subject of our play." Then with a flourish she is gone.

Now a single violin sounds. A high slow lament. And Pandora walks onto the stage. All the men in the audience stop breathing. She is stunning. She wears a long flowing white gown, such as the ancient Greeks must have worn, wrapped tightly around her body, leaving the arms exposed. Her breasts are accentuated by two thongs of leather wound over her shoulders and crossing over her chest. She moves slowly, walking barefoot, with the motion of a slow-moving wave, gently swaying as she makes her way to the centre of the stage. Her thick black hair is bound into a long single plait with more leather thongs. It hangs straight down her back, past her waist. Long enough to climb up. But her face is heavily veiled—as the face of the first woman, the most beautiful woman in the world, should be.

She walks to the front of the small stage, looking out beyond the audience, and then takes a deep breath, lifts her arms and breasts high as she does so. Every man in the hall rises slightly in their chairs with her. Then she begins to dance. A dance without music, but a dance that needs none. Slow graceful steps, with her hands moving in wide circles about her, then darting in close and shooting out again. Something wild and graceful in the moves.

She dances to the centre of the stage and then bends over low, swaying her hands right down to touch the floor. Then she stands up slowly, both hands running up her legs, climbing up her shins and thighs, lingering ever so slowly at her waist and then the fingers spread across her stomach until they come to rest under her breasts. She cups them for just an instant and then brings her hands up to her face, as if they are not her hands but the hands of her lover. The hands of every man there in the hall.

"Mein Gott!" one old man mumbles. Then he swallows very hard and feels his heart beating against his ribs. Wonders if he is going to die. Hopes it won't be before the end of the performance.

Pandora's dance continues. She comes to the front of the stage again, her arms floating out from her, and then she turns and twirls, moving back to the centre stage, going through the motions of the first woman exploring her new body. Each time a little bolder. Each time a little firmer. Each time she steps a little closer to the box at the side of the stage. The dim kerosene lamps throw shadows across the back of the stage as she dances. Huge dark shadows of her lithe figure, that twist and turn and move like some spectral fantasy in the men's minds.

Finally, she is next to the box and stops dancing. She reaches out and touches its lid. Runs her hands along the surface as if it is warm and pleasurable. She begins caressing the box. Running her fingers across it. Bringing her body up close and letting her hair fall upon it. Then she bends down and kisses the lid. Once and then once again. Then she places her hands on the clasp.

The hall is silent. Some men are sitting on the very edges of their chairs. Others have their hands in their laps, feeling the tingling need there. Pandora turns her head and for the very first time looks directly at the men in the audience. The feeling, for many of them, is like being shot in the sternum. Then she throws the lid of the chest open wide.

A sudden heavy drum beat sounds. A quick pow-pow-pow. Pandora reaches in both arms, deep into the chest and lifts something out. She turns her back to the audience to shield it. It is the evils that will plague the world, they know, and yet every man there wants to see what it is.

Then she spins and holds it aloft for everyone to see. It is a large sheet of paper. Blank paper. Some at the back lean forward and whisper, *"Was ist es?"*—what is it. Try to see if there is anything written on it. But there is nothing.

And Pandora's eyes smile as she steps forward and turns it slowly around to reveal it is a photograph of herself—which she holds out to the audience, offering it to them. Offering herself to them. At first nobody moves. Then one man in the front row stands up and makes a snatch for the photograph. The man beside him is only marginally slower and grabs the first man to stop him getting it. Then two men from the second row are jumping over their chairs to get there. Men up the back call out and stand to their feet. Push their way forward.

Suddenly the hall has become a battle-field. Men are shouting and locked in hand-to-hand combat, scrabbling to get to the front. Scrabbling to claim Pandora's prize. Some men scream at others to stand out of their way. Others push chairs aside. Some duck below the swinging limbs of larger men, while carefully edging forward. All of them are trying to get to the front of the hall where the photograph is. Where Pandora has been.

For Pandora has long since fled the stage. And the precious photograph—the source of all the world's evils—has been ripped to shreds by the many frantic hands that are fighting to grab hold of it.

Sergeant Gore walks past each of the six men and examines them closely. As if they are on parade. They stand stiffly to attention. Eyes forward, staring above the Sergeant's head, paying no heed to the drop behind them.

"Good," the Sergeant says. "Very good." He walks back along the line and turns to address them. "The Commandant has been talking to me. Called me in for a little talk. Let me know there are concerns at how things are going over in France. Concerns about what's being done for the war effort here. Has let me know just how serious it is." He pauses. "You won't find this printed in the newspapers. They keep this type of information away from the populace. Wouldn't want to panic them. But I know I can trust you each with it."

He watches as pride expands the men a little. "But I'm also telling you this so you'll know how much extra effort you are going to need to put into your training. It might be that you are called upon to become the last line of defence for this corner of the Empire." He pauses again. Lets the words sink in. Then he says it again. "The last line of defence." Then, "And that is what we are going to practice tonight—fighting with your backs to the walls. Single hand-to-hand combat."

Private Gunn is a little confused. Why has the Sergeant gotten them out here at night time to stand atop the small cliff if they are meant to be fighting against a wall? But he has learned enough not to question him. Learned to wait for the lesson to become apparent.

"I'm not going to tell you the rules, and I'm not even going to tell you where I will start, but I will attack each of you, one by one, and you must see if you can retain your footing on this land without being pushed off."

Now Private Gunn gets the point of it and turns to look at the Sergeant just in time to see him shoot out one arm and push Private Cooper off the edge. He was still standing at attention and Private Gunn hears his faint calls of alarm and surprise as he tumbles down the slope to the beach below.

"You never know when a surprise attack might come, nor where it might come from," says Sergeant Gore, and he feints at Private Smythe, who throws up his arms, but then the Sergeant kicks at the legs of the man next to him, catching him off balance, then he pushes him quickly over the edge too. Sends him tumbling to the sands below.

The Sergeant straightens up slowly. Watches the men carefully. Only four left now. All still standing at attention. But their eyes are on him. "Diversionary attacks aren't always what they seem," he says. He stands squarely in front of Private Strap. Looks at him. Dougie Strap licks his lips and shuffles his feet a little. Unsure whether he is allowed to lift his hands up yet. The Sergeant walks in close to him. Private Strap licks his lips again. Is thinking about what the Sergeant said about numerical supremacy. Wonders if they're meant to attack him in a group and are meant to overwhelm him that way. But he isn't sure. So he waits for the Sergeant to make the first move. It is one he doesn't expect. Sergeant Gore spins his head towards Private Gunn, as if to catch him doing something. Dougie Strap turns his head too. And he thinks for a moment that his mate is coming to help him. Is going to grab the Sergeant from that side.

But then he feels the fist in his chest. Feels it knocking him backwards. Feels himself sliding down the slope, unable to keep his footing. Falling. Hitting his head. Again and again. Landing with a thud in the sand by his two comrades. They help him to his feet and pull him clear. "Watch out," they say. "There'll be somebody else coming down in a moment."

Now there are only three. Sergeant Gore is smiling. "Who's gonna be next?" he asks. The three privates are looking at him, their concern clear on their faces.

Just to prove he can do it Sergeant Gore stands between two of them and sends first one and the other down the slope, shooting out a leg, and pushing at their torsos, tripping them over. First one side and then quickly the other. The men try and grab hold of him. Try not to fall. But they are too close to the edge. Too unwilling to fight back. They land on top of each other and call out in pain. Private Boote is certain his leg is broken.

Then it is only Private Gunn and Sergeant Gore. Facing each other on the small cliff top. Private Gunn tenses his leg muscles and waits for the Sergeant to come within reach. But the Sergeant is being cautious now. Gunn is much bigger and stronger than the others. A hulking country lad.

"Just you and me then, Gunn," he says.

Gunn says nothing. Still at attention. Eyes on the Sergeant. He watches him move to the left of him. Then to the right. Gunn turns a little to face him each time. Sergeant Gore doesn't like that. So he decides to handle him how the Generals always handled the enemy. Front on in full force. He leaps at Private Gunn and shoves with all his might. But Private Gunn is ready for him. The two men meet with a thud. Both pushing heavily. Chest to chest.

Sergeant Gore digs his boots into the dirt and heaves. But Private Gunn is like a brick wall. Refusing to be budged. He pushes back at the Sergeant, working his arms to get hold of him. And the Sergeant feels his feet slipping a little. Feels Private Gunn's strong arms encircling him. And Sergeant Gore feels a familiar stab of terror. Knows he is about to be surrounded. And he wants to call off the fight. Wants to fall to his knees and beg not to be hurt. But suddenly the ground behind Private Gunn gives way. One boot is suddenly slipping away into empty space. Then he is off balance. Sergeant Gore pushes mightily. Feels Gunn release his grip on him. Sees his arms waving in the air. Then hears him tumbling heavily down to the beach below.

The lesson concluded.

Arno is witness to a dream of Pandora that night. The man dreaming of her is standing in the dark, hidden in shadow, and Arno is trying to glimpse his face as he feels the passion and lust filling his body.

Pandora is dancing in a glade, dappled in soft light, oblivious to anyone watching her.

The sun is warm, even through the leaves and she is suddenly on the edge of a pond. She reaches out and tests the water with a toe. Then she bends over to reach out and brings a cup of cool water to her lips.

It pleases her and she begins undressing, to bathe in the pond.

She strips the light garments from her one by one, like removing veils, and casts them into the air, where they float like feathers to the ground.

The figure in the darkness is breathing heavily now, breath coming in heavy pants, as Pandora is piece by piece coming close to nakedness. But suddenly she stops and looks around. She has heard or sensed something. She clasps clothes to her bosom and takes a step away.

The man then steps out of the shadows and steps forward, becoming a beast, his features transforming quickly into a furry dark figure, filled with hunger for her body.

She screams and steps back into the pond as the beast pounces. His claws are like knives and his teeth are as sharp as daggers, but she is too quick for him. She dives into the water and the beast stops at the edge, howling in rage and frustration, as she is just beyond his grasp.

The beast turns and lashes at the trees and bushes, destroying the glade, and ripping her clothes to shreds, all the while screaming what he wants to do to her. Needs to do to her. But she is gone and the beast drops to the ground, panting as if he cannot breathe any more. Panting as if the desire is crushing him. Then he turns and slinks back to the shadows and is gone too.

Another dream of sexual frustration, but not of murder.

3
Another Day

Arno is waking along the wall before daylight, searching carefully for any trace of movement or sound ahead of him. But he sees nothing there today. No trace of violence or danger, or perhaps it is just obscured by the many dreams of passion that the dance of Pandora triggered in the men? He walks the walls and touches the cold stone and tells himself that if there is any danger about them, he will find it.

At breakfast Doctor Hertz is very late in arriving. The whole hall is waiting for him, but they know he has several new patients in the infirmary—cuts and bruises mostly, but also two broken limbs that needed setting last night. If the prison guards hadn't broken things up there might have been more. The men sit quietly, some reliving the battle in their minds, some replaying their part in it so it might have turned out differently. Some whispering questions, questions, questions to those around them. And all awaiting the doctor to make his entrance.

Finally, he strides in, looking rather tired, and takes a seat at the end of one table.

The whole hall is watching him—even if their heads aren't turned fully in that direction. They know what the men around him will ask him—the same question they have been asking each other last night and all morning— "*Wer war Pandora?*"—Who was Pandora? But nobody had known. The other actors didn't know. Herr Schröder, the orchestra conductor, didn't know. Even Herr Dubotzki the camp photographer said he didn't know. He said he didn't take the photograph she offered them. Told then that Doctor Hertz had taken it himself using his own small camera and that he had only requested that he develop and print it for him.

The men quizzed him over and over. Is there any way he could find out who she was? Did he still have the negative? Could he just make one extra print, perhaps, for a small fee?

Then somebody finally asked the unspoken question: what if Pandora had been a woman? A real woman. So many men had woken with a crick in their back from her having danced atop them all night long, but if she had been a real woman there would be no shame in their lustful dreams. The men looked into their porridge and think of that. So many had slept with the thought of her caressing them last night, that Arno felt she must now lived in the stone of the walls of the prison too, and perhaps she might balance out the nightmare beasts that live there, and prevent them from escaping somehow.

The idea of Pandora being a real woman started more questions. Who could it have been? Nurse Rosa? Surely not. One of the local women? Unlikely. They had to know! Who was she?

And then Doctor Hertz walked in. All eyes followed him, watching him sit down, watching the men around him question him casually, watching Doctor Hertz smile and slowly shake his head as the men about him frowned and placed their palms flat on the table and asked him again.

But he slowly shakes his head once more. The men clench their hands into fists and implore him. But he places his own palms on the table, shaking his head sternly and with finality. Then he rises, taking his meal, and walks out of the hall—taking their hopes with him. The men in the hall turn back to their own breakfasts, thinking that perhaps their porridge suddenly tastes a little bitter this morning.

After breakfast Arno is again standing at the prison gates looking at his watch. Again the guards are late. Again the internees stream outside when they are finally thrown open.

Arno, as ever, shields his eyes from the bright blueness of the ocean and looks around. So large. He breathes in the air of his native land and feels himself grow a little larger. Stronger. He turns his head slowly, looking for the smoking stacks of ships. Looking for anything new. Then he turns to make his way down to the beach. He has not gone far though when he hears sharp calls of excited voices ahead of him. The men closest to the beach are running down to the white sands, shouting and calling out.

He follows hurriedly and looks to where they are all pointing. There is something on the beach. Large and dark. A troop ship, is his first thought. But he checks himself and looks at the dark shape again. Sees it for what it actually is—a whale washed ashore.

Men around him are now shouting it out, *"Ein Walfisch!"* And like excited children they all run down to the sands to surround it.

By mid-morning almost all the internees are down on the beach. They are jumping in and out of the water, brandishing buckets and shovels and knives, eager to attack the dead whale that had beached itself in the night. Herr Kaufmann, a former New Guinea-based merchant, has declared the whale to be a sperm whale and its blubber worth a considerable amount if they flense it and boil it down. There is little they can do with the money, but the thought of it puts all the former businessmen into a state of excitement. And their excitement is infectious. Some men tally up rows of profit against the cost of transporting it to Kempsey or to Sydney, where it can be sold. Others look at the logistics of boiling down the blubber in the camp kitchens. The men could live on bread alone for a few days while it was done. And others try to oversee the organisation of the most able-bodied men into disciplined parties that will carve up the whale in small groups, flensing from one end to the other.

Once the word is out that they plan to skin the beast, men come running down the hill with any sharp implement they can find, ready to stick in and cut away any pound of flesh. Herr Kaufmann, who has appointed himself foreman for the whale flensing, based solely on his expertise in organising coolies on his plantation in New Guinea, shouts and rails at the men to no accord. They are quickly up to their arms in blood and blubber and digging deeper into the whale corpse, in a disorganised frenzy. They peel away the flesh and letting the blood pour into the shallow water about their feet.

The whale had obviously beached itself in the night at high tide, and the men are working to claim as much of the blubber as is possible before the tide comes back in again in the afternoon, removing their sudden treasure. They work right through lunch, shouting and laughing, as the guards in the watchtowers look down and shake their heads at them. And as they work the waters slowly rise about their ankles.

Two guards have come down to the beach and sit down, up above the sands, in the shade of a tree, with their rifles across their laps. Never having seen the men so active nor so well armed—they aren't sure what quite to do, and decided to keep their distances with a bullet in the chamber. Just in case.

The whale's body, cut and bleeding, seems to be slowly deflating as the men work. Wheelbarrows are brought down from the camp and the blubber is loaded in and carted slowly back up the hill to the kitchens. Men have Sperm blood all over their arms and through their hair, but keep working, stripping back the blubber and loading it into wheelbarrows.

Sweat and blood and sunshine seep into their eyes, but they wipe it away and keep at the attack. They laugh for the sheer joy of the work. One of the men, Gerhard Rohlfs, has climbed upon the whale's back and is cutting away the blubber there with a shovel, as if he is digging a shallow trench. He cries out suddenly, "I have found gold!" The men look up and laugh, shielding their eyes. And suddenly he is gone. They blink and wipe their brows and look again. His shovel is still there where he had stood but he is gone. Men walk from one side of the whale to the other to see where he has fallen off, but he is not there. He has disappeared.

Then another man climbs up on top of the whale, stepping cautiously closer to where Gerhard Rohlfs had been standing, and calls out, "He has fallen inside! He is inside the whale!"

Now there is consternation. The men hold up their knives and tools, but do not know what best to do with them. How to cut a man out of a whale? The animal has ribs like iron prison bars. Then Herr Kaufmann says, "We must save him. He will suffocate. We can go in through the whale's mouth or through the anus."

The men look at each other and quickly assemble near the whale's mouth.

As many as can fit there grab hold and heave, until they are able to lift the bulk just a little and open the mouth.

Herr Kaufmann steps up close and calls in, "Hallo!" As if shouting down a long dark tunnel. There is no response. He straightens up and says, "We must send somebody in. Somebody small and brave." He looks around as if seeking out the right man from amongst them. But while not wishing to be thought of as not being, many men puff out their chests and strain their shoulders so as to appear not small either.

Finally, Herr Kaufmann jabs his finger at one young man just a few years older than Arno. "You!" he says. "Herr Hess isn't it?"

"Heinz," says the young man slowly. "Karl Heinz." Herr Kaufmann frowns. He had wanted the young man to snap to attention. Perhaps click his bare heels.

"You will go into the whale and rescue Gerhard Rohlfs," he says.

Karl Heinz wrinkles his nose, as if giving this some very careful thought. The men, still holding open the whale's mouth, look back and forth from Karl Heinz to Herr Kaufmann, waiting to see if the young man is going to do it or not. Wanting somebody to move quickly. Straining from the effort of holding the weight of the whale's head.

Then one of the men towards the rear of the whale shouts. He jumps back as if a snake has slithered over his foot. A hand has emerged from some orifice low on the whale's side and has touched his foot. A human hand. He points at it and calls again. Quickly men run to the spot. Some take hold of the hand and others cut at the whale's stomach, cutting into the flesh and intestines, and slowly drag Gerhard Rohlfs free.

He staggers before them like somebody who has just been reborn. Blood and gore sticking to his body. He wipes at it and then looks up at the men around him. They stare silently. Then he throws his head back and laughs, a long ringing laugh that echoes off the distant prison walls and catches up all the men around him. They all burst out laughing as Gerhard throws himself into the ocean. He paddles out in the water and ducks his head under time and time again, scrubbing the gore and blood from his body, and leaping up out of the water and laughing.

The internees are now holding their sides. Are splashing each other in the shallows and are hooting like wild delinquents. They watch Gerhard rise up from the water and then sink down again, splash up and continue laughing at his escape from possible death. And they hear that laugh suddenly turn to a wild shriek. He jerks from the water and thrashes about. They see him leap to and fro and pound his way to the shallows—a look of abject terror on his face. Just like the look on Hans Eckert's face, think Arno. They see him stagger onto the beach clutching his leg. There is blood running from a nasty gash. And a man in the small wooden watchtower stands and calls out the word at the same time Gerhard says it, *"Haifisch!"*—"Shark!"

Men run from the water and stand high up on the sands, looking carefully for the dark shadows that are moving amongst the blood seeping into the water. One of the two soldiers comes down with his rifle held close and sees one of the shark's dorsal fin break the surface. Then a shark rams the tail end of the whale. The corpse moves as if it is still alive, twitching a little and trying to get out of the sharks' reach. The men all take a step further back up the beach.

Soon there is another frenzy, with perhaps five or six sharks feeding on the whale's corpse, attacking it higher and higher as the water rises around it. The internees and the guards stand around it in a wide arc, watching the violence silently. Then they hear the slow put-put-put of a small boat engine, making its way across the bay from South West Rocks. The men look up to see it is one of the small fishing boats from the township. It comes towards them very slowly.

"That's Gavin Hooks' boat," says a guard, when it is close enough to make out.

Gavin Hooks brings his boat in as close as he dares, then cuts the engine and looks out at the carnage in the water. Then he puts his hands to his mouth, forming a funnel and shouts, very slowly, "You—stupid—fuckin'—bastard—Huns!"

Gavin Hooks points at the whale and puts his hands back to his mouth and shouts, "These—bloody—sharks—and—blood—will—fuck—up—our—fishin'—in—the—bay—for—days!"

Herr Kaufmann asks one of the younger men nearby him to translate what the fisherman has said and then puffs out his cheeks indignantly and glares at the fisherman. Gavin Hooks sees him and lowers his hands a little as if waiting for some response, then calls, "Why—didn't—you—dopey—pricks—just—ask—us—to—tow—the—whale—out—to—sea!"

Again, Herr Kaufmann asks for a translation, and then has one of the men call back to Gavin Hooks in English. "It is a sperm whale. Is worth much for us."

"Sperm—whale?" calls Gavin Hooks. "Bull!—Shit!—This—is—a—Finn—whale!—Worth—bloody—nothin'!'"

The internees look at Herr Kaufmann out of the side of their eyes, waiting to see what he will say. *"Es is nicht wahr,"* he says—It is not true.

"Fuckin'—stupid—Hun—bastards!" Gavin Hooks calls again. Then the engine of his small boat restarts and he turns and makes his way slowly back across the bay.

The internees stand there, watching the sharks gorging themselves on the whale carcass for some time, and then, one by one, they turn and make their way back up to the prison, a heavier feeling upon their empty hands than any load of blubber they had carried up the hill that day.

At dinner that evening conversation has turned back to Hans Eckert. A word or two of information is whispered at one table and slowly spreads down the length of the hall, winding its way from table to table until all 400 men have heard it. But no one quite knows where it has originated from.

Arno is sitting at one of the tables at the end of the room, watching it travel around the hall. Horst is at his table, but is eating with his head down, not looking up at him. Herr Kaufmann sits next to Arno and seems eager to make up his lost fortunes with the men, by being the one who relays news to them from the table behind his back.

"It is said Hans Eckert was seen wondering around the compound on the night he took ill," he says.

"But it is forbidden to be in the compound at night."

"Some people wander around there in the dark," says Horst. Not looking up. Not looking at Arno.

"What was he doing?" asks another.

Herr Kaufmann then turns back to the table behind him to collect some more information. He looks back to his tablemates and says, "It is said that he was found by one of the guards in the first light. That they carried him to the infirmary where Doctor Hertz was called to examine him."

Arno knows this is not true, but says nothing. He had seen him killed in his cell. He had been by the walls when it was still dark, and the truck had been there already to fetch Herr Eckert's body from the infirmary.

"Poor fellow," says one of the old men, shaking his head. "He wasn't a bad chap."

"Did you know him?" asks Horst, barely looking up.

"As well as I know any of you here," he says.

"So you didn't know him at all," says Horst.

The old man splutters a little and looks across to Herr Kaufmann for support. He looks at Horst for a moment, and then says, "If you cannot talk without conflict, then it is better not to talk at all, you know."

Horst gives his agreement by not replying.

"So why do you think he would have been outside in the compound?" another man asks Herr Kaufmann.

"I'm sure the only person who knows that is Herr Eckert himself," he says.

And Horst adds, "And he's not speaking."

There is no concert that evening as the whale has consumed so much of the men's energies. Many go to their cells early to nurse their sore muscles and blistered hands. Others sit in the hall playing cards or talking, or just standing around the piano by the wall.

Arno however stands out in the yard under the southwest watchtower. The sky has gone from blue to blackness and he feels the stones behind his back turning dark and chill. He has had a new thought that the beast that slew Herr Eckert may have been the same beast that attacked Pandora, and it may have been created by the same man. One of the internees dreaming up their deaths as sure as if he were a murderer himself.

Arno tries to feel any remnants of that dream in the walls to help him identify it, but he's not able to concentrate this evening. He hears the sounds of waves outside the walls crashing against the breakwater, slowly wearing it down. Carrying it away. Bit by bit by bit.

After some time he opens his eyes and glances down at his watch. But he can no longer make out the time. He looks up again and can see stars in the sky. He tries to guess how long he has been standing there. He shakes his head a little to clear it, as it feels like he has been asleep. He shakes his limbs a little too, to rid the cramp in them. Then he sees something move out of the corner of his eye. He turns his head and stares towards it. Then he looks a little to the side, to improve his night vision. He can see something moving. Something dark, moving low and close to the ground. His first thought is that it is an animal. Something like a wolf. Something that has come out of the shadows there.

But the way it moves is not right. It scuttles. Like a giant dark crab. Or like a person, bent very low perhaps. Arno stands very still. He watches the dark figure move along the cell wall opposite him, then turn towards him. He leans back into the wall. Tries to still his breathing. And he thinks he sees a glint of light in the figure's hand. A claw? A knife? The murderer, he thinks, coming for him.

Then the dark figure moves right past him. As if he has been invisible. As if he has become a part of the rock wall. The figure reaches the foot of the wooden staircase and quickly runs up the stairs over Arno's head into the watchtower. Arno looks up and tries to hear any more sounds. Waits for the longest time, but can only hear the incessant beating of the waves breaking down the breakwater.

"Tell us about the front, Sergeant," says one of the men after the guard's evening meal. A keen-faced young local lad. Not long in uniform. The paleness of his neck showing where the hair has only recently been shorn. The redness around the throat where the rough woollen khaki uniform has been rubbing on it.

Sergeant Gore looks at him. Standing by the table where he has been watching a card game between two men. He likes to spend a bit of time each day in the men's barracks, getting to know them better. Getting them to know him.

"What's your name?" Sergeant Gore asks him.

"Horne," says the lad.

"Alright," he says. "I'll tell you a little about the front. What do you know already?"

The lad shrugs. "Just what I read in the newspaper. Just what I heard."

"Well you probably never heard this," says Sergeant Gore, and he waits until the card players have put down their cards. Waits until most of the men around him are staring at him. "A front happens when two armies meet each other. Before that it could be any place, just like here, trees and fields and a crop growing maybe. Or it could be a desolate strip of rocks and scrawny bushes. But then it becomes a battlefield. At Gallipoli we were landed in the dark, you see, the brass said it would enable us to get the jump on Johnny Turk. Enable us to creep right up on his defences before he even knew we were there. But it was chaos. Landing craft getting stuck in the shallows. Horses and donkeys screaming out as we tried to land them quietly, and so dark you couldn't see which way you were going. Couldn't see they'd landed us up against dirty great rock cliffs."

He pauses. Looks to see every man in the barracks is paying close attention. "Then when the first light came we saw how hopeless our position was. Saw it was like a fortress in front of us. And of course the Turks could see us, and they let us have it with everything they had. You've never seen anything like it. Shells going off all around. Bullets flying so close to your head you could hear them. Feel them sometimes. We dug into the cliffs and edged our way slowly upwards. Determined we'd get there. They threw everything they had at us, but we kept going. Would have reached the top and over-run them too if the brass didn't lose their nerve."

He's staring towards the roof now. "Men were dropping all around me. There'd be this sudden thud behind you and you'd know the man there had been hit. But I kept on. Led my men to a high point and then we dug in. Dug as deep as we could and let the Turks have it. Covering fire for our mates on the beaches. Helped as many get ashore as we could. Helped as many as possible dig their own trenches." The men closest to him see his jaw twitch as he talks.

He looks back towards Private Horne. Just looks at him.

"And?" the newcomer asks the Sergeant.

"That was it," says the Sergeant, "Except for the dirt and the flies and lice and the blood and the stink of shit and death and the lack of water and the lack of sleep and the constant shelling and seeing your mates getting shot out of all recognition, lying dead in their trenches like they were their graves you'd helped them dig, and each day the very landscape about you is blown to unknowable shapes and you can't even tell if the smashed up bodies around you belong to the Huns or your mates any more.

"The front at Gallipoli became just like the front in France," he says. "We were huddled in trenches in the mud, being shot slowly to shit by the Turks or the Huns and knowing that one of their bullets had our name on it, but never knowing which it was. And the maddening terror of that grips you worse than any winter's chill, I can tell you."

He stops. He's said it. Finally said it. He looks around the room. Takes in the faces of all the men watching him. Sees every one of them is staring at him closely. Even Simpson and Cutts-Smith. He's even said it to them.

"But," he says slowly, "when you suffer all that and still find the courage to stand up and attack the enemy one more time, then you know you're a soldier!"

Private Horne nods his head slowly, as if he actually understands something of that. But the Sergeant can see that Private Cutts-Smith is not so easily impressed by war stories.

He watches him turn his head away, showing the angry scarred side of his face to him.

Arno shares Gerhard Rohlfs' dream that night—clearly the most traumatised man in the prison. He is back inside the whale, but is unable to escape. The leviathan's skin has become translucent though, and he can see the vague shapes of people outside, calling to him. But he cannot answer them. He is captive inside the rib cage of the whale, the bones like tall ivory bars around him.

He can hear the muffled sounds of their talking, but has no way of letting them know he is still alive.

He hears them say they should find a way to cut the whale open and get his corpse out if he has died, or free him if he has not. He hears them say they could open the whale's mouth to reach him, but somebody has sewn the lips shut.

Then he hears the voices of Australian soldiers telling his comrades to move away from the whale, telling them it is illegal to try and enter the whale. Telling them that the whale is going to be towed out to sea, and left on a remote Pacific Island.

He hears his comrades ask if they will be told which island it is, so that they may travel there to free him, but the soldiers say the location is being kept secret and also that it will be illegal to visit the island.

He can hear the despair in his comrades' voices as they call out to him again, asking him to give them some sign that he is alive. And again he tries to call back to them, but still cannot make a sound loud enough to be heard. Then he reaches up and finds that his own lips have been sewn shut too. So even his screams at the terror of being imprisoned in the whale for endless years are silenced.

4
Another Day

Arno is standing by the walls of the prison the next morning as the first light starts to soften the darkness. He can feel so many dreams fading away into the stone, but none of them the violent and dangerous creature he is trying to find. None the murderer he is searching for. And he wonders, for an instant, if he isn't trapped in a dream of his own? All these years in internment just a passing moment of sleeping that he will wake from and find himself back in the worker's camp in Western Australia once more.

He lets the idea fall from him and then he thinks that if he still believed in prayer he would pray that this day was just like any other. That when the gates were thrown open the calmness would descend upon him and any change from the day before would be minor. He could survive that, he believes.

But when the guards eventually open the gates for the morning, after breakfast, the men stream out and find that their village of cafes and huts has been attacked in the night. Doors are kicked in. Mountain backdrops are pulled down and cut up. Furniture is thrown outside and smashed. And everything is covered in blood. It drips across the doorways as crudely as the blood on those posters of the beastly Hun they have all seen—a tall dark ogre-like figure, with a spiked German helmet, eating the hands off small children.

Men walk amongst the ruins in shock, picking up bits of canvas and wood that have been reduced from Alpine vistas to painted scraps. The destruction is too enormous for words for many of them. The proprietor of one of the cafes has dropped to his knees on the bloody and smashed up wood, trying to re-assemble it, like a man might when returning home to find a small crater where his family home had been. Some men sit in silence, amongst the wreckage of the cafes and bars and stare blankly at the reality of their situation that has been exposed. It is not a pleasant thing to contemplate.

As soon as he has heard the news Herr Herausgeber comes out to inspect the damage. He walks amongst the ruins with his notebook held out before him. "They are barbarians," he says aloud. "They are worse than barbarians. This is senseless vandalism. What have we ever done to offend them?"

Some men gather around him and mutter that the raiding party must have come through the dark forest, or else arrived by boat in the night, but either way the guards must have known they were coming. Must have seen something. Must have turned their heads away.

Then Captain Eaton appears, surrounded by a small handful of guards. He too inspects the damage. He shakes his head and tells the internees around him that he will ensure that the matter is taken up with the authorities in South West Rocks. "I will make sure that all efforts are made to apprehend the guilty parties," he tells the internees. "Such actions cannot be condoned."

The men listen to him respectfully. Some then go back to their cells to sit in darkness while others continue rebuilding their village—but both are certain that nothing else will be done about this. They are, after all, enemy aliens. They have affronted and threatened the local population by being German, and by being here. And they have no control over either.

Arno watches those men who have stayed behind go about their work trying to restore walls and windows. They scrub at the blood and mend broken supports, but he sees that they will never really be able to recreate the fantasy world they had constructed. Not now that it has been torn down and shown for what it really is. He also knows that Herr Herausgeber will run a large story about this in *Welt Am Montag*, deploring the destruction and lamenting that they are surrounded by hostile barbarians. But never once will he state that the war—that unspoken word—has finally crept right up to their isolated prison walls.

It is 11.05 by Arno's watch and Nurse Rosa has not come. He lies on the bed in the infirmary, looking down between his legs, imagining he can see her there, holding his feet. Pressing them against her strong thighs. Smiling to him. Turning them first one way. And then another. He wonders what has caused her to be late? Wonders how high the anti-German feeling in South West Rocks has grown? Wonders if they are stopping her from coming?

He props himself up on his elbows and looks around the small infirmary. It is empty again today. Those still recovering from the fight prefer to do it in their own cells. This room does not feel enough like an actual hospital room to encourage men to stay. It feels too much like a prison room. The cold stone walls. The high barred windows. The eternal quiet.

He lies back down and closes his eyes. If she is not coming today, he will recreate her in his mind before Doctor Hertz arrives to twist and bend his feet painfully. First, he imagines the whiteness of her uniform. The stiff starched material. Then her auburn hair, tied up neatly beneath her red cap. Then the shape of her face. The curve of her cheeks and nose. The shape of her eyes and lips. Then her neck, plunging down deeply beneath the uniform to her shoulders and breasts. He thinks carefully of the hidden curves of them. And the many secrets of her past that she also hides. He wonders what stories she could tell him if she chose to, as she massages her legs feet. Her hands have hold of one of his feet now, lifting it from the bed, working the muscles and tendons in it, rubbing her fingers over the skin firmly as she moves it one way and then the other, shaping it and straightening it.

He opens his eyes and sees her sitting there, holding one foot, looking down at him. *"Guten Morgen,"* she says.

"Guten Tag," he replies with a smile.

She smiles too. Just a little.

"You're late," he says.

"Ja." Now no smile.

"I thought something might have happened?"

"No." She puts his foot down and lifts the other. Looks past him. At the stone prison wall.

She is thinking of something far away, he thinks. Or somebody far away. And he wonders if she has a sweetheart. Somebody who is away at the war. Somebody who is fighting the Germans. Being shot at by them. How does that make her feel about working here, he wonders? And he wishes, not for the first time, that he could share her dreams and know what her fears and anxieties were. But also the things that brought her the most joy.

"Are you thinking of somebody?" he asks, stepping cautiously into no man's land.

"What?" she asks, looking back between his legs at him.

It is harder to ask the second time. "Are you thinking of somebody?" he says it again slowly.

"No," she says. "Just me." Still distant.

Arno nods. Wishes to bring her back to the present. Back to him. "Did you see what happened outside the walls?" he asks.

"Yes." She stops and puts his foot down. Looks at him coldly. Arno knows he has said the wrong thing and tries to make light of it. "A fierce storm might have done as much."

"No," she says, anger in her voice now. "It was done by men! Those angry ignorant hate-filled men!"

She puts her fist into her mouth, as if to stop anything emerging, then turns away from him.

Arno is searching for the words to make it alright, but he has none. He has not enough experience with women to really know where to begin. And when Doctor Hertz comes in and he sees Nurse Rosa is upset, Arno can only watch the easy way he goes to her and puts one hand on her arm. The other around her waist. He leads her to his office and sits her in a small chair there and pats her gently on the shoulder. Arno watches in fascination. Is it really so easy to reach out and touch a woman? he thinks. He can no longer remember.

Then Doctor Hertz closes the door and comes over to Arno. He looks up through his legs at the doctor and tells him, "We were just talking."

Doctor Hertz picks up one of his feet. Twists it sharply one way. Then twists it the other. Arno clamps his teeth together as Doctor Hertz says, "Talking sometimes causes pain too."

Herr Dubotzki is sitting in the dark in a small cell with the door locked tightly. He is staring at a blank sheet in front of him, as an image slowly starts to form. He moves the paper a little. Lets the developer run over it. Stares as the first shapes start to appear. A dark outline. Filling slowly. Then the soft grey of a face appearing. He watches carefully. He does not need a timer for this as he knows from experience when the print is ready. He watches as the face slowly solidifies, like coming towards him from a bright light, or out of the mist. The eyes are taking shape now, though the rest of the face is obscured by a veil. Now the detail of the figure's clothes are clearer, as are the curves of the arms and the breasts and the pattern of the dress.

He smiles and takes the print out of the developer tray, brings it up close to his face for an instant and then lowers it to the fixer. He has it. Has captured the tones and the look on Pandora's face forever.

He watches her floating under the fixer for some time and then lifts her out. He places her in water and lets her bathe in it. Then he lifts her out to dry. He admires her a moment and then reaches for another sheet of paper. It is like printing money, he thinks.

Arno is making his way around the compound, filling in time before lunch. He misses his morning's swim, but has little desire to go outside again and see the ruins there nor the bloodied whale remains on the beach. He has tried to find somewhere else to go other than his cell, while trying not to get caught up in the activities of the internees. He is feeling dislocated today, like he is on the edge of slipping into a dream, or a vision, as if the world made stone around him is not solid at all—but something he could pass through into another world.

The past, maybe. Or the future? Or another version of the present? It feels as if he could press up against the chill granite walls and pass right into them. Move his body through the chill stone and come out the other side in a world where Herr Eckert had never been murdered. Where the locals had not attacked the prison and destroyed their make-believe village. Where even if the world was still at war, it would be kept far away from this little corner of the world.

English language classes are being held in the hall, and they won't be out of there for another fifteen minutes or more, according to his watch. If he gets too close, he knows, they will call him in to take part, as his English is better than that of most of the internees. He has gone some days and made up nonsense words like bomblebee and discompute, and insisted they were real. But he has no interest in talking today.

He moves towards the washrooms and stops. Some of the members of the athletics club are showering and standing around in the sun there, puffing and panting. Their faces are red and sweaty and they grin at each other and laugh, mock boxing and slapping at each other's bare skin. They have been playing team sports. They are great advocates of team sports. It might have been football today—or tennis. They will play any sport except cricket. That is what the guards play. The club members never seem to tire of setting up a playing field, laying down the rules, carefully going through all the motions of training and rehearsals, and then attacking each other with great gusto. The actual game doesn't matter—it is only one part of the excitement.

He watches the men, bouncing on their strong legs and flexing their arm muscles for each other. At times they mock him for being a cripple and he responds by telling them that he won't take them with him when he escapes from the prison.

And then he wonders how much strength does a man need to kill another? Do you need to be an athlete, treating the death fight like a contest? The strong overcoming the weak? He has strong enough arms, he thinks. He leans forward a little onto his crutches, taking all the weight off his feet, holding himself up on his arms. If he were quick he could do it. If he were backed up against a wall, perhaps. A quick stab or thrust. That was all it took, surely. Doctor Hertz would know, he thinks. He lowers himself back onto his legs. Takes the weight off his arms now and lets his feet hold his weight. Then he ponders the mystery of why the doctor is covering up the killing? Is it just to protect morale, or something else?

He looks at the members of the athletics club again and wonders at the possibility of a world so different that he might have to defend himself from them. Had to fight them. He tries to imagine himself facing any one of them. Tries to imagine stabbing at their strong muscular bodies. But he feels he would never do it. He has a sudden understanding that killing is not all about strength of body, it is more about strength of hate.

He lowers his weight back onto the crutches. Perhaps the doctor isn't involved in the killing, he thinks. Surely there is nobody he hates. He is the most respected of all the inmates. He is the one the Commandant turns to when he needs to discuss the prisoners' welfare. And he is the one they all choose to take their concerns and complaints to the Commandant for them. But, he thinks, moving his body weight back to his feet again, like he is weighing up an argument, he is also the one who knows the most about death.

He turns and limps back across the yard, towards the infirmary. He stops and leans against the wall there. Touches the stone. Closes his eyes and tries to feel the world within. The worlds beyond. But it is only stone. And the doctor is a good man. A man who will keep his word to him and fix his feet one day after the war.

He turns again to go back across the yard, but as he does so a guard comes out of the infirmary, carrying boxes. He trips on one of Arno's outstretched crutches and falls heavily to the ground. He is back on his feet before Arno can even mutter an apology. "Bloody Hun!" he says. He dusts his uniform a little, and then steps up close—really close—and pokes Arno in the chest with one finger. "Would you like to try that again? Face to face with me?"

Arno stares at him as if he does not fully understand the guard's words, and tries to back away a little. But the guard follows him and Arno sees that one side of the man's face is badly scared with an angry red welt. "Come on," he says. "A coward are you?" And he pushes Arno so that he nearly tips over, but he waves his crutch around to stop him falling. The guard's eyes follow it carefully. Wary of it. Then he smiles, as if he has been challenged. He lifts his fists up and stares at Arno with hate in his eyes.

Arno shakes his head a little. "No," he says, but the guard is not interested in what he says.

"Hun bastard!" the guard says.

Arno wonders if the man would kill him if he had a knife in his hand. If it were night and he had come across him in the dark. If he has in fact already merged into the stone of the walls and come out in a different version of his world, where he is no longer so certain he will survive it.

"Enough!"

The guard turns.

Doctor Hertz is standing in the door of the infirmary. His voice sharp and abrupt. "It was an accident," says the doctor. "Leave the boy be."

The guard jerks his chin around a little, as if adjusting it, then gathers up his boxes and walks off to the main gate.

"Thank you," says Arno, and thinks to himself, I can survive this too.

The doctor just shrugs his shoulders. "There is enough fighting in the world already," he says, and goes back inside the infirmary.

Private Simpson stands in the watchtower breathing slowly and heavily. He is bored. Too many long afternoons where not much ever seems to happen have gotten into his blood. Even the novelty of the whale corpse and the destruction of the Hun's playhouses has worn off. He looks down to the whale's carcass and sees the red-stained sand and the dark circling shapes of the sharks there. He has watched them overly-long, picking on the remains there, and is now sickened by the sight of them. The leftovers of the whale corpse and all that blood reminds him too much of the western front.

He turns and looks into the prison yard instead. The internees are bored too. He can see that easily enough. These Germans are bored with internment as much as he is bored with guarding them. At the front every day had seemed a lifetime of hell, but here it is too much like living in limbo—days fading into weeks into months.

He wishes he was on night duty. It is easier in a way. You could have a smoke and a drink and nobody could see you. And you could even sneak away from the tower for a bit when you had to. Anything interesting around here happened at night. He knows that sure enough. The night was a little dangerous and he likes that.

He sighs heavily. Plays the game where he is a sniper, imagining his is picking the internees off one by one with his Lee Enfield as they ran around the prison yard like chooks with a fox amongst them. He smiles. Then he turns and looks out northwards over the breakwater, and thinks of those convicts who laboured away on it in the last century. It would have been a bugger of a job guarding them, he thinks. Murderers and thieves. But it would have been more lively than guarding these dozy Huns. He follows the direction of the breakwater and for the first time notices that if they had kept building it, and not stopped, they would have ended up reaching Freedom Island to the north west of the headland.

He puts his hands up around his head, and shades his eyes, so that he can't see the bloodstained beach. So he can't see the prison. And he stares along the direction of the breakwater, towards the distant green trees of Freedom Island.

It is sundown and Arno Friedrich stands under the southwest watchtower leaning against the granite stone, arms out wide, staring up at the sky, watching the colour go out of the world. He feels the darkness descending upon him like a mantle. He stands there as the first stars come out, and he thinks he would like to see the whole sky full of stars for once, stretching from horizon to horizon and unobstructed by tall prison walls.

And he feels a touch of menace stirring within the walls, as if a dream or nightmare within is striving to escape. He stays by the wall for some time, as the feeling fades, and then he grips his crutches tightly and begins making his way around the prison. He goes along past the cell blocks and hears an argument coming out of one cell. He tries to make out which barred window cell it is coming from. Tries to make out the words. But all he can distinguish are the dark edges of anger in the voices.

He tilts his head back. Discerns it is coming from a second floor cell. Perhaps two cell mates, having forgotten that if you could not talk without conflict then it is better not to talk at all. He stands there and listens to the anger grow softer and then fade away until all he can hear is the low rumble of the distant grumbling surf on the breakwater.

Camaraderie makes for good comrades, Arno thinks, repeating the camp motto, and he continues on. Then he stops. He had felt something. Like swimming through a cold current in the ocean. He takes one small step backwards and then looks around. Listens. There is a soft clink behind him. He presses close to the wall and peers into the darkness. Listens for the sound again. It was something like the sound of a metal knife on stone. Then he hears it again. Much softer. Higher up. As if the noise is floating away into the sky.

He stays where he is and listens carefully. Thinks of the guard who wanted to fight him. Wonders what he will do if somebody confronts him in the darkness? Wonders if he could defend himself? Wonders if he imaginings are running away from him?

He turns and takes a slow and careful step forward. Then stops and listens again. Nothing. Then another slow step forward. He has just about convinced himself it was nothing but a random sound amplified by his imagination, when he hears the footsteps. Quite close. He turns his head as the figure reaches out and grabs him. He feels his heart leap out of his mouth. But a heavy hand clamps over his lips. A face is close to his own. Eyes staring at him hard.

"What are you doing out here?" Doctor Hertz demands.

Arno has to swallow several times and shake his head a little until the doctor lowers his hand. But Arno doesn't know how to answer him.

"Why are you here?" the doctor hisses again.

He is unable to tell him. "I'm just walking," Arno says.

The doctor stares at him as if looking for the real truth in Arno's face. But he unable to see it in the dim light. Then the doctor says, "It is not allowed after dark."

"I thought I heard somebody behind me," says Arno, and turns his head back the way he has come. Trying to shake the doctor's stare from him.

"Hmm," says the doctor and lets him go. "You should be inside," he hisses, then hurries off into the darkness. In the direction Arno had indicated.

That night the orchestra plays Wagner. It is heroic and fills the men with pride. They sit tall in their chairs with their chests puffed out. They would have stood and sang but for the guards at the back of the hall. After the fracas of the last concert the Commander has sent three armed guards in to keep a lid on the internees' excesses. The guards slouch against the walls and look disinterested. "Peasants," Herr Herausgeber mumbles to those around him.

The orchestra is playing excerpts from the opera *Tannhäuser,* the story of the heroic singer and poet who is torn between his love for a princess and the goddess Venus. After half an hour the players rise to a loud applause and take several ovations. Now the audience sits forward on their chairs, waiting for Scheherazade to appear.

She enters the stage from the left, her arms floating around her like a bird in flight. Her veils are kept high and tight. The guards perk up a little and watch her delicate movements with wide-eyed appreciation. She announces to the audience that tonight there will be a short play based on the German hero Tannhäuser. She briefly outlines the plot, of the hero who left his home in Germany to make a pilgrimage to Rome, but ends up at the court of Venus, the Queen of Love, where he lives a life of earthly pleasure. But after many years, torn by remorse, he escapes her court to complete his pilgrimage.

Scheherazade then slowly unfastens one dark veil and lets it drift to her feet, then she spins on the spot and lets her arms fly her from the stage.

The men in the audience sit expectantly. The sound of a single flute is heard. And then Tannhäuser enters from the right of stage. He is a tall man, dressed in the clothes of a Prussian guardsman. He strides to the centre of the stage and he proclaims his good-heartedness and loyalty to his Emperor, and his need to make a pilgrimage to a distant land. Then he strides on, over tall mountains and across rivers and oceans and along long dry roads, until his destination is in sight. But then the flute music returns. This time more melodic. More inviting.

He turns and follows it, looking for the source of the music, as if it might be a bird hiding in a high tree. But suddenly the music changes and it becomes a military march and Tannhäuser turns to see two soldiers in khaki appear and take his arms. They drag him to a distant castle, and fling him inside a cell. He looks around, then stares out the barred windows, lamenting that he has been captured and imprisoned for no reason.

But then the flute music returns. High and melodic, dancing around him. And he turns to see Venus, goddess of Love. She is gorgeous. Long blonde hair and a loose-fitting harem costume. And she is surrounded by young maidens who rush to Tannhäuser's side. They run their hands over his broad shoulders and feel the muscles in his arms. They bring him gently over to Venus and she walks around him slowly, her hips leading her steps. She admires him and asks him to lie down beside her on soft cushions. Tells him to enjoy the warm sunshine and food. Tells him to give himself over to decadence and to her care.

At first he refuses. But she runs her hand across the side of his face. Places her fingers on his chest. Guides his hands towards her own face and chest. And then pulls him down on the cushions beside her. The flute music rises as Tannhäuser shuts his eyes as if falling into a deep sleep.

The lights around Tannhäuser dim, to indicate the passing of many years. And when the lights rise again he is still asleep, Venus and her maidens draped around him like thick vines. The flute can no longer be heard, but in the distance is the sound of approaching footsteps. Marching boots. The sound gets closer and closer and then another tall Prussian soldier enters. He is dressed exactly like Tannhäuser, as if he is his *doppelgänger*. His other self. He enters the court of Venus and sees Tannhäuser asleep and bends down to touch him. So close he could almost be kissing him. Tannhäuser's eyes open and he looks around him. And he is revolted by what he sees.

He carefully peels himself free from the sleeping goddess, but she wakes as he tries to step away and she calls for her guards. The two khaki-clad soldiers return and Tannhäuser and his double dispatch them with one blow each. Then they make their escape from the castle and, arm in arm, together resume their pilgrimage. The flute music rises triumphantly filling the stage with Wagner's theme, and the audience rise to their feet in applause.

The three guards look at each other carefully. Certain there was something objectionable in the play, but not able to say just what it was.

"What do you think?" one private asks, leaning towards the man next to him.

"Bloody operas," he says. "My dad saw one once."

"What'd you reckon of those sheilas though?"

"I'd root her if she wasn't a Hun."

"Bloody Huns," the other replies.

Arno lies on his bunk later that evening, jotting single words down in his diary. So many pages have only two or three words on them. *Pelikan*. Or *Stihmboht*—steamboat. To mark the only things different that had happened on those days. But now he is filling pages with words. Phrases and short sentences. All mixed and jumbled. Still the clipped language of internment, but there are so many new things to write about. So many things are disrupting his desire for the safety of sameness. And then he hears the shouts of two men in the corridor. There is a cry followed by the loud grunts and slaps of men locked in battle. Horst turns over on his bunk, listens to the sound and then lays his head on his pillow again, as if it is nothing new to him.

Arno grabs his crutches and limps over to the cell door. He can see that men from all the cells are moving out into the corridor now. He can see them all looking in the same direction. Herr Schwarz, leader of the athletics club, and another man, Wilhelm Heinecke, are locked there in battle, hurling grunted curses at each other. They cling together as if they are trying to squeeze the life out of each other, and then break apart. Swaying wildly, Ernst Schwarz curls a fist and swings at his opponent. But the blow goes wide, flying through the air. Herr Heinecke blinks rapidly, trying to follow the fist, and he nearly stumbles right into it. Ernst Schwarz, overbalanced from his swing, then falls forward, landing on top of his opponent. They both fall to the ground, a sudden tangle of flailing limbs. And Arno realises they are both drunk.

The internees watch the two assailants regain their feet and circle each other, looking for an opening. Trying to find some weak point in their enemy's defence. Trying to determine just where to begin their assault anew. But both men appear evenly matched in fury and drunkenness, and it looks like they are going to trade ineffectual blows for a long time.

Then suddenly they both charge at each other. They clash head on, fists flailing, and then grabbing, seizing each other tightly. They stand together like a pair of maddened dancers, cursing and panting and then suddenly break apart again, and fall to the floor once more. Herr von Krupp, standing like a Medieval Baron, steps between them. He slaps them both heavily on the face with an open palm, knocking the men back from the force of it. Ernst Schwarz jumps up and looks at him with hate and anger in his eyes, but von Krupp quickly slaps him again. The sound echoes down the corridor. Then Ernst Schwarz steps back and lowers his eyes.

"Fools!" von Krupp hisses at them both. "Why do you waste your energies fighting each other?"

He is about to say something else when the sound of running boots is heard. The men in the corridor part and two guards run in, rifles levelled at their chests. "What's going on?" one of them demands.

Von Krupp steps forward and smiles. "Just two men letting off a bit of steam," he says.

The soldier quickly takes in the situation. "Fighting is forbidden."

"Yes," says the von Krupp, "but we are organising a boxing tournament, which is permitted."

The soldier looks at him, then nods. Just a little.

"These two just cannot wait," von Krupp says, and waves his hand dismissively at the two men behind him. The soldier looks at the two men and then back at von Krupp. "I think it would make for interesting entertainment, don't you think?" he asks the guard.

"It would," the man agrees. "I enjoy a good match."

"Then the next time these two fight you shall see one."

The guard stands there a moment, thinking, and then says, "Yes. Alright then. But no more outbursts or the Commandant will hear of it."

"You have my word," says Herr von Krupp, as if he were the commanding officer of the internees. The two soldiers turn and slowly walk back down the cell corridor.

"You disgrace the German nationality," says von Krupp, turning to the two men, then he looks up to glare at all the men in the corridor until they all look away and go back into their cells. Arno too turns from his gaze and is surprised to see Horst standing behind him. Hears him mutter softly, "Pompous Prussian arsehole."

Private Simpson is tired and wishes Gunn would shut up. He's just like the other boof-headed locals, he thinks. They don't know nothin' about the war but forever wishing they did. He turns on his bunk and digs his head deeper into his pillow. He's going on again about the Hun and what Sergeant Gore has told him about them, how he's going to be over there before the year's end, keen to get to the fight before it's all over.

Simpson lifts his head off the pillow and says, "Give it a rest Gunn, you're a bloody idiot!"

Private Gunn stops in mid-sentence. His face reddens a little. He's never sure what to make of Private Simpson. He respects him, like all the veterans, but he tends to make fun of him, as if his enthusiasm is something to be ashamed of.

"What's the matter?" he asks Simpson.

Simpson sits up and looks at him. "For Chrissakes!" he says. He sees Gunn is cleaning and stripping his rifle. Again. He plays with it more than he plays with himself. "Just give it a rest!" he says. "I'm trying to sleep."

Gunn frowns a little, uncertain, and keeps working on the rifle. Snapping the metal pieces together. Taking them apart.

"And put the bloody rifle away," says Simpson. "It wants to go to bed too."

"Gotta be ready," says Gunn. "The Sergeant says a good soldier's always prepared."

Simpson stares at him. "So you reckon the enemy might walk in here one night?" he asks.

Gunn gives a shrug. "Might do," he says.

"And you'll be ready for them?" Simpson asks.

"Yep," says Gunn.

"With your rifle in pieces?"

Gunn turns a little redder. He isn't sure why Simpson is making fun of him. "I'm just keen to get into the fight, I reckon," he says. "Keen to shoot some Huns."

"Keen to get bloody killed," says Simpson.

"Not if I train properly. The Sergeant's been giving some of us extra training. Getting us ready to face the enemy."

"Let me tell you something," says Private Simpson. "The Sergeant is bloody mad and anybody who listens to what he says is bloody mad too!"

And Private Gunn looks down at the rifle in his hands. He feels his face and neck burning, but keeps working on the weapon. And he wonders if it is not as easy as he had thought to tell who is the enemy.

Arno is sharing a dream of an internee named Klaus Peter. His previous dreams have been about picnics with his family in German forests, when he was younger, and losing something important—money or keys or something—and searching everywhere for them but not being able to find them. And as the dream progresses, he finds he is alone and then has trouble even remembering what it was he had been so fervently searching for. And then he is struggling to even remember where he is, as if everything including his sense of understanding is being taken from him.

But tonight the dream goes in a different direction. Herr Peter is not younger. He is as Arno knows him—a middle-aged man with a plump red face that looks like he is forever on the verge of shouting something obscene at everyone about him. But his face changes in this dream. It is pale and riven with fear. The forest he is in is dark and menacing, and all the trees are misshapen and sharp. And there is something else in the forest, stalking him. Some dark shape that moves through the shadows around him, and growls with a deep low and hungry sound.

Herr Peter tries to run from the beast, but stumbles into branches that pluck at him. Roots and stones seem to rise up to trip him and brambles ensnare his legs and arms. He kicks and swipes at them, trying to clear a path, trying to fight his way free, but the more he struggles the more they entangle him. Then the dark shadow is so close he can feel its breath chilling the air about him. The beast turns the air to ice. Turns Herr Peter's fear to terror.

He spins this way and that to try and make out the creature, to see where it is. But all he can see is movement in the shadows. Then he sees it. The shape of a large wolf. On all fours. Then standing upright like a man. Then gone.

Herr Peter's legs have turned to jelly, unable to hold him upright, and he falls to the ground. He falls and falls and falls into darkness, where he is ensnared tightly in brambles. He cannot move. He is naked and the thorns cut into his flesh. Blood is all along his limbs and torso like tiny blooms.

Then the wolf is beside him. Is upon him. Is devouring him. Its claws ripping at his flesh, stripping it away to uncover a small scared boy hiding within. The child stares up at the beast—in the sudden awareness that it was his fear of this thing that he had lost and now remembers fully. He knows this for only an instant as it opens its mouth, all teeth and maw, and pounces on him.

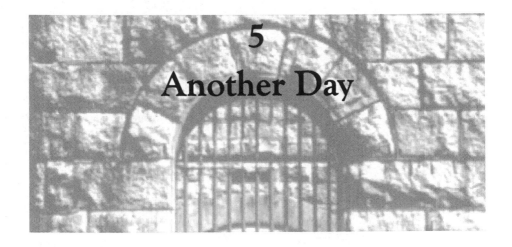

5
Another Day

Arno watches the sky slowly turn blue overhead and fill the world with light once more. He leans up against the chill granite walls for some time, trying to find a trace of the violence of last night's dream. But he cannot. As if it has not returned to the imprisoning stone. As if nothing is the same as it once was.

He then makes his way slowly around the walls. He stops to listen to Herr Schröder singing Wagner in his cell. Listens to the soft mumbles of Herr Voigt reciting his rosary. Listens to the kitchen staff clinking pots and pans and smells the warm aroma of newly-baked bread. Just like any other day, he thinks. Hopes. But feels it will not be.

On the way back into the hall he is stopped by the guard with the red scar on half his face who had tried to pick a fight with him. He puts his hand on Arno's chest and then leans close to him and says, "You've been seen wandering the yard when you shouldn't be."

Arno looks at him but says nothing, as if he still doesn't understand him. The guard lifts his hand and places one finger against his nose. "If you know what's good for you, you'll give it up, okay?"

Then he places his finger on Arno's chest and pushes him until he stumbles back a little. "It could be very dangerous," the guard says. "Very, very dangerous."

After breakfast the men are assembled for roll call. In the first months of internment roll call had been every morning. Then it was every second day. And now it has been reduced to once a week—or on any special occasion that prompts the Commandant to assert his authority—such as today. Over 400 men are assembled in the yard, spread around the walls, waiting for Commandant Fort, followed closely by Sergeant Gore, and a pair or two of extra guards, to pace slowly along the path from the main gate to stand before them and address them. Like a celebrant at a mass.

Arno looks at them and recalls that when they had first assembled they were dressed so well, in linen suits and hats, and now they are wearing faded and oft-mended clothes and similar white cloth hats. They are slowly becoming convicts, he thinks.

The Commandant eventually appears and takes up his position, near the washrooms, and holds up several sheets of paper. Then he begins reading the names typed out on them. Arno, like many of the men around him, leans against the granite wall, feeling the sun warming the rock behind them. The Sergeant has often tried to get them to stand to attention for the duration of the roll call, but at times like this, as he marches up and down their line, barking orders at them to stand level and straight, they appear to have great trouble with the English language.

Arno closes his eyes, waiting for his name to be called—knowing that there are about 50 or so men ahead of him alphabetically. Then the Commandant finally calls, "Friedrich, Arno."

He leans forward a little and calls, *"Hier!"* Then leans back against the warm rock wall again, waiting for the ritual to end. Listening to the Commandant make his way slowly down the list. Listening for one name in particular.

"Müntzer, Fredrik?"

"Hier."

"Neisser, Hermann?"

"Hier."

It is a matter of pride and defiance for the internees to answer in German, knowing that the guards cannot tell the difference in the words.

"Neumann, Johann?"

"Hier."

"Opel, Fritz?"

"Hier."

Arno leans heavily onto his crutches. Feels he is suddenly much heavier and wearier than he has ever been before. Feels he needs to go back to his bunk for the day, like Horst does. Then he wishes he were able to go to the beach and swim. Wishes he had not had the run in with the guard. Wishes Herr Eckert hadn't been murdered. Wishes this day was not going to be marked by any new changes.

"Peter, Klaus?"

Again. "Peter, Klaus?"

Arno closes his eyes, listening carefully.

The Commandant stands silently waiting for somebody to answer. Heads are slowly turned back and forward, looking for Herr Peter amongst them.

"Peter, Klaus?" Once more.

Still no answer. The Commandant beckons two of the guards over to him and then sends them into the cell blocks to conduct a quick search. The internees stand in the morning sun waiting. The Commandant refuses to progress further down his list until Herr Peter is located.

The guards come running back after a few minutes and shake their heads. The Commandant looks around in annoyance. He repeats the name a final time, "Peter, Klaus?" Still no answer.

He calls two more guards over to him. Now four men clump off in different directions around the compound. Into the wash house. Into the infirmary. Into the kitchen.

Arno looks about him. Internees are still glancing around, as if Klaus Peter might be somehow standing amongst them when he had not been there a moment ago. But nobody can see him. If they had to conjure him up they would create a professor of Romantic Literature, living and teaching in Singapore when the war had come for him. He was a thin man, slightly bald. He wrote poetry that he never shared with anybody and had asthma. And he had been one of the theatre troupe, and had played one of Venus' maidens the night before.

The four soldiers soon return, one by one, and report to the Commandant, shaking their heads. He looks down at his lists of paper. Thinks hard for a moment and then calls out, "Who is Klaus Peter's cell-mate?"

A man steps forward. Herr Klees. Once a manager for a shipping company who is now thought of as a skilled tailor. He has his shoulders back, standing to attention. The Commandant beckons him to come forward and he passes the list of names to the Sergeant. He then leads Herr Klees towards the guardhouse to question him.

"Piper, Wilhelm," shouts the Sergeant in a voice that echoes loudly around the yard.

"Hier."

They find Klaus Peter shortly after they have finally opened the prison gates for the day. One of the internees sees him and reports it to a guard. His body has been thrown onto the breakwater like a broken chunk of granite. The legs are gone where the sharks have reached them at high tide. The guards carry the bloody remains away and herd the internees back into the compound, locking the gates once more.

A few men, like Arno, who had reached the beach early, had also seen the remains of drag marks along the sand leading to the breakwater. Inside the prison rumours and supposition scuttle up and down the corridors. By lunchtime the stories say that

Herr Peter had been very depressed. He had been very drunk last night. He had been murdered. He had been thrown to the sharks, but they had not finished the job. He had left his cell late in the night. Only a guard could have carried his body out of the compound.

The internees look out through the high barred windows, at the khaki-clad men with rifles on the watchtowers. Only a guard! And the solid stone cells do not seem as secure as they had once felt.

In the early afternoon Arno makes his way over to the infirmary. The morning's commotion had caused him to miss his daily session with Nurse Rosa, but he hopes she is still there. Hopes she might still massage his legs for him, and talk to him a little. But she is not there. Intern Meyer is minding the infirmary and looks very jumpy when Arno arrives. He smiles and tells Arno to come in and lie on the bed. Arno says it doesn't matter. Says he has been looking for Nurse Rosa, and asks if intern Meyer knows where she is. "She's not been in today," he says. "And Doctor Hertz has gone into Kempsey with the Commandant. They have taken the remains of Herr Peter in the back of an army truck." He shrugs a little, trying unsuccessfully to make it seem routine. "They have gone to see the officials there. To make out the death certificate, you know."

Arno nods. He sits down and looks around the small room and tries to think of something to ask intern Meyer. But he doesn't know him very well. Yet it is Meyer who first asks a question, "Do you get on well with Nurse Rosa?"

"Yes," says Arno. "Very well."

"Oh?" asks intern Meyer.

"We have lots of conversations, you know."

Intern Meyer nods. "She has been massaging your legs for almost two years now, *ja?*"

Arno thinks carefully and says, "It makes nearly 300 hours."

"So long?"

"Yes. Put together it would be over 12 full days."

Intern Meyer smiles. "You are a very precise person."

Arno nods. "There is much time for precision here."

"You are also a very lucky person," says Meyer.

Arno looks down at his crutches and doesn't say anything.

"I think she likes you," says intern Meyer.

Arno can feel a warm blush rising up his neck. He looks down at his watch. 2.18. Looks back up at the bare stone wall. "Do you think so?"

"Of course."

Arno is about to say that he thinks she likes Doctor Hertz more, but he doesn't want that thought confirmed. He just sits there and lets the heat continue to rise around his collar, feeling the burning pleasure of it.

Then suddenly a dark shape fills the door. Arno looks up quickly, thinking it might be the guard again who had threatened him. But it is an internee. A thick-set man named Smitz. One of the athletes. One of the boxing club. He rubs his large hands together and says, "I am looking for Nurse Rosa."

"She is not here," says intern Meyer.

Smitz looks at both Arno and Meyer. Sniffs deeply. Then turns his head a little and spits outside. "Well you two boys tell her when she comes back that I came looking for her. Tell her that I want a special appointment with her." He steps closer into the room and puts his hands on his hips. "You understand me?"

Neither Arno nor intern Meyer reply.

"You tell her that?"

"She is not here," says intern Meyer again. Smitz takes a step closer towards him. "But you must tell her." He says it quietly, so his meaning is very clear.

"She might be back tomorrow," intern Meyer says. "When the doctor is back."

Smitz takes a step back. Then says, "I'm not afraid of the doctor."

"Can I tell him that too?" asks intern Meyer. And Smitz's hand suddenly strikes out, hitting him in the chest. The blow knocks him back against the wall and intern Meyer stays there, hugging the stone for support. Then Smitz sniffs again. He rolls spit around in his mouth, then turns to Arno. "Better look after your friend," he says. "He could do with some nursing."

"That was an excellent attack," Arno says. "You are wasted here and should be in the trenches in France."

He can see Herr Smitz trying to decide if that is a compliment or an insult and then sees the man shrug, turn and steps back outside. He spits noisily again and is gone.

"Are you all right?" Arno asks Intern Meyer.

But he doesn't turn from the wall. Just says, "I'll be okay. Please leave."

Arno finds Herr Herausgeber in the small cell that is his newspaper office. He is very disturbed by the death of Herr Peter, and tells Arno that he is sure there will be a lot of trouble because of it. He has been thinking of writing something in his newspaper about it, but he is not sure what to say.

"Death is a very difficult topic to handle," he tells Arno. "You can craft your words carefully, thinking you have them just right, but you find that when your readers get them they have suddenly changed and taken on new meanings." He picks up a sheet of paper with a single column of type on it, and holds the words up to the light to examine them.

And Arno is filled with a sudden need to tell him what he knows about

Herr Eckert and Herr Peter, and he knows both men were murdered in some way, and that the doctor is aware of it. But Herr Herausgeber is not a good listener and is already talking again. "There will be trouble for all of us because of this, you mark my words," he says, with his head bent down over columns of type laid out on a small desk before him. He has scissors and paste and is moving the words around before him. Creating an article. Creating his own versions of realities. "The Commandant should put a stop to it at once!" he says.

"Put a stop to what?" asks Arno.

Herr Herausgeber turns his head a little to regard Arno. "The alcohol smuggling of course."

Arno shakes his head a little. "What?" he asks.

Now Herr Herausgeber turns fully to regard him. "Don't tell me you don't know?" he asks.

"No," says Arno.

Herr Herausgeber sighs heavily. "You are the most amazing boy. You see so many things and yet you must be the only person in the camp, including the Commandant, who does not know. For months the guards have been smuggling alcohol in for some of the men. It is stored in the watchtowers and they make their transactions in secret in the night. They pay good money for it. But a high price. Too high a price it now seems."

"Do you mean Herr Peter was involved in it?"

"So it appears, although I had believed it was restricted to the members of the Wolf Pack."

Again Arno shakes his head a little. "What?" he asks.

Herr Herausgeber turns back to his words. "And don't try and tell me you didn't know of the Wolf Pack in the camp."

Arno doesn't even try to reply. Everybody talks about the gangs that are active in the large internment camps at Holsworthy near Sydney, organising sedition and causing trouble for the guards whenever they could. But he had no idea they had a presence here. And Arno has that sudden giddy feeling again, that he has emerged from the stone of the walls into a different world to the one he had left.

But then it all becomes suddenly clear to him. It is Herr von Krupp and the athletics club, he thinks. They are the Wolf Pack. That explains his power over the other men. But the doctor? What is his influence? "Who is the leader?" he asks Herr Herausgeber.

But the editor does not reply. Instead he lifts up a sheet of text and says, "Wait until the men read this. The German forces have made great advances on the Western Front. They will overrun the Allies' lines soon. Push them right out of France."

Arno does not need to read it. He has read it all before. Every issue of *Welt am Montag* predicts that the great last push is about to take place. And yet the war goes on—without the word *war* ever being mentioned.

"They will push them right back to England," he says. "Then the German navy will invade England while the airships bomb London. They will conquer the British army and then they will return to the Pacific Ocean. You mark my words, one morning you will walk out the front gates and you will see a dozen ships out there on the horizon, steaming towards the headland here. And we will stream out the gates to welcome them."

"Why was Herr Peter killed?" Arno asks him.

Herr Herausgeber lays down the copy he is working on and turns to look at Arno. "Because the guards fear us. Because they know we shall defeat them. Because they know one day those ships will appear on the horizon. Because they know that Germany is far stronger than they pretend." And he waves his hand dismissively at the pile of Australian newspapers stacked on a chair. Some of the guards sell him old papers to search through for stories for *Welt am Montag*. Arno picks up the top copy and looks at it. The Australians are still fighting over conscription he sees—as if there isn't anything more important to fight over. The other stories are of allied victories in France. German troops demoralised. British war production at an all-time high.

There are photographs from the front. Brave Tommies standing over German trenches waving a British flag. Dead German soldiers lying in the mud. Limbs missing. Blood oozing into the soil. Arno looks at the faces of the dead men. Dark and lifeless. Like Herr Peter. Looks at the faces of the Tommies. Grinning bad teeth. Wild eyes. Mad looking. He wonders if the German troops had looked as mad before they were killed.

Herr Herausgeber looks around and sees Arno is absorbed in the newspapers. "Don't believe anything you read in them," he says quickly. "It's all propaganda. Designed to keep morale high. Designed to make them hate us more."

"Do you think that is why the people over at South West Rocks hate us so much?" asks Arno. "Why they smash our huts? Because they are told to?"

Herr Herausgeber looks back to his words. Cuts out some more and rearranges them. "Yes and no," he says. "They don't only hate us because of the propaganda and the thoughts of their family members who are fighting and being wounded or killed in the war—even though they never stop to think that we too have family members fighting and dying in the war. They also hate us because of the truth of this camp."

"What truth is that?" asks Arno.

"The truth that we get three meals a day. Meat every day. Sun shine and exercise."

"I don't understand," says Arno. "What do you mean?"

"Do you know how their people are being treated in Germany?" he asks Arno. "The prisoners there. Do you think they get meat to eat even once a week? Do you suppose they even get fed well? Or regular exercise? Did you know that there are over one million internees and prisoners in Germany? Living in conditions that make Holsworthy seem pleasant."

Arno hadn't thought of it before. But he knows Herr Herausgeber is right. And he knows the people of South West Rocks know it too, and hate the Germans in the old prison for their sheltered lifestyle. And then he has a sudden image in his mind of the body of Herr Peter dashed onto the hard rocks of the breakwater and the local fisherman Gavin Hooks and his mates standing over him. Holding a British flag. Smiling. Wild eyes. Mad looking.

Arno puts the newspaper down and turns to look at the photos stuck all over the stone walls. Internees swimming on the beach. Internees queued up for breakfast. Men playing tennis. Men sitting on the balcony of a small cafe. Men on the stage of the theatre. Men waving happily at the camera. It is more than just half the world removed from the war, he thinks.

"If you believe even a small bit of what you read in the Australian newspapers," Herr Herausgeber says, "Allied internees are living in labour camps."

But Arno isn't listening any more. His attention has been caught by one photograph pinned up on the editor's wall. Amongst the many photographs there is one he has never seen before—a shot of Hans Eckert dressed like a woman, smiling seductively at the camera. One strap of his or her dress is hanging off the shoulder and one hand is cupped under a breast. And he notes there is a new backdrop of a ship in the background, sailing towards her—or him.

Doctor Hertz returns with the Commandant in the late afternoon. He is met in the dining hall by a delegation of internees led by Herr von Krupp. They talk together for a short time and then the doctor leads them back to see the Commandant. Internees sit in the dining hall or stand around in the compound near the gate, waiting for them to emerge. They are well practised at waiting.

And leaving Herr Herausgeber's office Arno Friedrich limps out into the yard and sees Nurse Rosa is there, sitting on a wooden chair outside the infirmary building. She must have just arrived, he thinks. He watches her lean back against the wall, her eyes closed, her head tilted up to the sun. Arno draws back a little and stares around. The yard there is empty. He looks back to her. Sees her arms lay relaxed in her lap, palms upwards, and her legs are crossed at the feet, with her long white skirt lifted just a little to let the sun onto her legs. The sun shines so brightly off her white uniform that it appears to give an aura to her body. This is how the great painters would have envisaged apparitions of angels, he thinks. Just like this.

He wishes he were standing closer to her, but doesn't want to disturb her. He has never seen her looking so at ease. So unguarded. So given over to pleasure. She smiles, moving her head a little, as the warm sun plays around her neck.

Arno moves his head a little too. Just the way she has. Smiles too. Wishes again he were closer. Sitting next to her. Sharing her pleasure. Watching her face up close. Studying that slight smile upon her lips and examining the set of her arms and legs. Holding his just the same. Perhaps even holding out his hand, so that she would take it in hers. Those long fingers settling in his own like a fragile bird's wing, he thinks. He will write this scene in his diary, he determines. Retell the story so that he is sitting beside her.

There is a sudden noise behind him and he turns to see three men walking out of the dining hall. They are upon him quickly and noisily walk past, towards the Commandant's office, where most of the men have gathered. Arno turns back towards Nurse Rosa, but she has flown. Gone like a startled bird.

Doctor Hertz and the delegation have negotiated with the Commandant for over an hour and emerged triumphant, with permission to erect a memorial to their dead comrades on a high point on the headland, looking out to sea. The word spreads around the compound quickly, gathering enthusiasm. There is an impromptu meeting in the hall and some men volunteer to cart stone from the old quarry used by the convicts, others begin sketching designs. Those with building experience quickly begin debating the best way to build the structure, and others begin drafting the words to go onto the tombstones.

Doctor Hertz is glad of the distraction. The men are so obsessed with the memorial that nobody has asked him what was the cause of Herr Peter's death. Nobody has asked whether he was dead before the sharks got to him, and nobody has asked him how Herr Peter might have gotten outside the prison walls. But he has practiced his answer anyway. "Causes of death are not always what they seem. We should wait for the final results of the full examination."

Such is the infectious zeal with their project, that the first work party makes their way up to the headland that same afternoon. About fifty men, with wheelbarrows and carts descend upon the old quarry, where the convicts of the previous century had slaved away chipping off great chunks of granite for the breakwater. They gather up granite blocks, sweating in the late sunshine, cursing and abusing the heavy stone which skins their hands and cuts their fingers. Then they struggle up the hill with their burdens.

Others, up at the high point on the headland chose the exact plot of land, facing out to sea, and then others set to digging. Herr von Krupp strides around amongst the men, like the Kaiser inspecting his troops. He nods with satisfaction as they dig the foundations and oversees the first cart of granite as it reaches them. Smiles as they sing battle songs while they work.

By the time the sun is low behind them and the guards are calling them back into the prison, they have dug what resembles a fortified trench that is deep enough for a man to crouch in, with granite blocks piled around like battlements. The internees look at each other in great satisfaction and slap backs and rub blistered palms as they make their way back down the hill with the long strides of victory.

"A good start," they say. "But tomorrow—tomorrow we will really make some progress."

The guards stand in the watchtowers and at their barracks further down the headland, watching the Germans return to the prison, and once more they shake their heads. "Silly blood Huns," they say, trying to put the increasing gulf between them into words.

Captain Eaton sits in his office late into the evening, drumming his fingers on his desk as if it might actually distract him from the news in front of him. The portrait of the King silently watches him, as if it knows otherwise. He has an official telegram from the Department of Defence before him. The Sergeant had hand-delivered it to him and stood to attention in his office, waiting for him to open it, as if he knew what was in it already. But the Captain had dismissed him, not wanting to share bad news, or his reaction to it, with anyone. For telegrams during times of war always contain bad news—the death of a family member or being dismissed from your post. When he opened the telegram though he was surprised by its content. New internees were being sent to him within a few days. Prisoners of war. Make preparations. Await further instructions.

That was all it said. He reads it over a few times to pick up the real meaning between the sparse words. Prisoners of war! He wonders who they would be. Officers, of course. Perhaps those from the German raider *Emden,* sunk in the Indian Ocean by the Australian cruiser *Sydney* at the end of 1914. The papers had been full of that story at the time, like it had been a major victory akin to recapturing Belgium or driving the Turks out of Gallipoli.

But military prisoners in the camp will mean significant changes to the way the camp is run. Stricter security. More discipline. Less access outside the prison walls. He will have to dust off the many memos he has received about enforcing stricter controls over the internees' lives—limiting freedom of movement, ensuring no pro-German sentiments are being expressed in the camp.

He imagines a delegation from the Department of Defence will accompany the new prisoners to examine how strictly he has been following all the directives he has received to date, to ensure the prison is suitable for military prisoners. And they will not be pleased with what they find.

So that is the choice he now faces. Should he comply with the directives that have been sent to him, which will also please his wife, in restricting the liberties of the civilians under his charge—or should he risk the disapprobation of the Army and the Department by following his conscience? He drums his fingers on the desk again. If he does not follow the orders of the Army he will risk losing his position, but if he does, he will lose what he believes to be right.

That war could be so morally traumatic for one so far from the front confounds him. He would pray for guidance if he had been a man who found any solace in prayer. As a young man he had toyed with joining the church, drawn to its doctrines of forgiveness, before admitting to himself that he did not have the faith for it. The Captain scowls and wonders if the choices that the front-line officers have to make are actually any easier?

The sun has set and Arno stands by the prison walls under the southwest watchtower, watching the colour going out of the sky, and feeling the rock behind him turning chill and dark. He feels himself turning chill and dark too. There are too many changes to his world to keep up with, and he wishes he had the power to control them, to keep things as stable and safe as he once believed he could.

The nights are noticeably colder now with winter upon them, though the internees mock the winter here and say it has none of the strength of a German winter that toughens the soul. They say an Australian would never survive the chill grip of a real German winter. Arno shivers a little in the night air and wonders if he would survive one.

Keeping his eyes out for any movement ahead of him or behind him, he slowly limps forward and ponders how much of this world of internment that he thought he understood has been kept hidden from him. Then he sees a figure ahead of him and stops. A man is standing there, as if waiting for him. Arno looks at him carefully to see if it is a guard, or perhaps Doctor Hertz, but the figure is too thin and is standing there with his head bowed. Arno takes a cautious step closer and the figure looks up at him and then throws its arms up in alarm and leaps back into the shadows of the wall.

Arno, just as startled, steps back and hits his head against the wall. And he feels a momentary rush of fear, as if sharing something with that dark figure. But then it is gone and he is alone by the wall, thinking he has come close to understanding something but has failed to grasp it.

The guard in the watchtower above him glances down into the prison yard and sees some movement along the dark wall. He leans out a little to peer more closely. There is somebody down there in the shadows below him, he thinks. He grips his rifle a little tighter and raises it. Stares into the blackness. Cautious. Like he remembers staring out into no man's land each night while on watch in France. Eyes flickering between every imagined darkened movement. Looking for the ever-possible signs of a German raiding party, creeping forward to slit his throat in the dark. Being attuned to danger keeps him alive.

He leans a little further out still, and one foot touches the bottles at his feet and two clink together. It makes him jump. It sounds to his ears like the sound of a gun bolt being drawn. Then reason catches up to his imagination and he lowers his rifle and breathes out quickly. He watches the figure below increase his pace and seeing the strange gait carry him around the corner of the cellblock, he recognises the figure. It is only that mad cripple, limping around the walls again. Somebody ought to put a stop to that, he thinks.

Scheherazade dances onto the stage that evening and tells the men that the play to be performed for them will be accompanied by the full orchestra performance—a piece by Richard Strauss—the Opera of Salome the temptress.

The internees applaud politely and the Commandant, seated down the back of the hall, recrosses his legs and looks to the soldier on his left who has given him a full and detailed description of the performance of the previous evening. He does not wish to close the theatre down, but it may be time for a bit of judicious censorship, he suspects.

Scheherazade spins on the spot and says to the men, "Salome was the dark opposite of Scheherazade. I dance and tell stories to evade death—but Salome dances and tells stories that lead to death." Then she spins again and reaches down to the hem of her dress, lifting it over her head in one quick movement, revealing a new costume beneath. A full dark dress, with glittering gems and diamonds around the bodice. Her head is adorned with light veils. The face veil very short. More of her eyes can now be seen. Darkly outlined in kohl and her lips are full and dark red. Her movements change too. She now leads with her hips more. Holds her arms out wide as if inviting an embrace. Shaking her shoulders and breasts more. Smiling to the men in the audience in an enticing way.

The Commandant recrosses his legs yet again, then sits a little further forward on his chair. He is distracted by trying to imagine his wife dancing for him like that. The small orchestra begins the overture as the other players emerge onto the stage. King Herod is dressed like an Arabian king—but in khaki. His wife, Herodias, is by his side, and some assembled Roman soldiers stand about them. Their daughter, Salome, dances rather than walks onto the stage. King Herod and his wife, heavily made up in theatre face paint, wave to the company around them, holding goblets in their hands, enjoying themselves. But Salome dances away from them, to the side of the stage, where there is a prison door. She leans in, full of curiosity, and then inside of the cell is lit. There is a tall man inside, head lifted up to the heavens. He is wearing the costume of Siegfried, the German hero, but everyone knows he is John the Baptist.

Salome is intrigued by this man. Her body language, the commandant sees, shows that never has she seen such a fine and noble being, unbowed by the powers of Rome, and unbowed by the lustful cruelties of her step-father. She hums a melody and sways her hips back and forward as she walks around the cell, admiring the man's body from all angles.

Finally she sings, *"Lass mich deinen Mund küssen!"*—Let me kiss your mouth!

But John the Baptist does not take his eyes away from the heavens and sings. *"Ich will dich nich ansehn. Du bist verflucht."*—I do not wish to look upon you. You are accursed.

And, the Commandant sees, Salome's eyes narrow. Her bottom lip pouts. Her head sinks low towards her shoulders and she spits at John/Siegfried. But she keeps circling him. Keeps admiring his body.

Then the king calls to her, "Salome." And she turns to him, her face petulant as he sings, *"Wie schön ist die Prinzessin Salome heute abend!"*—How beautiful the Princess Salome is tonight.

She looks at him with disdain as he sings to her, *"Tanz für mich Salome. Wenn du für mich tanzest, kannst do von mire begehren, was du willst, ich werde es dir begen."*—Dance for me Salome. If you dance for me, you may ask me for anything you desire, and I will give it to you.

Then she tilts her head to one side and looks at John the Baptist staring up to heaven. Looks at the King. Sees his lustful eyes on her. And she replies that she will dance only if he will grant her a promise. The King takes a long drink from his goblet and agrees. Then he takes a seat and awaits the performance. Salome steps slowly out of her sandals and pushes them aside with one foot. She waits for the orchestra to surround her with the slow swaying dance of the seven veils. Then she begins moving. First her hips. Wide circles. And then her arms rise slowly about her. Her pale hands like two small birds, rising above her and flapping gently. Then she ducks her head a little and begins moving. Slowly towards King Herod. His wife looks away, not pleased with the way her daughter is flirting with her stepfather the King. But King Herod is transfixed. He crosses his legs. Recrosses them and sits further forward on his seat. Swallows hard and his mouth falls open. It is clear that his wife Herodias never danced for him like this.

Salome keeps advancing slowly towards him. Following the waltzing flow of the music, smiling as she glimpses King Herod's lust, then hides her face again. The two white birds fly in front of her features, masking her eyes as her hips move forward, closer and closer to the King.

Then she steps back and turns away. She dances a few steps from him and suddenly spins back. Takes one of the veils from around her head and shoulders, and unwraps it. She advances upon the king once more and drops the veil at his feet. Then she turns and retreats. Advances again. Lays another veil at his feet. A little closer each time. A little closer to the king's reach.

He is now sitting fully forward in his chair, almost tipping from it, his hands gripping the khaki robes tightly about his throat. She retreats from him and advances seven times. Seven veils lay at his feet and she stands before him with nothing left to remove but her clothes.

Then the music stops—just as Salome is so close to him that he could reach out and cup her breasts in his hands. Press his lips into her belly button. Kiss her flesh and bite her on those fleshy hips that are now stilled before him.

Slowly he sits back in his chair. Blinks. Looks at the men around him. But does not look at his wife. He smiles. And Salome also smiles. Waits for King Herod to remember his promise, and he sings, *"Was willst du haben?"*— What is it you want?

And Salome's hips sway just a little bit, as she replies, *"Den Kopf des Jachanaan!"*—the head of John!

Herod recoils from her request and says no, it cannot be. But Salome steps closer to him—closer within reach—and pointedly tells him he has promised it. Tells him that everyone has witnessed it.

Again Herod says he cannot. And again Salome steps closer. So close that Herod cannot breathe without tasting her perfume. So close he cannot turn his head in any direction away from her. So close he cannot deny her. He waves his hand in agreement, and then sinks his head into his hands.

Salome spins and her eyes have become narrow slits of vengeance. She calls to the guards who drag John from his cell and lead him off-stage. The heavy sound of an axe falling is heard and then one soldier returns with John's head on a silver platter.

Salome holds the platter before her, as if mocking the remains of the great hero, and then she leans forward and kisses the lips of the severed head. The guards and Herod are so revolted, and Herod so appalled at how she has played him and what he has allowed to be done, that he orders them to seize her. The music crescendos and cymbals crash as they fling her into John's empty cell. Then the lights dim. The play is ended.

The cast rise together and bow to the audience. And the audience rises and applauds them, loudly but well behaved. The Commandant rises with them, taking his hands from their firm grip of his khaki lapels, and also applauds. Then when the clapping is slowing, he nods to the men next to him and exits the hall, perhaps the only man there not thinking of the beauty of Salome—but rather of the folly of Herod.

Heavy rain has begun lashing down upon the metal prison roof in the night with a sound like a thousand horses charging across a plain towards them. Arno wakes to the sound and looks at his watch. It is exactly midnight. And he writes in his diary—the Witching Hour. It is the first heavy rain that has fallen for some months and it falls with a fury they have never previously experienced.

Arno eventually falls asleep again and a dream comes to him from Herr Schwarz—the leader of the athletics team. He is a young boy lost in the woods, and is afraid of the dark and afraid of snakes and spiders and lizards, and afraid of other creatures that he could not even begin to identify. But when there is a crackling of branches behind him, it is not an animal that emerges, but an old woman. She sees the young boy and her face breaks into a gap-toothed grin.

"Hello," she says. "What is your name?"

But the boy is too afraid to answer her.

"Don't be afraid of me," she says. "I was once young and beautiful."

Then he tells her that his name is Hans.

"I once knew a little boy named Hans," she says. "He was my house guest, but he did not behave very well and he and his sister pushed me into my oven to burn, and then ran away."

The young boy does not know what to say to this. "Are you a witch?" he finally asks.

And she bursts out laughing. A shrill laugh that makes his legs tremble and his stomach shrink in tightly.

"No, I am not a witch. I am a princess. But I have lived alone in these woods for many years for having done something very bad to a man I loved. But love makes you mad sometimes." She looks at him to see if he understands—but can see that he still thinks she might be a witch.

"If I was a witch I would not be so friendly," she says. "If I was a witch

I would kill you and cook you up and eat you."

"What would you kill me with?" the boy asks softly, because it needs asking.

"I would cut off your head with a knife like this," says the old woman, and lifts the cloth from the basket she is carrying, and pulls out a large bayonet and laughs as the boy runs off into the darkness.

6
Another Day

By morning's light it is still raining heavily. Arno stands in the hall and watches the men fetch their breakfast quickly and huddle together at the benches, feeling the chill damp wind enter through each barred window. Then they hurry back to their cells, to crawl back under their blankets. Some men remain and stand in the main doorway, staring out into the yard, watching the rain bombarding the dirt and turning it slowly to mud. Then they too wander away.

Arno has stood in the doorway to the hall since before 7.00 that morning, staring out at the walls, feeling that deep need within him to walk over and touch them. Just to see if he can find any traces of a dream of the murderer. Or any indication of further violence.

Yet he doesn't move.

Some men come hurrying across to the hall, having been rounded up by their Lutheran Minister, Pastor Fischer. It is Sunday today, and he has been going from cell to cell to rouse the men to attend his service. He is a pale-faced man with a chin in full retreat from his mouth, ill-suited to ministering to the demands and troubles of so many men. His dreams are often filled with memories of life in the seminary, which was the only time in his life he felt particularly close to God. Not since leaving its confines has he felt the same. And truth be known, he would prefer to spend his time in isolation, writing on theology. But that is not the world he now lives in—and it shows in his inability to even draw men to his services on a rainy day. But it is hard to sustain faith, yet alone the routines of belief in this world. Very few men have followed him and Arno watches them assemble on the benches of the make-shift place of worship, and bow their heads. The sound of the Pastor's words are drowned out by the rain beating down upon the prison roof—and no one fully hears his preaching of hope and the need for faith during times of adversity. Arno watches him struggles on though, perhaps believing that his words are bringing some meaning to somebody, even if only himself.

He turns and goes back to his cell. He sits on his bunk and presses his palms flat against the stones there, and feels a chill dampness in them. Then he wraps himself tightly in his blanket, and looks up to the thin window. He can feel the cold air coming in and winding its chill touch around them. Then he takes up his diary and writes how he had walked the walls in the rain. Braved the elements to do his duty. Even though he had not.

Horst has developed a cold in the night and he lies on his bunk, wrapped tightly, shivering and sniffling. Every now and then he emits an enormous sneeze that echoes around the small cell like a gun being discharged. And each time he sneezes Arno mumbles, *"Gesundheit."* It is the closest they have had to a conversation for some time.

There are few men out in the corridor as most have gathered in their cells in small groups, hiding from the elements or the Sunday service, talking or playing cards, or just huddled under their blankets, trying to return to sleep through the lassitude of a wet Sunday in internment.

Herr Kaufmann, walking back to his cell after the morning's service is finally done, puts his head into Arno's cell and says, "This rain is good news, yes? It should wash away the blood and guts on the beach, making it safer to swim again."

Arno looks up at him. The optimistic smile on his face is like an actor's painted mask, he thinks. "Yes," he says. But Herr Kaufmann has gone before the words are even said. Arno wonders what else the rain will wash away? It might wash all the colour from the outside world, he thinks. It will certainly wash away any blood stains left behind by Herr Eckert and Herr Peter.

He closes his eyes and tries to picture the blueness of the ocean in his mind, but all he can conjure is a deep grey. He looks back across to Horst and watches him shiver. Then he sneezes again—an almighty shot. *"Gesundheit,"* Arno says. Horst says nothing.

And Arno is tempted to ask Horst what he thinks about as he lies there alone on his bunk during the days. His wife? His children? Does he dream of flying away from the prison perhaps? Or does he think of dying there? Like the two men already dead. Then Arno suddenly says, "I believe Herr Peter died out in the compound in the middle of the night."

Horst slowly rolls over on his bunk and looks at him. He sniffles a little, then says, "Yes. He often left his cell in the night." His eyes are red and weepy, and Arno sees just how ill the older man is.

Arno sits forward on his bed. "What do you mean?"

"Herr Peter regularly left his cell late in the night. Often not returning again until near the morning." And Arno understands he is sharing his cell with a man that he does not really know at all.

"Why?" asks Arno, but can see from Horst's face that it is the wrong question to ask him. "I mean, how do you know?"

Horst rubs his watery eyes, as if he's too tired for spite today, and says, "Franz, his cell-mate told me."

Arno knows Franz Grübber as a tall thick-set man. An Austrian. And an active member of the athletics club. An unlikely cell mate for Herr Peter, whose interests in life were more classical, although Arno had always suspected he had too strong an interest in watching other men bathing down on the beach, reflected in his dreams of swimming with young boys in a large bath. He had also heard some of the men calling him "decadent"—in a deriding tone. But all he can ask Horst, again, is, "Why?"

"Maybe he was a member of the Wolf Pack," says Horst, then sneezes again. Another sudden shot echoing loudly around the cell. Then he ducks his head back into his blankets to signal the conversation is ended.

Arno lies back down on his bunk and pulls his own blankets over his head. He opens his diary inside his little cave and writes that name there, *Wolfsrudel*, as if it is very secret and dangerous. As if it needs to be kept hidden.

Herr Dubotzki is sitting in the dark of his small cell. The door is tightly sealed. Locked from the inside. He is staring at a blank sheet in front of him. Watching as an image starts to form. He moves the paper a little with his tweezers and lets the developer run over it. He stares carefully as an outline forms. Sees the soft grey of a face appearing. Watches the face slowly solidify. Like it is stepping out of the darkness around it. The eyes are taking shape now, and the mouth. Then the more subtle tones around the cheeks and nose. It is a face he knows well. Pandora's face—but without the veil. He knows just what it would be worth to him to sell the photo in the prison. But he knows there would be a higher price he would have to pay. He holds the print down in the tray before him, refusing to let the face surface to the air. Holds it down as the features darken and the background fills out completely. Then the face ages to a deep grey. And finally to black. He takes the print out of the developer and drops it into a bin at his feet, filled with other darkened images. He smiles to himself as he takes a clean sheet of photographic paper. Just one more, he thinks.

Doctor Hertz has a frock over one arm and a pair of women's stockings in the other. "Try the dark dress," he says.

Fritz Fuchs, a young engineer with a thin and bony body, sighs and pulls the blue dress over his head. He is becoming bored with this. All the dress changing. The make-up. The wigs. The padded breasts. He is wondering if he still wants to be an actor. But the doctor has confidence in him. He has told him that he can shape him into a great actor. Fritz Fuchs isn't so sure. The doctor has told him he has perfect bone structure to play a woman, and is trying to get him to stand and walk like a woman.

They are in the small infirmary, where much of the rehearsing is done. It is private and less intimidating, the doctor has assured him. Costumes and accessories are spread out over the beds and intern Meyer stands to one side of the room, disinterestedly cleaning some jars.

"How is this?" Fritz asks, adopting a pose. Doctor Hertz adjusts the dress, sets the wig straight and then walks around him. He takes up one of his hands and sets it on his hip. Bends the fingers out a little. Then grabs his shoulder and massages it as if it were clay, and he were reshaping it. He relaxes the muscles there and bends it to the shape he wants. Then he takes up Fritz's other arm and holds it by the wrist, moving the hand back and forth in a soft swaying motion.

Then he stands back, like a sculptor, admiring his work, sizing up the line and angle. He steps in close again and places a hand under Fritz Fuchs's chin, and tilts the head back a little. Then he turns it on a slight angle. He steps away and looks at it. Frowns. Steps in closer and puts Fritz's hands on his hips. Moves them a little. One side slightly higher than the other. Steps back. Looks again at his creation. Smiles.

"*Ja,*" he says. "*Es ist gut.*" Then he says. "Walk for me."

Fritz takes several steps across the room and turns his head to look at the doctor as he goes. But the doctor is shaking his head. *"Nein, nein, nein,"* he says. "Women don't walk like that. They glide."

Fritz Fuchs pulls a face. "My sisters never glided," he says. "They walked like this."

"Acting is not about becoming the women you remember," the doctor says. "It is about becoming the women you imagine."

Fritz considers that. "Here," says the doctor. "Meyer. Show him how it is done."

Meyer puts down the jars he is cleaning and without saying a word he walks over to the wall and takes down a long apron. He ties it around his waist and then stands with his back to them for a moment. Then he turns around slowly. His face and posture have changed completely. His chin is tilted up and he holds his hands slightly away from his body. He looks around the room, as if sizing up its space, not looking at any of the people there—and then he walks. No, he glides. Right across the room, from one side to the other and back. Fritz Fuchs is astounded. The transformation is so consummate that he feels he is watching a woman. Meyer stops at the wall again, with his back to them, and lets his posture drop as he turns back into the doctor's intern. He doesn't even smile. Just walks back to the jars and begins cleaning where he left off.

Fritz Fuchs claps, soft and slowly. *"Sehr gut,"* he says. "Yes. It is much easier to understand when you see it before you."

Arno looks at his watch. 3.20pm. He listens to the rain. It has let up a little, but is still falling as incessantly as afternoon boredom. He looks over at Horst. He is dozing noisily, heaving great sighs as he breathes. Arno looks at his watch again. It is still 3.20. He has his diary in front of him. He has been staring at the empty page but cannot quite capture what to write. As if words are beyond him today. He counts the stone blocks up the wall to the roof—one to twelve. Then back down again—twelve to one. Then he looks at his watch again. 3.20. He lifts it to his ear to listen to it. Tic—tic—tic. He watches the long minute hand to see if he can observe it moving. He counts the seconds in his head 1—2—3… The count fades away somewhere in the twenties and he turns to look out the cell door. Somebody is pacing in the corridor. Walking down towards the hall, then back again. He tries not to look at his watch anymore. Tries not to count the stones in the wall again. Tries not to think of the look on Herr Eckert's face again. 3.20. And he once more wonders which of his cell mates might be a killer—and if he is even aware of it?

Commandant Eaton is sitting in his office with Sergeant Gore before him. The Captain has demanded that he produce a list of suspects for the two murders, and is not happy to be told by the Sergeant that he has been unable to identify any. "Even someone that we can investigate more thoroughly in order to clear their name would be progress," the Captain says. "For if you can't manage it, we will be forced to accede to the Military Police." The Captain has practised this line to hide the desperation from his voice.

Sergeant Gore stares back at him in consternation for a moment, and then has to check himself to stop a sly grin spreading across his face. He recognises a bluff when he sees one—even if not at first. The Captain will have a lot more to lose from the MPs giving them a visit than he will. Though the thought of them searching through the barracks fills him with unease. He looks at the Captain and suddenly finds that he has a common interest with him.

"Righto," he says. "Here's my thinking on the matter. It was a feud that was imported into the camp—not one that was created here, like the way the Turks and Germans fight in Holsworthy for no other reason than being Turks and Germans. We've got Jews and Christians and competing businessmen in here, and some who have brought wealth with them and some who haven't—and that just sets the ground for jealously and conflict."

"Go on," says the Captain, all too aware that people who are brutalised tend to be those that brutalise others in turn, but not convinced that any of the men in his care could be said to have been driven to such extremes.

"Well, to my mind there are only two things a man decides it is worth killing for—a woman or money," says the Sergeant.

The Captain says nothing but he is thinking that there is some logic in what the Sergeant says, even if his imagination is limited by only two incentives to murder.

"And since there ain't no women here, the disagreement must have been about money. If we follow the trails of the Huns' money around the prison I reckon we'll find our murderer."

The Captain considers that and watches the way the Sergeant looks up at the portrait of the King over his head. "Continue that line of investigation then, Sergeant," Captain Eaton says. "And let me know what you find." He is not confident that the Sergeant's line of reasoning will identify the killer, and he wonders if that is because he does not want to believe that any of the men are capable of acting like the beastly Huns they are all too-often portrayed as. It would only prove his wife right to find one was a murderer.

"Yes, sir," Sergeant Gore says, and snaps a salute at his commanding officers. He then turns and leaves the office, thinking that if it were easier to find someone to blame the murder on than to find no one, then that's what he'd have to do. The only real decision then was who he should find, because he does not want to look where his instincts tell him the murderer will actually be found.

There is no performance that evening, being a Sunday, but all the inmates are treated to a long drumming concert on the metal roof of the cell wings, as the rain has still not let up. Chill damp air continues to creep in through their barred windows, and men don heavy coats and wrap themselves in their blankets. Horst had not risen all day, except for a quick trip to the latrine. He is still shivering and sneezing.

All down the corridor, as internees enter or exit their cells, swinging open the barred doors, Arno can hear the same joke being repeated over and over, "Close that door, it's freezing in here!"

Arno plays out in his head walking around the prison yard, touching the stone walls and trying to feel the dreams stirring within. For only a madman would be out tonight in weather like this, he thinks.

Private Cutts-Smith is in the southwest watchtower looking out into the dark rain. He curses the weather. There is a wind blowing the icy drops into the tower that catches him wherever he stands. He curses the rain. Then he curses the army. Then he curses the Huns.

"Bastards," he mutters. This is not much better than being on patrol in the trenches. Feet in cold water. Feeling the rot in his boots. Shivering and staring into the night until his eyes feel they have turned to ice. Just waiting for the flares to go up. Waiting for the whistles to sound. Knowing an attack is getting closer. He can recall feeling at times that the corpses out in no man's land were creeping towards them, as the rotting and putrid stench of them drifted in, as if warning them of an enemy attack. He would lift his rifle and lean out into the darkness, wishing he could use it to part the curtains of rain. Wishing he could see the men advancing upon him. Wondering if he should fire off a flare just in case. Wondering if it would have much effect on the rain that beats down on his metal helmet like falling clods of earth after a shell burst. It would make him deaf to all noise. Blot out the advance of the Hun, sneaking up on him to slit his throat.

He wipes the streams of water from his face and stares out into the darkness again. Shivers. Wishes he'd put on his sheepskin jerkin. Thinks for a moment he can see movement out there. The shape of a man running around the corner of the cellblock. Running across the compound towards him. Coming for him, to slit his throat. He looks around for a flare gun. Thinks, if only he could see them he would be able to pick them off before they got him. Then sniffs the air for that warning smell of corpses.

Arno dreams of death that night. Not another murder though. This dream belongs to a German industrial engineer named Schmiedecker, and is of the man's father, walking along a bush track, begging passers-by to be godfather to his newborn child. But the man is so poor that no one is willing to agree to it.

Not until Death comes along the path, clad in black robes, and says that he will be godfather to the child, and as a gift he will give the boy the ability to see who will live and who will die. The father is very thankful and praises Death for his kindness. But as the boy grows older he finds the gift is also a curse. He is a young man now and becomes a soldier, in charge of a troop of men. And he is ordered to lead them into combat. But when he looks at them he can see that they will all die.

In the dream, Herr Schmiedecker, the soldier, chooses to run away rather than lead the soldiers to their deaths. But he is then stumbling through a muddy no man's land and is surrounded by enemy soldiers. They capture him and throw him into a prisoner of war camp. And even there he is haunted by the gift, for when he looks at the faces of any of his fellow internees, he sees that are all fated to die as well. And this time there is nowhere to run away to.

7
Another Day

The next morning the sun is out, shining brightly, just like it does on most days. Arno has been at the wall before sunrise, standing on the damp ground and pressing himself hard against the chill stone, ensuring that there is no trace of violence within. Hoping for a day that will bring no major change. Nothing new. Just one more day like any other.

But of course it is not.

After breakfast and another protracted roll call the internees are lined up at the gates with shovels on shoulders or wheelbarrows in hands and regulation white canvas hats on heads. They are ready for a solid day's labour working on the monument. The guard comes out of the guardhouse and sees the men assembled for work and thinks for a moment to make a joke of it. But he can't quite form the right words in his head and so he just spits to the side and unlocks the gates.

The internees stream out, splashing through puddles, some heading up the hill and some making their way to the quarry. Arno lets them push past him and then swings himself forward to take in the expanse of blue ocean. He feels himself calming at the sight of it. It seems so much bluer today. Bluer than it has ever been before. Larger than it has ever been before. He holds up his hands to shield his eyes from the enormity of it and then slowly turns his head to take it all in.

There are no ships steaming towards them today. No fishing boats out on the sea. And he turns away from the direction the other men are taking and makes his way down to the beach. There are no remains of the whale left there. The storm has washed them out into the bay, where the ocean's strong current will have dragged them far away, obliterating them more thoroughly than the sharks had.

He tilts his head back and breaths in the scent of distant eucalypts and salt air. It smells like freedom to him. Arno then makes his way right down onto the sand. It is all pock-marked with the force of the rain and is wet like the tide had risen half-way up the cliffs in the night. He swings his way down towards the water, noting that his are the only feet prints there. His crutches sink deeply into the damp sand as he moves, and he continues right up to the water's edge. He lets the sun embrace him. Warm him. Lets the breeze off the water clear his mind a little.

Then the turns and looks back up on to the headland. He can see the internees making their way up the hill there like an advancing party of soldiers, holding shovels across their shoulders like they might hold rifles. Advancing on the enemy's positions on the high point. Walking quickly. Occasionally slipping in the mud in their haste.

Arno turns again and looks out across the bay. He searches for any sign of dark shadows swimming beneath the water. He knows there will be nobody in the little watchtower chair on the beach today, but resolves to swim anyway.

He slowly undresses and lays his clothes in a small pile near his crutches. Lays his watch in his canvas hat on top of them all. Looks at the time. 9.12. He thinks what a perfect day it will be today. He limps slowly out into the water. Feels the chill of it. Colder than he could remember it ever having been before. He wades out until it is around his thighs, then, taking a deep breath, he lowers himself quickly up to his neck. His testicles strategically retreat. The chill forces his breath out and he begins paddling his arms in the water. Kicking his legs and moving around. Getting the blood moving to warm his body.

Then he turns over and begins swimming. Slow strong strokes that carry him out into the bay. The further he swims the colder the currents are, but he keeps on. He swims until he is level with the end of the breakwater and can feel the first strong pull of the ocean's current tugging at his legs. Then he turns and looks back to the prison. He sees the dark silhouette of the watchtowers and he sees the small shapes of men in the distance, toiling with blocks of granite, carting them slowly up the hill.

He chooses to imagine it is the convicts of the last century he is watching, toiling futilely on the breakwater. Then chooses to imagine that if he turns and keeps swimming he could swim forever.

Herr von Krupp is pleased with the day's progress on the hilltop. He arrived with the first men there that morning to find that the trenches they had dug for their memorial's foundations were flooded and had collapsed, and many of the blocks of granite they had placed there had slid down the hill as the soil under them turned to mud.

But they were undaunted. They bailed the foundation trenches and then dug out the mud. They threw fresh soil into the base and carted more granite from the quarry. They toiled on. For Herr von Krupp has a clear vision of what this monument will look like. It will be a fine memorial to the fallen—and not just to those who have died in the prison, but those German heroes who had sacrificed themselves for the Fatherland in Europe and Africa and German New Guinea.

Though God help that no more men should die here at Trial Bay.

Sergeant Gore is in the eastern watchtower. Private Gunn is beside him, standing fast to attention. He hopes the Sergeant isn't looking too closely at his uniform as he knows it is pretty scruffy today. His top two buttons are undone too. He had been hoping for a quiet cigarette up here in the tower alone. Hadn't expected the Sergeant to suddenly appear before him. The Sergeant almost never climbs up into the watchtowers. But Sergeant Gore isn't watching Private Gunn. He has his field glasses tightly up to his eyes and is staring up the hill, watching the internees there. He does not like the way they are banding together. Does not like the precision with which they are working. Does not like this sudden burst of enemy activity at all.

Private Gunn takes the opportunity to lean his rifle quietly against the side of the watchtower and bring his hands up to fasten his buttons. He almost has the second of them done up when the Sergeant lowers his field glasses and turns back to him. Gunn grabs up his rifle and lowers his chin a little to cover the last undone button.

Sergeant Gore holds out the glasses to him. "Take these," he says. "I want you to keep a very close eye on what's happening up there. I'll be back every half hour for a report."

"Yes sir!" says Private Gunn, and takes the field glasses. He looks at them curiously for he has never used them before.

"Do you know how to use them?"

"Yes sir!" says Private Gunn.

The Sergeant nods. "Good man," he says. Gunn smiles and watches the Sergeant make his way back down into the yard. Then he lifts the field glasses to his eyes. He isn't sure what to see through them. He moves them around until he sees the German internees up on the hill. They appear closer, but less well defined. He squints and blurs his eyes, but can't get them to focus properly. He can't see the features of any of the men clearly. Then an idea takes his fancy that he might be spotting for artillery in France. A little higher. Further to the left. Pow. He lowers the glasses for a moment and the full panorama of the headland and the ocean fills his vision gain, making him a little giddy. He lifts the glasses back up once more. He isn't quite sure how to work them and isn't quite sure what he's meant to be watching, but he is sure the Sergeant will be back soon asking for a report, so he keeps them trained on the men up on the hill. So, he watches them toiling up the slope and digging in the mud—but what he sees is that he might have a chance for a quick cigarette after all.

At 10.58 Arno is lying on the bed in the infirmary, waiting for Nurse Rosa. "Just a moment," she calls from the small room next door. "You're a little early."

He looks at his watch again, and looks around the bare room. He thinks perhaps he can detect a faint smell of her in the air around him. Perhaps. Then she comes into the room and puts her hands on her hips. She smiles broadly and says, "What is your hurry today?" She is in a good mood.

"I'm always in a hurry to see such a happy pretty face," he says boldly.

"Ha!" she says, and sits down and picks up one of his feet. She presses it against the starched white uniform by her thigh and begins massaging it. Arno looks at her between his legs and closes his eyes. He knows he's smiling broadly himself but he doesn't care.

Then he opens his eyes again. He decides he prefers to watch her today. She looks up and sees his idiot stare. "And what are you grinning at?" she asks him.

He shrugs. "You."

"Why me?"

"There's no one else to look at in here."

"Tsk-tsk," she says, and looks down at his feet as he fidgets a little with his trousers. He moves the waistband around a little, trying to make it look like he's making them more comfortable. "You should be thinking of your girlfriend, not me," she says.

"What girlfriend?"

She looks back at him. "You must have had many girlfriends before you came here." He shrugs again and tries to remember the name of one girl back in Western Australia. Tries to remember her face. The soft touch of the cloth of her dress when it brushed against him. White with a fine red ribbon woven into the hem. He recalls the feeling of her though. One day he stood so close to her bare freckled shoulders that it made him giddy—reaching out his hand and feeling how warm and soft the skin was. It was just that one time, but he had dreamed of touching her like that many nights, and of her touching him. Until that night he looked up and saw the six dark angels around his bed with their bayonets poised. He thought at first they had come to punish him for lusting after an Australian girl. Thought that her bigoted father might have sent them.

He remembers that he had once thought of her every day—in the old world—but now he can't even remember her face or her name. "Let's talk about something else," he says.

"Like what?"

"One of your secrets."

She stops massaging him and says, "What makes you think I have secrets?"

"I have always thought you must have a great many of them."

"Well—I do have one," she says.

"Yes?" asks Arno.

She leans forward and says in a soft and confidential voice, "Do you know what I heard from Doctor Hertz about the men from the *Emden*?"

During lunchtime, *Welt am Montag* is distributed throughout the camp. Herr Herausgeber is proud to be the one who shares news with the whole camp, as he is proud to be the one that controls the news. He walks amongst the rows of benches laying the thin eight-paged newspaper on the tables beside those men who have subscribed to it. For their payments they get to read its news first, and in the camp news is a commodity to be waited for, and savoured—even when it is mostly already known. But there are usually a few bits that are really quite new.

The copies will then slowly make their way down to the rest of the men, like a chewed-over block of dried meat, less valued each time it is passed to another man. But when it appears newly printed, men snatch it up eagerly, ignoring their meals and devouring the words in front of them. Savouring each phrase of their mother tongue. They read some parts out loud to their table comrades, smiling at the way German victories are reported in camouflaged language. Or they laugh at the obviously satirical way Australian news is reported—such as stories of sheep flocks increasing but beer production being rationed. And they always enjoy the theatre reviews, so full of hyperbole. But each reader becomes a little more solemn when they read the obituary notices for Herr Eckert and Herr Peter. The newspaper eulogises them as great heroes, and summarises their lives outside the prison—in the old world—expressing confidence at the greatness each man would have achieved in his field, had they not been interned. The men read those words several times over and then turn back to their meal—sated on words for the moment and content to pick over the articles again and again and again in the privacy of their cells.

Herr Kaufmann, who is a subscriber and is sitting beside Arno, tells him that the obituary report says that Doctor Hertz has been officially informed that Herr Peter's death has been attributed to an accident. It was determined that he had fallen from the wall and had seriously injured himself, and had then stumbled along the breakwater where he had fallen again, and there had been attacked by the sharks. His body was then carried back up onto the breakwater by the strong tide. He reads out each word in the report very carefully and precisely, as if it is important that he himself believes it. But Arno does not believe it and asks Herr Kaufmann, "So there is nothing in the newspaper about the *Emden* officers coming here?"

It is all he needs to say and word quickly overtakes the newspapers being passed around, leaping from table to table. "*Emden* officers are coming here!" This is something so new and so compelling that copies of the newspaper are now being left unread on tables. Herr Herausgeber grinds his fists as he hears the rumour, and thinks for an instant that he should take all the newspapers back from the ungrateful men and then reprint it with the *Emden* story. But he knows it is too late. This is a different type of news—something that he has no control over.

After lunch, while the labourers return to the hill on the headland, Arno makes his way back to his cell and finds Horst is sleeping. His breathing is laboured and heavy. Arno has told him that he should go to the infirmary for his fever, but Horst has refused. He says Arno can go there and have his feet massaged, or any other part of him he cared for, but he would not be going.

Horst looks much worse today. Arno has told him that he should at least go out into the sunshine and try to dry the infection out of his lungs. But Horst wrapped himself tighter in his blanket and rolled over towards the wall. Fell asleep. And didn't once taunt Arno about his poor German.

Arno steps over and looks at him now. There is heavy spittle hanging out his mouth and mucus blowing from his nose when he snores. Arno reaches out and puts his fingers gently on Horst's brow. It is a peculiar feeling, for it is the first time he has ever touched him. The skin feels hot. Clammy and hot. Arno runs his fingers slowly around the edges of Horst's face and wonders if he can feel that in his sleep and imagine it might be his wife. He pulls his hand back and takes up the blanket to tuck it a little tighter around Horst's neck. And then he sees a book there. Between Horst and the wall. He thinks it not a safe place to put a book and he picks it up, meaning to put it onto the shelf above his bed. And then he sees the photo sticking out of it. It is probably a picture of Horst's unseen wife and children, he thinks, and he pulls it out to look at it. But it is not Horst's wife. It is a small photograph of Pandora, as she had danced for the men in the hall. He looks at it and feels his own skin turning hot. Then he opens the book and lets it fan open in his palm. It is a diary like his own, full of small tightly scrawled Gothic print. And there are photographs between the pages. He pulls out another. It is a picture of a woman, heavily made up, leaning against a chair. One hand is held up beside her face. Her long hair is tied back behind her head. There is a look of boredom on her face. Sensual boredom, Arno thinks. A look he has seen before. Then he knows where. The women's face. It is Klaus Peter.

Horst suddenly coughs and turns on his pillow. Arno quickly puts the photos back in the book and slips it down beside Horst's head, then turns and leaves the cell, the ground feeling just a little giddying beneath his feet.

Sergeant Gore is alone with the Dark Knights. Just him and his six chosen, in the remains of an old stone store building that the convicts built outside the prison walls. The darkness within is dissipated by a single candle and he is whipping them into a frenzy, talking loudly, above the sound of rain falling outside.

"The Hun was the first one to use gas," he says. "He had no principles about how ungodly a weapon it was. At first they used to lay out long pipes and pump it towards our trenches, but sometimes the Good Lord would turn the wind back towards them and they'd get a mighty dose of their own medicine."

The six chosen smile and chuckle, despite being cold and wet.

"But the Hun is crafty," Sergeant Gore says. "He then loaded it into shells and shot it at our boys from many miles away."

The men curse the Hun's ingenuity in warfare.

"But he is crafty because he is a coward," Sergeant Gore says. "He is notorious for trickery and deceit. Did you know that the cruiser *Emden* had been disguised as a merchant vessel." He looks around the group. "The captain had a false funnel constructed to disguise the ship. Too many merchant vessels were lured falsely into their doom because of Hun trickery."

"Did they fire gas shells at them?" asks Private Strap.

Sergeant Gore turns and looks at him. Sees his question was serious. "Gas is not effective at sea because of the high winds," he tells him. "It is most effective inside a confined space." Private Strap nods his head very slowly, as if that is a statement he is committing to his memory forever.

"Hun officers are skilled in deceit and treachery," he tells them, "and you'd all be advised to keep a very, very close watch on our new guests. It's my bet that they'll be up to something before very long."

The six men nod their heads eagerly. It is happening at last. The war is coming to them!

The truck with the *Emden* officers arrives in the middle of the afternoon. The men working on the memorial on the hill pause to watch it drive out of the dark forest and up the thin road. They lean on their shovels and follow its slow progress up to the prison gates. They see a small squad of guards emerge from the guard house, and, peering harder now, shielding their eyes from the sun, watch carefully as four men climb down from the truck and be led into the prison at close gun point.

The internees look at the rock and dirt at their feet and then look at Herr von Krupp. And one by one they shoulder their shovels and make their way down the hill back towards the prison.

The *Emden* officers are standing in a small group together, with their Captain in front, as they have stood every time they had been transferred over the past three years. Commandant Eaton comes out to greet them, but he does not shake their hands. The four men look around the empty prison yard and look at each other.

"I trust your journey here was not unpleasant," the Commandant says.

"There was some small trouble at the township," says Captain von Müller. "Many protesters. Some throwing rocks. Apparently, many of the locals do not want us here."

He has a thin face with a pointed nose, and high cheekbones. And Captain Eaton thinks he has seen the like in a Biblical painting somewhere. Perhaps one of the ancient kings. Perhaps. "Yes," he says. "There is a certain amount of antagonism from the local people. They tolerate the internees, but are less accepting of actual prisoners of war who have engaged in military activities against them."

"I don't recall ever shelling this tiny hamlet," says von Müller. "Did we ever raid here, Wolff?" he asks one of the lieutenants behind him.

"No sir," the surliest looking of them says. "I'm sure I would have advised it a waste of shells."

The Commandant's face reddens a little. He sees this man has the most piercing blue eyes—and his hair is so fair it is almost white. He also sees a twinkle of danger in the man's eyes, undimmed by almost three years of captivity. "We are used to a well-regulated and organised lifestyle here," he tells his new prisoners. "Life is not hard, but you will be expected to follow the regulations and not cause any disruptions."

Captain von Müller makes the slightest of bows, and then asks, "You have many men here?"

"Over four hundred men," says the Commandant proudly.

The four officers look around the compound once more. They run their eyes over the rows of cells and their many barred windows. Captain Eaton sees their backs stiffen a little and suspects they have been in small cells before, and they know what to expect of them.

Then Captain von Müller turns his head towards the gates. He hears the sound of many feet approaching. Men in shabby work clothes are walking up the road to the gate, holding shovels and tools in their hands, with ugly white canvas hats on their heads.

"What is this?" asks von Müller. "A reception committee of your country-men? Come to smash down the walls to send us back to Holsworthy?"

The Commandant says nothing until the first of the men have reached the gates and stand there, lowering their tools and staring at the four new arrivals. He waits until he can see the unease in the four officers. Waits until the crowd has built to a menacing size, far outnumbering the guards. Then he says, "Captain von Müller, lieutenants Wolff, Bärr and Kat, these are your countrymen, not mine."

The *Emden* officers are handed over to Herr von Krupp for a tour around the prison. He thanks the Commandant with a sharp click of his heels and leads the men around the walls. At every corner it seems there is an internee, aged or overweight, waiting to shake hands with the sailors.

Herr von Krupp leads them through the kitchens. Through the infirmary. Introduces them to Dr Hertz. Shows them the washrooms. The workshops where the internees mend clothes or shoes. The hall where the orchestra practises. The cell where Herr Herausgeber produces the newspaper, and finally into the great hall where he sits them at a table with coffee and buns waiting for them.

Captain von Müller is polite, but his fellow officers appear less tolerant, and finally the youngest lieutenant, a tall man with very close-cropped blond hair, says, "Yes, yes, you have shown us everything except our quarters. Will you show us them please?"

"Forgive me," says Herr von Krupp. "You are undoubtedly tired after your journey and would welcome a rest before dinner. Let me escort you myself." He waits for the four officers to rise and leads them down one cellblock—to the far end, where two cells have recently been emptied of brooms and buckets for them.

"We are expected to make our own furniture and beddings," explains Herr von Krupp, "but we have proved quite enterprising in this, even charging the authorities for our labours." He smiles as he talks, as if this is a victory over the enemy to be proud of. "But of course we won't expect you to have to make your own furniture. We are honoured to provide this to brave German officers like yourselves."

"Yes, yes," says the Lieutenant. "Thank you. I would like to rest now." And he strides into one of the cells and closes the door. Von Müller and von Krupp look at him through the bars and von Müller says, "Lieutenant Wolff finds that incarceration brings out the worst in him, which you may find too."

"I'm sure he will find that he is only amongst friends and comrades here," says von Krupp.

"Yes," says the Captain. "I'm sure that if he finds nothing else in this godforsaken outpost he will at least find that." Then he bows a little to von Krupp and opens the door and goes into the cell with the young lieutenant.

The officers don't emerge from their cells again until dinnertime when Herr von Krupp personally escorts them into the dining hall. He has members of the athletics club ready there to take control, and when the four new arrivals enter the hall all the internees rise and applaud them. The officers look self-consciously at each other and ask Herr von Krupp to please ask the men to stop.

Herr von Krupp nods and strides to the front of the hall, holding up his hands for silence. The applause dies down and he says, in a strong voice, "Gentlemen, we are honoured to have heroes of the German Empire amongst us. I trust they will find our humble meals fitting and our entertainment worthy of the sacrifices they have made for the Fatherland."

All eyes then turn to Captain von Müller. The internees stand by their places, waiting for his stirring words. Waiting for his fine speech. But he simply says, "Please do not treat us any different from the rest of you." Then he sits at the table. The internees stand there for several long moments before they too begin taking their seats again.

Doctor Hertz sits opposite Captain von Müller, as if he has important things to discuss with him. But before he can say anything, Herr Herausgeber squeezes himself onto the end of the table, and asks, "What news from the front?"

Captain von Müller stares at the editor as if he has said something quite preposterous. "I hear there is going to be a big push any day now," Herr Herausgeber insists. "I hear our troops are preparing for the final assault that will carry them all the way to Paris. I hear they have created new guns that can reach London from Berlin."

Still Captain von Müller just stares at him.

"I hear they are amassing a fleet to sail to South East Asia to reoccupy German territories. You know the German raider *Wolf* is already active in the Indian and Pacific oceans, sinking allied shipping. The fleet will recapture German New Guinea and will sail right down to Sydney. They will sink the Australian navy ships and land on the shores of the prison here. Liberating us all."

"You hear all this?" asks von Müller.

"We hear many things…" begins Herr Herausgeber, but von Krupp is now beside him, and cuts him off. "This is Herr Herausgeber, the editor of our camp newspaper," he says.

"I'm sorry," says Captain von Müller to him. "I have heard none of these things."

Herr Herausgeber looks surprised. "You have not?"

Then Lieutenant Wolff leans a little over the table and bares his teeth as if he were going to bite him, and says, "We have been prisoners since 1914. We have been living in small cells on the Cocos Islands, then in several tropical backwaters, and for the last two years in that infernal heat and dust of Holsworthy—what news of the front do you think we have?"

Herr Herausgeber looks hurt. Then the Captain smiles to him. A weary smile. "I'm sorry," he says. "I have heard none of these things yet, but if I hear of them now I will certainly let you know."

Herr Herausgeber sits back a little and nods his thanks. *'Danke.'* Then he just sits there with his hands holding tightly onto the edge of the table, as if it were a life preserver, holding them all afloat in a wide rough sea.

A rno stands under the southwest watchtower as darkness descends. He touches the rock wall at his back and thinks of all the changes of that day that have distinguished it from any other. He thinks of Horst's infection, which has not cleared up. He thinks of the *Emden* officers. Thinks of the way the internees are reacting to them. The way the guards are subtlety treating them all like military prisoners now. He thinks of the memorial to the dead. And he thinks of the way the truth about the deaths will be buried with them unless he can discover it.

He stands there with his back to the stone wall, and ponders what other secrets are hidden in the cold rock before leaning forward and making his slow way around his nightly circuit, seeing shades and shadows scuttle away in front of him, long before he reaches them, and wondering what unsettling things he might dream that night. Wondering if any two days will ever be the same again.

Dinner has been cleared away, and the hall readied for the evening concert. The audience sit waiting for the orchestra to gather. They know tonight will be special and the four *Emden* officers are seated at the very front of the hall. Herr von Krupp sits on one side of them and Herr Schwarz on the other. They keep leaning across and telling the officers that they are in for a pleasant surprise. The officers nod politely and look back and forward at each other, clearly not needing words between themselves.

Then the orchestra walks out and takes their seats, as solemn as if they are the Berlin philharmonic. Herr Schröder the conductor then comes out and gives a short bow. Without a word he turns to the players and lifts his baton aloft. He holds it there a moment, then brings it swiftly down. Boom. The drum beats a single loud note and the strings leap in to follow it, thrumming strongly. The men in the hall smile. They know this one well. Wagner! The Ring of the Rhine Maidens!

The strings carry the rhythm, then the brass comes in—loud! The drums roll. The brass roars again—the sounds of the Germanic gods. The *Emden* officers smile. The strings take up the rhythm again. A fast beat like a forced march. Then the brass returns. Strong and stirring. The flight of the Walküries. The audience thrums with the music, letting it carry them aloft. Bearing them to the hall of the gods.

Now three maidens come on stage. Not the Rhine Maidens in their long flowing robes and hair that swims like the Rhine's current—three tall women in ancient battle dress. They wear brass bustiers and helmets and carry swords or spears by their side. These are the Walküries, handmaidens to the gods, who will carry the fallen heroes up to the skies.

The four *Emden* officers sit forward on their chairs. Stunned. *"Mein Gott!"* says Lieutenant Wolff. It has clearly been a long time since he has seen women up close—and an even longer time since he has seen any women like these. The three Walküries stride around the stage and then step in close and clash their swords and spears together. Then they turn to the audience and hold their weapons aloft, as if challenging them. Then all too quickly they stride from the stage.

The drums are still rolling and the brass instruments blaring as they go—but the *Emden* men no longer notice the music. They sit transfixed in their chairs as if they have just seen a vision.

Then the music stops and the conductor raises his baton once again. He brings it down quickly and the strings and brass come in together. The battle march of Siegmund the hero. On cue, he strides on stage dressed in armour and carrying a sword that shines and sparkles under the stage lights. He holds it aloft as the trumpets blare out a welcome for him.

He bows to the audience, to acknowledge them, and then out of the corner of his eyes he sees a soldier sneaking up on him. A man dressed in khaki, wearing a helmet that looks like a British tin hat. The man has a spear, and wields it like it is a rifle and bayonet. He tries to stab Siegmund in the back, but Siegmund is too fast and parries it away with his sword. Then another soldier enters from the other side and also tries to stab him in the back. But he wheels and parries him too. Then a third soldier enters. Lieutenant Wolff looks across at Captain von Müller, who does not seem to mind their poetic licence with the plot. He folds his arms and smiles.

The three soldiers have Siegmund surrounded now and are pressing him closely when the trumpets blare once more. It is flight of the Walküries again. Then one of the battle maidens strides in and throws herself between Siegmund and his attackers. She parries their blows with her sword and drives them back, giving him the opportunity to recover and attack while his enemy are disorganised. He strikes one down. Then a second. Then a third. They fall at his feet and he holds his sword aloft in victory. The trumpets and horns blare.

Then Siegmund the hero turns to Brünnhilde, the Walküre who has saved him. He takes her in his arms. He presses his face close to hers and looks into her eyes. He leans forward to kiss her and the audience leans forward on their seats too, arm muscles tensing where they imagine holding her. Then the drum rolls heavily again. The horns blare an angry sound. It is the rage of Wotan, father of the gods, for Brünnhilde has broken her vows to him never to interfere in a human's battle.

Thunder and lightning rings out from the orchestra and Brünnhilde and Siegmund are struck and fall to the ground.

A curtain falls and the orchestra sounds the roar of the gods as the strings then carry the march of time onwards. The curtains lift and Brünnhilde is lying on a pyre of rocks. Her shield is on her breasts, and she is surrounded by a ring of imitation flames. The men in the hall stare at her in wonder, seeing just how beautiful and noble she is in death. And ashamed that they had ever deserted her for the seductive charms of Pandora or Salome, each man there tonight is willing to brave those flames to waken her with a kiss. But it is Siegfried who strides onto the stage. Siegfried the son of Siegmund, dressed as a Prussian soldier, in long white trousers, tall leather boots, and wearing a tall brass and silver military helmet, who bravely walks up to the flames towards the sleeping maiden within.

But the anger of the gods will not be denied and waves of drum rolls and trumpets blares the warnings of Wotan. Yet Siegfried will defy even Wotan to reach Brünnhilde, who has sacrificed her life for him. He waves his sword about him, banishing the sounds. Then he swipes at the flames and strides through them. He is beside Brünnhilde now and looks down at her sleeping form. He lifts her shield from her. Lifts her helmet, and finds long flowing golden hair that falls about her shoulders. He lifts her breastplate and sees the soft curve of her bosom. He gently reaches out and touches it. Runs his hands along her body. Touches her face. Her neck. Her waist. The men in the audience are breathing rapidly like the soft beat of the violins. Then he leans down and kisses her. Lieutenant Wolff licks his lips and crosses his legs. Can feel the heat around his collar. The desire in his loins. The hardening between his legs. And Brünnhilde opens her eyes. She sees her hero and sits up and presses her body to his. They hold each other in a tight embrace and the curtain falls as the final triumphant chords sound.

The audience all stand, clapping and stamping their feet, louder than any thunder and lightning. Louder than the anger of the gods. Each of them ready to fly up to the heavens with Brünnhilde by their sides.

Von Krupp turns to von Müller and asks, "What do you think, Captain?"

And von Müller is lost for words. He is still applauding. Then Wolff leans across and asks, "Who was that woman? She was exquisite. I must meet her."

"You already have," says von Krupp with a smirk. But the officers are confused. They don't understand.

Now the curtain rises again and the players come out to take a bow. Wolff turns back to watch them. He looks at the three maidens and fastens his eyes on Brünnhilde. She smiles back at him. He wishes he suddenly had a bouquet of flowers to jump up onto the stage with to press into her hands. To press himself into her arms. To run his hands over her body.

"She is exquisite," he says again.

Then the players take off their helmets and wigs. Von Müller stops clapping. And Wolff's face turns dark. He no longer sees Brünnhilde. He is staring into the face of Jacob Meyer.

Von Krupp slaps him on the shoulder. "What do you think of that?" he asks.

But Wolff knocks his hand down. "This is an insult!" he says. "You have insulted the German military with this deception. You have denigrated yourself. You have no dignity. An insult!" he shouts loud enough for all the men in the hall to hear, and then he leads the four officers out of the hall.

Private Simpson, in the guard tower, hears the applause suddenly stop. Hears a single shout of anger. Watches the four German sailors march out of the hall into the yard. Stop. Realise they must go back through the hall to reach their cellblock. Turn in consternation and wave their hands in the air.

He smiles to himself. He has seen the same look on the faces of new guards who have watched one of the internees' concerts without being told beforehand. He shakes his head a little and smiles to himself. Poor old Fritz, he thinks mockingly. But it would have been a hell of a bigger surprise if any of those German sailors had gotten one of those beauties back to his cell for a bit of slap and tickle. That would have had them more than just stomping confusedly around the prison yard.

Sergeant Gore looks around carefully. It is dark out tonight and the air is chill. But the enemy are out there somewhere ahead of him. His guts are churning and he feels his bowels loosening. Feels the cold fingers of fear inside him, trying to claw their way out through his insides. But he won't allow it.

He crawls forward a little on his stomach. His rifle is held close. He thinks he can see a man crouching ahead of him, but then sees it is a log. He breathes in and out quickly to still his heart. But it has little effect. He feels the churning in his guts again. The fear trying to get out his arse now.

He rolls over to the bushes and urgently drags his trousers down. It was like this at Gallipoli, he thinks. An urgent need to shit every time he faced battle. Dysentery, he'd tell his officer. Bad case of dysentery. And why should anybody doubt him? Everybody had it sooner or later. But for him it was every time they had to go over the top.

He squats in the mud and shits. Rivers of it. Shit and blood and guts all pouring out of him. He can't believe it. He wants to scream. But doesn't want them to hear him. It's his cowardice emerging from him, he knows. Stinking and slithering about him. He tries to get to his feet, but slips. Falls in the filth. Tries to rise again. Falls face down. Is suddenly drowning in it. Trying to lift his arms. Trying to call for help. Then the flare goes up. And he's illuminated there in the stink of his own cowardice as he's surrounded by soldiers of both sides. All staring at him in disgust. Raising their rifles at him. All of them. Preferring to shoot him than to help him.

Then he sits up and shouts aloud! Grabs the blankets and throws them from the bed. Sits there a moment panting until he knows he has been dreaming.

That same dream again.

8
Another Day

Arno Friedrich makes his way around the prison walls early the next morning, wondering whether the sky is actually a different shade of blue today. It has been a long night. Horst is still very ill and is still refusing to go to the infirmary. He still coughs and talks in his sleep. And Arno woke up many times in the night, disturbed by so many different dreams, as if they are all seeping out of the walls together now, like the prison walls were crumbling under their assault. There was Sergeant Gore's dreaming of dying in blood and shit. Another dream of a child being stolen by the devil. An erotic fight with Brünnhilde. And another dream of walking in a dark forest, holding a tall man's hand tightly, then losing him. Of being a child—alone and afraid. Sitting on a cold stone wall, like a row of tombstones. Then another dream of the prisoners of the old century, carting rocks out onto the breakwater, trying to lay a path right across the bay, piling the granite blocks up high like battlements that they hid behind when enemy soldiers attacked them with machine guns. Then he was looking up to see enemy ships gathered on the horizon, firing at them, and as the men at the battlements fell their bodies were piled onto the breakwater, as blocks of stone. And Arno was one of them. But then he was a part of a wall facing into a thin cell, looking at photographs of a corpse on the thin bunk. Herr Eckert. Herr Peter. Himself.

He woke cold and stiff and could not quite shake off that feeling of having turned into granite until he was moving around the prison walls, waiting for the sunlight to arrive and set the world to right once more.

After breakfast and roll call, Arno stands by the front gate, mingling with the other men and waiting for the guards to arrive and free them. Some of the older men have towels on their arms, ready to go down to the beach. Some have building equipment, ready to continue repairing their villages. The remainder have shovels and barrows, ready to continue work on the monument. The three groups stand slightly apart from each other, not meeting the eyes of anyone not in their own division, but all staring impatiently out beyond the gates.

Arno, standing with the bathers, looks around to see which group the *Emden* officers have joined. But they are not to be seen. Perhaps they have found that the internees are not the fellow countrymen they have claimed to be, he thinks.

Finally the guard emerges from the stone guardhouse and stares at the men. He is the big red-headed boy. He can see the anticipation on their faces. Their eagerness to get out of the prison. He shakes his head a little and mutters something to himself, then slowly unlocks the gates, fussing over the ancient metal key, fitting it just so, and turning it carefully. Then he steps back and lets them swing the gates open and stream out, ungrateful not to even thank him for his efforts. He shakes his head again and returns to his duties.

Arno follows the internees, letting them surge ahead of him. He stops and looks out at the wide blue ocean and shields his eyes. He turns his head slowly to take it all in and sees that the day is different already for there is a ship out there near the horizon. Probably a cargo ship from Sydney, he thinks, though it is too distant to be certain. It could be anything. He takes several deep breaths and lets the scent and taste of the land and the sea fill his senses. Feels he is again in a world that he understands.

The *Emden* officers emerge from the prison a short time later, escorted by a single guard. He walks some twenty paces behind them, his rifle slung over his shoulder, paying more attention to the thin cigarette he is smoking than to the four men. They stroll to the end of the headland and look down on the remains of the breakwater. Then they walk along the western side of the prison and looked down on the beach. They see the old men walking briskly on the sand and see one man swimming out far into the bay. Then they walk around the eastern wall where the men are repairing their huts.

Herr Herausgeber sees them and strides over. "Welcome to our small German village," he says. The four officers regard the huts and backdrops curiously, waiting for Herr Herausgeber to tell them more. But instead he guides them over towards one hut and then calls for Herr Dubotzki and tells him to fetch his camera. He tells the officers he would like him to take a photograph of them.

They look at the each other, as is their habit, and Lieutenant Wolff shrugs his shoulders, and then Captain von Müller agrees. Herr Herausgeber sits them on the veranda of one of the restored facades. It is a small alpine café and they sit at a wooden table and Herr Herausgeber places empty beer steins in front of them. Lieutenant Wolff lifts the stein to his lips, pretends to drink, and then says, "This beer has gone off. It is at least twenty years old!" The other officers laugh. Herr Dubotzki returns and fusses and moves his camera around, saying he has to get the light just right. Then he asks some men to refit the backdrop that had not been rehung behind the cafe. The four officers turn in their chairs to watch two men raise up a painted scene of alpine mountains behind them, showing tree-covered slopes topped in snow.

"What are you doing?" asks Lieutenant Wolff.

"Creating the photograph," says Herr Dubotzki. "It must look just right."

"It must look just right like what?" asks Lieutenant Wolff, examining the drab-painted background behind them.

"Like Germany!" says Herr Herausgeber. "We will give you each a copy to hang on the walls of your cell, and you can imagine you were in Germany."

The four officers look at each other again. "Make an extra print to send to the Commandant at Holsworthy then," says Lieutenant Wolff.

"That's good," says Herr Dubotzki, looking at the backdrop. "Now can you all turn towards the camera." The officers look towards him. "I can see four naval officers sitting at an outdoor cafe in the southern mountains," he says, describing the scene he is looking at through his lens.

But the four officers, looking out past the photographer, see dark prison walls, a wide blue bay, bounded by a headland covered in thick bushland and gum trees.

"Think of Germany," says Herr Dubotzki. "You must think of Germany or it will show in your eyes."

The four officers squint a little as they stare out beyond the camera, but they have not yet learned the art of delusion like the internees have.

Arno emerges from the sea and looks at his watch. 9.42. He shivers and shakes the water from himself. He wishes the sun had more warmth. Then he dries himself and dresses before making his way back up to the prison. He pauses at the top of the slope to watch the internees hauling rocks up to the monument on the top of the hill. And he wonders how many years it might take before it is worn down by the forces working against it, like the breakwater.

The four *Emden* officers pause when they have reached the front gate again. "Where should we go now?" asks Captain von Müller. And Lieutenant Wolff points to the top of the hill. They nod and set off. Their guard pulls a long face and follows them.

Von Krupp is quick to wave to them when he sees them coming. *"Guten Morgen,"* he calls, before they are even within hearing distance. He waves again until the four men change their course a little and head towards him.

"This is to be our memorial to the fallen," he says proudly, when they reach him. He points at the trench in the ground that is almost filled with stone. And he unrolls some drawings, having suddenly forgotten his well-rehearsed lines, showing what the granite monolith will look like upon its completion.

Von Müller leans in close to examine the work and smiles politely. The other three officers walk around watching the men digging and dragging rocks. Von Krupp then turns and waves his arm out over the ocean. "It is a glorious view, yes? From the front of the memorial you will only be able to see ocean. Not this accursed land and not this accursed prison."

"Yes," von Müller agrees. "It will be a fine view."

"We will put the names of the fallen on tombstones around it," von Krupp says. "Eckert and Peter."

"How did they die?" Wolff asks him, stepping forward.

Von Krupp blinks. "Herr Peter had a bad fall and was mauled by sharks and Herr Eckert died of heart disease," he says.

"That is really too bad," says Wolff. And he looks down at the plans a moment. Watches the men working. Then asks, "So nobody has been shot or stabbed?"

Von Krupp narrows his eyes. "What do you mean?" He sees the men around him have slowed their working and turned a little to listen.

"And nobody has been blown to pieces?" Wolff asks.

Von Krupp tilts his head back. He thinks he knows now what the Lieutenant is getting at, for over 130 men died on the *Emden* when it was shelled by the *Sydney*. He knows that they were the officers' close comrades who had stood beside them in battle. Wolff was reminding him that they were military men and the internees were not. "We are ready to fight for the Fatherland when it comes to it," von Krupp says softly.

"Then why not kill the guard there?" asks Wolff, tilting his head towards the guard, who stands looking out to sea, not paying too much attention to his prisoners and their German gasbagging. Von Müller and the other three officers turn their heads a little and look out to sea too, as if they can see something way out there near the single ship on the horizon, letting von Krupp know they are not going to offer him any help, but neither will they side with Wolff against him.

Von Krupp looks from Wolff to the guard. He also sees all the internees are closely watching him. He knows he has to tread very carefully, so he licks his lips and says, "We have been keeping ourselves in readiness. Waiting for men such as yourselves to lead us. To show us how it is done."

"Yes," says Wolff cheerfully. "We might just show you one day." And he turns and walks down to the prison. The guard turns to see if the other three officers are going to follow him. Isn't sure whether he should go after Wolff or not. He looks back and forward between them. Captain von

Müller shrugs and follows Wolff, but says to von Krupp in English as he passes him. "Yes, they will certainly see this memorial from many miles out at sea."

After the German officers are safely back inside the prison their guard reports to the Sergeant, who quizzes him as to what the four men have done, asking for every small detail. The guard tells him about the photograph and about the visit to the headland. The Sergeant has him repeat every detail of that twice, and then sits there stroking his chin for some time. He thanks the guard and then goes to his window. He has a partial view of the internees up there on the hill, toiling away.

He then he goes to the Commandant's office, knocks before being bid to enter, salutes the portrait of the King, and repeats the story. Telling it as he sees it. Glad to have something to deflect the Captain's questions about providing a murder suspect. The Commandant makes notes on a pad as the Sergeant speaks and also quizzes him on several points.

Then he in turn thanks the Sergeant and dismisses him. Then he curses quietly, wondering how he will get out of having to report this to the Department of Defence.

Arno stands in the yard and looks at his watch. It is 10.55. Almost time to be at the infirmary. But he is watching the four new officers. They stand in the yard together as if not sure where to go. As if quite lost amongst the close confines of the prison. Three of the men turn and go into the hall, and one stays there, smoking a cigarette, walking around and looking up over the walls, like he is searching for something. He comes very close to Arno and looks at him quickly. Arno says, *"Guten Morgen.* You are a sailor from the freighter *Bummsen*, yes?"* But the Lieutenant doesn't even respond to his jibe—just keeps looking up over the walls.

And then Nurse Rosa comes out of the infirmary. She waves to Arno and calls, "I'll just be a minute. You can go in and lie down and wait for me."

Arno sees the Lieutenant's head snap around. Sees him stare at her. Arno raises his hand slowly and calls back to her, "I'm just coming." He grips his crutches and tries to swing very casually past the Lieutenant. Arno sees his eyes are staring at the retreating form of Nurse Rosa fixedly. He sees the sudden fire in them, smouldering like a hungry beast, and that knowledge nearly trips him up.

Arno looks at his watch. 11.47. He stands in Herr Herausgeber's small cell, looking at all the photos on the walls and reading over some of his articles lying around on the bench top. Nurse Rosa had seemed too distracted to talk much today. There was so much he wanted to tell her. About the officers. About Horst. About the photographs he had found. But she kept returning the conversation to their practiced lines, and then finally asked him if he could be quiet today. She didn't explain more than that, just worked away on his feet in silence.

So Arno has come to talk to Herr Herausgeber instead. He wants to ask him what he knows about some of those photos. What else he knows about Herr Peter and Herr Eckert. What else he can tell him about the Wolf Pack. He suspects that Herr Herausgeber knows enough to help him identify the killer in the camp, but is just too distracted to see it.

But Herr Herausgeber is not there.

Arno looks carefully at each photograph on the wall and tries to reconcile what he sees in each one with the men he knows. They seem so different. Black and white men on the beach or in the cellblocks. Men in the yard. Queuing for breakfast. Sitting in the alpine village. Dressed as sailors by a backdrop of a ship. Posing as women. So much fantasy. Like Herr Herausgeber's editorials, he thinks.

Arno then wonders how people would think of them all, many years from now. He imagines people might be standing like this, examining the flat black and white people in the pictures who looked like they were carved out of the flat black and white rock walls behind them. He reaches up and runs his fingers over the many photographs there before him, and suddenly plucks one from the wall. It is the photograph of Pandora that Horst had in his cell. And Arno holds it up very close, looking carefully at the eyes and the curve of the face behind the veils. He is certain there is something very familiar to it, but unable to quite place who it is.

Then there is a noise behind him. He turns around and sees it is the Sergeant of the guards. He stares at Arno with a look of suspicion on his face, as if he knows what he is up to. As if he has come to apprehend him. But he says, "I am looking for Mister Herausgeber."

"He is not here," says Arno. "I was looking for him too."

The Sergeant frowns, as if he is doesn't trust what Arno has said, then says, "Tell him I want to see him." And is gone.

Private Gunn is sitting in the guardhouse with Private Cutts-Smith. He doesn't like his company, and even looking at that red scar across his face makes him shiver, but he knows the shift will pass soon enough. If he just keeps still and shuts up it'll be all right. But it's hard not to talk to another bloke right there beside you. So he's taking his rifle apart again. Cleaning and checking each part. Reassembling it carefully. Determined not to talk too much. Not to get on Cutts-Smith's nerves.

"Whada ya reckon of them new Huns?" he says eventually.

Private Cutts-Smith looks at him, turning the good side of his wounded face to him. "They seem a bit strange to me. Seem to keep to themselves too much. But so would I if I was dumped into this mad-house."

Private Gunn smiles, "Yeah, I know what you mean."

Private Cutts-Smith doubts it very much.

"You know what I heard?" asks Gunn.

"What?" asks Cutts-Smith.

"I heard there's gonna be trouble about them."

"What trouble?"

"Amongst the Huns."

"Says who?"

"Says the Sergeant."

Private Cutts-Smith looks at him hard, the scarred side of his face framing his glare. "What kind of trouble?"

"Don't know rightly. Something about different factions amongst them."

"Bull!" says Private Cutts-Smith. "They all keep together too much."

"Well," says Gunn, "the Sergeant has got us keeping a close eye on them. He's even got contacts amongst them. Spies, if you like. He reckons the Huns aren't as united and all chummy as you might think. Reckons the new blokes won't put up with some of the rot the others are carrying on with. Reckons these officers were trouble-makers in Holsworthy. Reckons there'll be trouble here."

Private Cutts-Smith stares at him and thinks. Private Gunn tries to look away from the scar and looks down to his rifle again and keeps taking it apart.

"So you're determined to be ready for 'em with your rifle all in bits again are ya?"

But Private Gunn doesn't answer. He just keeps his head down and starts reassembling his rifle, and wishes he'd never said anything in the first place.

Lunch is mutton and tomato soup. The weary builders and workers eat without talking. They are feeling the tiredness in their arms and legs. Feeling the ache of muscles long unaccustomed to hard work. They flex their biceps and stretch their backs as they sit there. And they smile at the pleasure of it.

Herr von Krupp is again seated with the *Emden* officers, although he no longer tries to make conversation with them. He concentrates on his meal while Herr Schwarz leads the discussion. "We have been training," he says to the four men. "We call it an athletics club, but we are readying ourselves for the day of action."

"How many men?" asks Wolff, not taking his eyes from his meal.

"Twenty-two," says Schwarz. "Strong and well-disciplined."

"And what is this day of action you refer to?" Wolff asks, still not looking up.

Schwarz looks at Wolff and then looks around the table, as if the answer has been there before him a moment ago and has suddenly disappeared. "Why—for the day we are needed," he says.

"Needed for what?" asks Wolff.

Schwarz looks pained. "Action," he says.

Wolff nods. "Do you drill with guns?"

"Of course not."

"Do you have weapons?"

"We have other things," says Schwarz in a low voice. "And we control the camp with them."

Now the Captain looks up. Looks genuinely interested. "But who controls you?" asks Wolff. "This aristocratic dandy here?" he gestures towards von Krupp.

Von Krupp looks back at him and glares. "That is an insult!" he says softly.

"No," says Wolff. "This is an insult!" And he reaches over and tips von Krupp's plate into his face.

Von Krupp leaps up and bares his teeth. "Now," he says aloud, so that all the men in the hall can hear. "Now it is time you were taught a lesson in discipline."

Wolff stands up and looks back at von Krupp in contempt. "Will you read me a book on it at bed time perhaps?"

Von Krupp turns to Captain Müller to see what he is going to do, but the Captain just looks up, slightly amused. It is obvious he lets Wolff run on a very long leash. Von Krupp says, "I'm sure your Captain will understand that this is just between us." And he steps away from the bench and lifts his fists to assume a boxing stance. Wolff looks at him for a moment—like he is going to leave him standing there—and then he too steps away from the bench.

"Stop!" calls a sudden voice from the entrance, and von Krupp turns his head to see a red-headed soldier walking in, holding his rifle out. "No fighting!" he calls.

"No," says von Krupp to the guard, without lowering his stance. "This is the boxing match we promised you." The guard looks at Lieutenant Wolff, keeps his eyes on him, curls his lip a little and then nods his head in assent.

Von Krupp smiles. He stands half a head higher than Wolff. He is much older, but he has seen the *Emden* officers have led a life of idleness in confinement, and have not worked to improve their strength daily. "You will pay dearly, for your insult," he says. Then immediately he falls to his knees. Wolff has booted him in the shin.

"It is not fair," shouts Schwarz pushing forward. "That is against the rules."

"There are no rules in battle," says Wolff, circling von Krupp as he rises, his face flushed with anger. He takes two wild swings at Wolff and then realises he is being led into a trap. If he loses his temper he will lose both the fight and his support, and he needs to win both.

He steps back two paces and then assumes a boxer's stance again. Wolff cautiously copies him. He looks at von Krupp's confident stance. His large fists. Knows he is facing a trained boxer. But also knows he is no fighter. He permits himself the faintest of grins as he goes in for the taller man—low and hard. Von Krupp steps back as he advances, blocks his first punch and then hits him in the face. His hand comes back tingling.

Now it is Wolff's turn to step back. He puts the back of his hand up to his lip. Looks at it. Looks at von Krupp and spits onto the table beside von Krupp's meal. "First blood," he says.

Von Krupp says nothing. He keeps his guard high and advances slowly on Wolff. But Wolff stays his ground for he is where he wants to be. He waits until von Krupp is close, then he grabs a metal plate off the table and quickly slashes at von Krupp with it. It catches him sharply on one hand and splatters food across his front. Red tomato stains spread across his chest. Von Krupp feels the heat of them. Pulls his wounded fist in close.

Wolff steps in quickly now and slashes at his enemy's face. Mustard flies off and catches the elder man in the eyes. Von Krupp throws up his hands to wipe it clear and calls out, "I cannot see." And at the same time he tries to grab the plate from Wolff. It is a mistake. He is too slow to realise the fight is no longer a boxing match. Wolff is in very close now. Driving the plate into his jaw. Then he drops it to the floor. Grabs von Krupp. Hugs him close. Holds him in a tight embrace. Drives one knee up between von Krupp's legs. Feels it connect with his balls. The taller man slumps and Wolff snarls into his face.

Von Krupp is looking into the hungry jaws of the naval officer, tasting the blood in his own mouth. Tasting the fear. He struggles to stand back up. Struggles violently to break free. But Wolff's grip cannot be broken.

"That's enough of that," says the guard, stepping closer and motioning with his rifle. Lieutenant Wolff lets go of von Krupp and realises he has been holding him on his feet. He watches him fall to the floor amongst the remains of the meal. Wolff turns to the guard, and says loudly, "Yes, you're right. I think everyone will agree that is quite enough."

Horst has not been at lunch and Arno returns to their cell to seek him out. He is still rolled over in his blankets against the wall, sniffing heavily. Arno asks, "How are you feeling?" But Horst does not reply.

Arno swings over closer to him. A sickly stink rises off him. "Horst?" He asks and puts one hand out to touch his face. But it is no longer hot. It is now cold and damp. Horst sniffs some more and pulls the blanket higher, tunnelling down lower. And Arno realises he is crying, his sorrow seeping into the cell walls.

"What is wrong?" he asks. But Horst says nothing. "Horst!" Arno repeats again. "What is wrong? I will fetch doctor Hertz!"

"No," says Horst, and slowly rolls over. Arno looks at his face. His eyes are red and bruised looking. His face puffy. And when he speaks Arno can smell the alcohol. "Don't do that!"

Arno stands there a moment and then asks again, "What has happened?"

And Horst's face falls apart before his eyes—the skin cracks and the eyes shrivel up in pain and his mouth bursts open. He says, "I'm so miserable."

Arno puts a hand on his shoulder. "It's the prison," he says.

"No," says Horst. "It's more than that. It's everything." He looks down and then says, "I'm so ashamed of myself."

"Of what?" asks Arno. But Horst doesn't answer him directly. "What would Maria and the children think of me? I miss them so much. So much it hurts. But how can I ever be with them again?" Then he reaches under the blanket pulls up a clear unmarked bottle and drinks the few drops still remaining in it.

Arno reaches over and takes the empty bottle. "Where did you get this?" he asks, peering into it, as if it might contain some answer to what Horst is raving about, and some answers to all his unanswered questions.

But Horst shakes his head. "I can't tell you that."

"Why?" asks Arno.

"I just can't."

"I won't tell anybody else. I swear it."

"Would you swear it on your very life?" asks Horst, and turns back to the wall when Arno cannot answer that.

Arno sits there for some time and then says softly, "I wish I could take you with me when I go. I wish I could take you all with me."

A rno stands under the southwest watchtower at dusk, watching the colour fading out of the whole world as the chill of night wraps itself about him. The darkness descends quicker, he thinks, and he looks up to see the first stars appearing, like tiny holes in the blackness. Those small lights of the heavens that steered ancient mariners across the oceans. But from inside the prison they could steer you nowhere.

He leans back against the cold granite wall, and tries to feel what is stirring within. It is something dangerous, he feels that may well help him identify the beast or creature that stalks amongst them. But then he thinks, what if he cannot actually protect everyone as he has long imagined, and all he can do is witness the deaths, his strange ability not a gift but a curse.

He turns his head a little and listens for a soft footstep above him. There is none and he realises the guard is absent this evening. He wonders where he has gone? Wonders if it has something to do with the alcohol and the Wolf Pack and the deaths and the photographs of the dead men? He is certain they are all connected in some way, and he is sure that if he could only put all the events together in a way that might make sense to him, he could still prevent more deaths.

He needs to believe that.

He leans onto his crutches and begins making his way down the wall. Then he stops and sees up as the dark shape detaches itself from the shadows in front of him. He waits for it to see him and retreat into the darkness again, but it takes several quick steps towards him and slashes with something sharp. Arno stumbles back. His crutch takes the brunt of the blow. It is a large knife, and it is stuck in the wooden support of his crutch. He struggles to hold onto the crutch as his attacker tries to pull it free and then Arno lets the crutch go, sending his attacker stumbling backwards. The man curses and regains his footing while Arno takes another step back. He tries to press himself into the wall. Watches the man come at him again. Sees he has the knife free in his hand. Is much slower this time. More careful. The blade is held back, ready for the deathblow. Then, unexpectedly, he makes a choking sound and drops the knife. It takes Arno a moment to realise that another person has him from behind. Arno hears the heavy kick of boots. A deep grunt. Then he sees his attacker fall to the ground and sees a tall figure kicking at him.

Wolff then stops and looks around furtively, then holds his hand out to Arno. "Come," he says. "Quick. The guards will come."

Arno bends over to pick up his crutch and has a quick glimpse of his attacker. He can see he is still moving, trying to get to his feet again. He limps off back towards the cellblock with Lieutenant Wolff. Neither speak until they are at the door to the hall. Then Wolff suddenly turns on him. "Do you know who that was who attacked you?" he asks.

"No," says Arno. Regardless.

The Lieutenant nods. "Lucky for you I was following you, huh?"

Arno wants to ask him why he was following him. But all he says is, "*Ja.*"

"Okay," says the Lieutenant. "Now you owe me big, huh?"

Again all Arno says is, "*Ja.*" But he had seen enough of his attacker to believe it was one of the other men of the *Emden*.

He has witnessed just another performance.

The concert that evening is introduced by Scheherazade. She dances to the centre of the stage and carefully unwraps a veil. She tells the audience that tonight they will witness the fall of those who had set themselves above most mortals and it is a play with a moral—as all plays should have. The orchestra strikes up a long deep chord and she announces, Wagner's Götterdämmerung—the Twilight of the gods.

She drops the veil to the stage and flees as the music builds to a higher and higher pitch. And then Wotan, the highest of gods, dressed like the Emperor of Germany, strides onto the stage. His face is heavy and solemn. He addresses the audience and tells them that he has promised the goddess Freia to the giants who have built his fortress Valhalla. He would rather offer the giants gold, but the warrior Siegfried has the Rhine gold and upon his fate hangs the fate of the gods.

Then he strides off stage.

Siegfried, the tall brave Prussian soldier, now enters, holding Brünnhilde by his side. He pledges his devotion to her and tells her he must set forth to battle, but he gives her the ring of Rhine gold to wear. She places it upon her finger and waves farewell as he marches away.

Siegfried now comes into a strange world. It is a dark wood, where dark shapes flit in the background. The growls of wild beasts can be heard, but Siegfried pays them no heed, and continues on until he comes upon a German soldier. The man immediately recognises the hero and goes to great lengths to win his favour, offering him food and a place to sleep. Siegfried is greatly pleased to meet a fellow countryman and soldier, and shares his meal with him. After eating he yawns and the soldier prepares a bed for him on the ground. Siegfried thanks his new friend and lays down to sleep.

The soldier then dances around the hero, for he wants to win Brünnhilde for himself and will kill Siegfried to obtain her. But he finds he cannot kill the great hero while he is sleeping. So he rouses Siegfried to drink some broth, and as he lifts it to his lips the soldier plunges his bayonet between Siegfried's shoulder blades. The hero falls to the ground, dying, calling Brünnhilde's name. The soldier then throws off his uniform to reveal a khaki uniform below, and he calls his troops to his side. More men in khaki then enter and rally about him to celebrate the death of Siegfried, the only one who could prevent the fall of the gods.

The soldiers then drag the fair Brünnhilde on stage as their prisoner, manhandling her and laughing as they do. They build a large fire around Siegfried's body and set it alight. But Siegfried's followers have followed their leader, and several Prussian soldiers come on stage and call on the khaki-clad soldiers to prepare to fight to the death. They prepare to engage the enemy, but when they see Siegfried is dead they are filled with despair and are easily beaten.

As the pyre burns the Emperor Wotan appears in the flames, for the halls of Valhalla are also burning. The Emperor sinks beneath the flames as the khaki-clad soldiers laugh and point. Then they lift Brünnhilde to her feet, determined to have their sport with her too—but she breaks from their grip and leaps onto the pyre, determined to die with her love rather than submit to them.

With a roar of anger more khaki soldiers run on the stage. Holding their rifles before them. The inert form of Siegfried comes back to life as two soldiers grab him by the arms. Sergeant Gore is at the forefront and he demands the play be stopped. The audience rise up in their chairs. The Prussian soldiers rise up from death and level their painted wooden guns at their guards. The hall is silent. Two armies staring at each other on the verge of battle. One soldier clacks the bolt on his rifle loudly. The sound echoes around and around the hall like the absent drum roll that at this point should tell of the death of the gods.

The spell is broken and the internees lower their play weapons.

Captain Eaton sits at his desk, all too aware of the King looking over his shoulder as he opens the top-secret envelope. Whatever it is, it has been deemed too secret to send by cable, and too secret to dispatch by post. A driver had brought it to his office and would not hand it over until it had been signed for.

So he sits in his office with the door closed. Sits and studies the envelope with its top-secret stamps across it. He shoves a small knife into the envelope and slits the document open.

He reads it slowly and carefully. It has been typed on thin paper, each full-stop punctuating a hole in the document like a tiny bullet hole. The Department of Defence is advising him of the presence of a German raider operating in the Pacific Ocean—suspected by intelligence officers to be the *Wolf*, whose presence has been flagged by British naval intelligence after it attacked ships off South Africa. The message states, in terse language, that six US cargo ships have disappeared on route to Australia and another four have been sunk by explosions in or near Australian waters. Mines being laid by the raider are thought to be responsible. A freighter, the *Cumberland,* hit a mine south of Eden on the New South Wales coast, and had to be beached by its crew.

The ship is believed to be using fake funnels and demountable decking to change its appearance.

The Department of Defence is trying to control wild speculation in the newspapers by blaming the loss of vessels on German-born terrorists who it claims are working in Australian naval yards, and planting bombs on ships. This has led to major anti-German sentiment in newspapers, and growing anti-German sentiment amongst the public. Sometimes extreme.

Then the point of the top-secret message. Military intelligence is concerned that German militia or civilians in captivity could be signalling the raider, and providing information on allied shipping. As such, extra vigilance needed to be adopted towards any such enemy aliens in captivity, while the Department of Defence assessed how best to control the situation.

Captain Eaton folds the message and slips it back into the envelope. Control the situation! That doesn't fill him with confidence. He suspects that the Government's propaganda efforts would lead to them losing control of the situation. It doesn't seem particularly feasible that any of the internees in his care are in touch with a mystery raider. But it does seem feasible that the anti-German sentiment they are fostering will put all the men under his care at risk.

If so, the solid stone walls of the old prison may prove more use to him in keeping the angry locals out than keeping the internees in.

Arno feels this dream vividly, like he is not just sharing it or watching it, but is actually in it. The dreamer is Herr von Krupp, and he and Arno are in a dark place. There are shadow and skeleton branches all about them. They are afraid. He can feel the older man's terror. Something is chasing them and they are looking for shelter. They hear a wild howl and spin on the spot. It seems to be coming from all sides at once. They must flee.

Their feet stumble as they try to make their way through the darkness, trying to find a path, trying to find some light. And then, up ahead, they see a break in the trees and brambles. They emerge into a clearing. And recognise it at once. They are at the forest's edge over-looking the prison. There is a rustling at their feet. Maybe a snake. Or maybe a giant spider. They step out of the forest and run again. Arno's crutches swing wildly as he tries to race on. Then that howl again, a little closer. They run faster now, still stumbling, but not falling over, thank God. They need to reach the safety of those stone walls ahead of them.

They run right up to the gates and shout out to the guards inside to open them and let them in. But there is no sign of anybody. No lights on inside the prison. Nobody at the guard's quarters outside the walls. They grab the heavy barred gates and push and pull on them, trying to get them open.

Then the howl. Very close. A sound of panting. They don't even turn their heads for the heavy gate is starting to move. So very slowly edging open. They push harder. Can feel their blood pounding so heavily that it hurts behind their eyeballs. They will push until their bodies break from the effort of it, but finally the gate is open enough to squeeze through.

Then they turn to try and push it closed again. It seems heavier. They strain until they feel the bones of their backs click. It is not shut fully, but it will be enough. Surely. Then there is a loud roar and a crash as the dark creature outside, the beast without, throws itself against the gate. It howls in rage and hunger and they step back away from the gate. They turn and run further into the prison, into the darkest corner they can find by the wall. They press themselves against the stone there and feel the coldness of it against their bodies. Feel their fearful sweat turn chill on their skin.

They close their eyes and listen for the beast. It has gone quiet. Perhaps circling around the walls trying to find another way in. Perhaps looking for faults or cracks in the old stone walls that it can use to climb them.

They open their eyes again and feel their hearts slowing. Feeling they are safe for the moment. They look about and wonder where all the other internees are. But the prison looks empty. Like they have arrived in a different era. Or moved into a different world, where they do not live in the prison.

But then they feel something stirring beside them. They feel the very walls starting to throb and come to life. And to their horror they see the beast pushing itself out of the stone walls, where it has perhaps lived all the time, a product of their boredom and fear and anger and desperation. And slowly it detaches itself and stands before them. It looks like Herr von Krupp, but larger. The face is distorted into a long muzzle with long sharp teeth. And the hands are huge claws. Each talon the size of a bayonet. The creature looks at them and howls, so close it stops their hearts beating.

Then it reaches out one large claw and sinks its talons into the flesh of their necks.

Their blood-choked screams join the beast's howl, echoing around and around the dark walls of their prison—until the dream fades away to nothing. Absolutely nothing.

9
Another Day

Arno Friedrich found Herr von Krupp's body, early the next morning, lying where it had been attacked in the dream, in the shadows of the wall. He stared at the corpse, hoping it would fade away into the stone, as the light of the new day filled the sky around the prison. He could now clearly see the dark red of the wounds and the paleness of the dead man's skin. The closeness of the corpse made him shiver and he was tempted to reach out and touch him—to see what the skin felt like and to try and detect if anything of the man was left there.

He was disappointed that he had witnessed another murder and still did not know who was conjuring the beasts that killed so savagely. He had shared Herr von Krupp's terror at his moment of death but was not able to help him. And he thinks that perhaps he is seeing it wrong, that it is not the dreams of somebody else who creates the beast he sees, but what if he is witness to the last moments of the slain, who have conjured the beasts themselves? For where else does a man go at that moment of death, when one's life ceases to be, or seeps out of the body, but into the shadows of dreams?

But if that were so, and he ever left these walls, might he suddenly find he was confronted with the dreams of the dozens and hundreds and thousands of men dying every single day? That would be unendurable and he would prefer this life of internment to it.

So many things he didn't know, but it felt like all the clues were there in front of him, waiting for him to understand it all.

He then looks up and sees the guard in the southwest watchtower there, staring fixedly out to sea. And Arno wonders if he could be seen in the shadows of the wall there. He also wonders if he should call out to him and alert him to the killing. But instead he turns and made his way around to the infirmary, where there is a light on. Intern Meyer is there alone.

"Where is Doctor Hertz?" Arno asks him.

Meyer turns and looks at him. A little startled. "What's the problem?" he asks.

Arno bites his lip and wonders whether to tell him. Then the doctor is suddenly standing behind him. "What is it?" he asks. A little breathless.

"Herr von Krupp," says Arno. "He's dead." The doctor looks at Meyer. "Killed," says Arno.

"Show me," says the doctor, and lets Arno lead him back around the wall until Arno is pointing at the corpse lying there in the shadows. Doctor Hertz and Meyer both bend down to examine it, and Arno looks up to see that the sentry in the watchtower is now looking carefully down at them.

The general assembly is called before breakfast. Armed guards stand all around the yard and Commandant Fort walks back and forward as he talks to the men, fidgeting with his pistol holster. First, he announces the death of Herr von Krupp. Then he warns there will be an official inquiry into the killing. He warns that he has been made aware of power factions within the prison and that he will not tolerate such behaviour or provocations of violence.

Then he announces that all extra privileges will be cancelled or curtailed. There will be no more concerts in the evenings until further notice and no one will be allowed outside the prison walls anymore. All the internees will be treated as prisoners of war!

Arno takes a short sharp breath. The Commandant has said the unspoken word aloud. Has released it into the prison.

Then the Commandant tells his prisoners that before they consider forming a delegation to come and complain to him, that they should address such complaints through the American Consul in Sydney who represents their interests, who will forward their concerns on to him.

He then paces away, leaving the shocked internees to try and understand just how very much their world has suddenly changed.

"Hey, kid," Lieutenant Wolff calls to Arno, and beckons him over to where he stands. Arno swings his way over to the officer. Men are wandering all around the prison yard, like ships without a rudder, no longer certain where to go at that time of the day.

"Yes?" Arno asks.

The Lieutenant stares at him a moment. Says nothing. Then asks, "What was your name?"

"Arno."

"Ja. Arno." He looks around the yard a bit and then turns back to him. "Tell me, what is that Nurse like?"

"What do you mean?" Arno asks.

"Do you think it'd be worth my while calling in sick tomorrow?"

Arno doesn't know what to say.

"They tell me that nobody has ever gotten into her pants, but if anybody has, it would be you. Is that right?"

Arno feels the heat rising around his collar. Feels his blood rising like a king tide. He looks down at the ground. "She massages my legs and feet," he says, stumbling over the words.

"Yeah—I think I'll get her to massage mine too. Afterwards." He tilts his head and licks his lips, as if tasting something. "Yeah," he says. "I think I'll get her to do that too." He looks back at Arno. "Okay, thanks kid. Put in a good word for me, okay. You owe me one, remember!"

Arno nods his head a little. He doesn't want to agree, but says, "Sure." And is immediately angry at himself for it.

"Thanks," says the Lieutenant, and he then winks at Arno and saunters off.

Herr Herausgeber stops Arno as he passes the door to his cell, as if the editor has been standing there waiting for him all morning. He beckons with his finger for Arno to follow him inside. "Big news," he says, with a bright smile on his face. Arno is tempted to keep walking, but follows him into his cell.

"There will be a big offensive in the next few days," Herr Herausgeber says. "This is the one that will sweep the British troops out of their trenches and into the sea."

Arno looks at him, unable to summon up the energy to confirm the fantasy today. Herr Herausgeber says, with great enthusiasm, "I'll bet you wish you were at the front now, wearing the uniform of the Empire, fighting for the Kaiser, yes?"

Arno doesn't answer, for he is thinking not of the glory of fighting for the Kaiser but of the stories of blood and slaughter that he has heard whispered in the cafes outside the walls. Soft words of bullets and gas and heavy feet bogged down by mud, unable to leap over the cracks and trenches in the ground. Words never spoken aloud in the prison, but spoken nevertheless.

"Yes," he says. Then he turns away and runs his eyes over the photographs fastened to the walls of the office once more, and thinks the history of the internment camp is caught there. They show men lined up at the kitchen for breakfast. Men in the dining hall. Many of the actors in costumes. Tall proud Prussian grenadiers and guardsmen. And men staring listlessly at the camera as they mope around the cellblocks. And one of them is probably of a murderer. He wonders if, when they finally catch him, they will look closely at the prints and say they could see it in his face all along.

Then Arno turns back to Herr Herausgeber and asks him, for the first time, "But what if these stories are wrong?"

And Herr Herausgeber smiles and wags his finger at Arno. "You are so mischievous," he says. "I know it. I hear the things you tell some of the other men. But this," he says, tapping his finger on the article he is working on, "is the truth, and you know it and I know it." Then he lifts his hand and asks, "Do you know what else I have heard?" Suddenly whispering.

"What?" asks Arno, prepared for another fantasy.

"I have heard that a German raider has been sighted cruising up and down the coast."

"A raider?"

"Yes. It is called the *Wolf*. It has sunk several ships already. And the authorities believe that somebody in the prison has a radio and is in secret contact with it. They believe that there is a plan to raid the prison. Land on the beach in the bay and liberate us all. Carry us back to Germany."

Arno watches the editor's face carefully as he talks. "A raider?" he asks again.

"Yes." Then he lowers his voice even further. "If you talk to our friends from the *Emden* you might find they know more than they are letting on." And then he winks, very slow and carefully.

"Is that what you are writing?" Arno asks him, indicating the article before him.

"Oh no," he says. "This is a piece on the death of Herr von Krupp. Another very tragic accident."

Arno turns some words over in his mouth, as if tasting them, and then says, "It wasn't an accident. I found his body. He was killed by somebody in the camp. As were Herr Peter and Herr Eckert."

Herr Herausgeber looks directly at him. Then says, "I'm quite sure you're right."

Arno blinks. Then again. "Then why don't you write that?" he asks.

Herr Herausgeber shakes his head. "They would never let me print it."

"The authorities?"

"They are the least of my worries."

Then Herr Herausgeber lowers his head a little and looks at Arno over the top of his glasses. "Arno, my boy, things are rarely as simple or as obvious as they seem." Arno nods his head a little, as if it is the first truth he has ever heard from Herr Herausgeber. "Think of it this way," the elder man says, "many years from now, when this madness has passed us by, we will be nothing but a curious memory, like those convicts of the last century. And the only thing they will know of us will be from the records we have kept. The photographs. The newspaper. And so on."

"But..." says Arno, pointing at the photographs and the columns of type strewn around, "It's not the truth. It's not how it is."

"It's one truth," says Herr Herausgeber. "And it's a truth that we can create, not one that is created for us." He points at the Australian newspapers piled in the corner. Arno turns and looks at them. He knows what they say of the Germans. That they are raping and murdering. That they are barbarians. That they are set on destroying civilisation.

Arno turns back to Herr Herausgeber. "Or think of it this way," he tells Arno. "You want to have legs that work like everybody else's—it's simple. Have Herr Dubotzki take a photo of you standing on the beach with the athletics club. You could be a runner. Forever."

Arno thinks about that. He nods his head once more and leaning heavily on his crutches makes his way back out into the corridor.

Nurse Rosa turns and sees Lieutenant Wolff standing in the door. "Can I help you?" she asks.

"Yes," says the Lieutenant, "My name is Wolff. Lieutenant Wolff."

"You're one of the *Emden* men," Nurse Rosa says.

"Yes. That's right," says the lieutenant, stepping into the infirmary room.

"How can I help you?" Nurse Rosa asks again. She holds a basket in her hand. Fruit and bread. She puts it down on the bench beside her.

"Were you going somewhere?" he asks.

"Nowhere special," she says.

Wolff smiles. So she can see what big teeth he has. "I've got this ache," he says. "And Arno tells me you've got the most sensitive fingers in the camp."

"You are a friend of Arno's?" she asks.

"Sure," says Wolff. "We're great friends." He steps further into the room, takes off his cap and toys with it in his fingers.

Nurse Rosa watches him carefully. Not sure about him.

"He doesn't have many friends in the camp," she says.

"We're both loners," he says. "That's the attraction I guess." And he takes a step closer to Nurse Rosa. Turns the cap again. So she can see what big hands he has. "Ever feel that? Immediate attraction to somebody?"

She moves back a little. "Perhaps," she says.

Wolff lays his hat down on the bench beside her. He can see her tense as he leans closer to her. "Arno says you're the only person who can help me," he says.

"Help you with what?" she asks.

"Some things aren't easy to put into words," he says, still smiling.

"Such as what?"

"Well," says Wolff, "I could tell you you're the most beautiful woman I've ever seen easily enough. I could ask you to run away with me. Break out of here together and sail away into the sunrise—far away from this stupid place—I could do that easily enough. But that's not my problem."

He watches her shoulders loosen a little. Watches the curiosity thread its way through her body. Watches her turn her head a little to regard him.

"So what is your problem?"

"This ache I've got."

"Where is it?"

"All over."

"What kind of an ache?"

"An ache for a beautiful woman," he says, and steps up close enough to hold her. Stares into her eyes. Sees the red colour rising up her throat. Grabs her suddenly and presses his lips to hers. Stares into her eyes as he kisses her. Pushes his tongue just a little way into her mouth. Runs it across her teeth. Starts pushing one knee between her legs. Sliding one hand up her stomach towards her breasts. Feels her lack of resistance to him.

"Lieutenant!" snaps a sudden voice behind him. Loud and sharp. A voice full of command. And anger. Wolff breaks away and turns to see Doctor Hertz standing in the doorway. He glares at Wolff and at Nurse Rosa. She pushes herself away from him and tries to rearrange her red cap and her cape, straightening her uniform, but keeps her eyes down, refusing to look up at him.

There is deep anger in the doctor's voice as he says to Wolff, "I think you should leave immediately!"

Lieutenant Wolff just smiles. "I'm sorry," he says. "Next time I'll make an appointment." He picks up his cap, winks at Nurse Rosa and strides slowly out the door, back out into the prison yard. Doctor Hertz doesn't even turn to watch him leave, his fierce gaze is squarely on Nurse Rosa.

The Commandant has finally given permission for Herr von Krupp's body to be buried on the headland. He had left the delegation waiting for over an hour before he even agreed to meet them, and then it was only on the condition that they not discuss the new regulations he was imposing upon them.

The men, led by Herr Schwarz, agreed and came straight to the point. They would like to be able to continue work on the monument and they would like to be able to bury Herr von Krupp under it. The Commandant wouldn't give them an answer straight away and told them he would consider it. But he prefers the men were occupied at hard labour rather than getting up to trouble inside the prison, so he agreed.

He sits in his office now, beneath the icons of Empire, his shoulders bent. He has failed these men, he thinks. He has not protected them from the violence of the war. He has not even managed to keep them all alive. He suspects the next cable he gets from the Department of Defence will be informing him of his dismissal. Three deaths under his care, and no clear suspect.

Sergeant Gore has suggested to him that very morning that he needs an altogether tougher line with the internees if he is to protect his position. His advice was to conscript the internees into building the breakwater. Taking up where the convicts had left off. He told Captain Eaton that this will keep them too worn out for their concerts and their riots and fights, and that it will prove to the Germans who are the victors and who are the vanquished.

But the Commandant knows that those types of stories will eventually get into the press. The Department of Defence will be just as upset with him for that. So he agreed for work to continue on the monument instead, and he agreed that Herr von Krupp's body could be buried there.

Not that different from toiling on the breakwater really, he thinks.

And he wonders how the internees here would be treated if men like Sergeant Gore were in command of them? For he knows there are far more men like the Sergeant in uniform than men like himself. He turns and looks out his single window of frosted glass, watching a figure walk past, body all distorted in little mosaic shapes of light. And he notes that even his own window has bars on it.

Lieutenant Wolff corners Arno in the yard after a desultory and quiet lunch. "Okay," he says. "I think it's time to tell me about your little escape plan."

"What escape plan?" asks Arno.

Wolff shakes his head and leans closer to Arno. Presses him up against the granite wall. "Now I know you've got a plan," he says.

"Why do you think you know?" asks Arno, wondering who Wolff might have been talking to. The German officer's eyes are as blue and icy as a deep northern sea.

"If you didn't have one you'd have denied it," he says. "And I can see it in your face. You are the only one out of all these men in here who has that look of escape written on him."

"What look?" asks Arno.

"That faraway look. Like you're staring out over the horizon, even when you're inside the prison walls."

Arno says nothing. Neither yes nor no. He does not trust Wolff and does not trust himself to say anything.

"I thought you were my friend," says Wolff, stepping even closer and placing one hand on Arno's shoulder. The other he presses into his stomach, one finger extended, as if it were a gun. Or a knife. "I'd be very disappointed if I found out you weren't my friend," he says.

Arno feels the hard rock wall behind him. The threat before him. And ever so slowly he nods his head.

"You've got an escape plan alright," says Wolff. "I've seen you out in the yard checking out the walls in the darkness."

Arno has no answer for that.

"Yes," says Wolff, and he slaps Arno on the cheek—a friendly blow, but one that leaves his cheek red and sore nevertheless. "You need to remember who your friends are, yes?" And he turns and walks away as if he couldn't really care about Arno's escape plans or not, but just wanted him to know he knew.

Night falls over the prison, turning the tall granite walls dark and chill. Arno is not at the walls tonight for a guard has led him back to the cell block at rifle point and told him he is not allowed to wander the yard after dark.

Arno protested that it was just turning dark. The guard looked up at the sky and waited a moment, then indicated the first stars. "It's dark now," he said, and then gestured towards the cellblock with his rifle. "March."

Arno tried to explain to the man how vital it was that he be by the walls as darkness fell, but the words started sounding absurd to his own ears before he'd even fully spoken them. Like they were another language. So Arno sits on his bunk looking at Horst, who is sitting opposite him, with his blanket wrapped tightly around him. He is coughing like he has been gassed and Arno can see that he has lost a lot of weight. He says to Horst, "Do you know what you look like?"

"What?" asked Horst between coughs, glancing up at him.

"Like the photographs of soldiers who've been to the front."

Horst laughs, then bends over coughing again. "Do you think the Kaiser would give me a medal?" he gasps.

"Does the Kaiser even know you're here?" asks Arno.

"According to the Wolf Pack he does," says Horst. Then he stops laughing and his face turns sullen. He pulls his blanket tighter around his shoulders and ducks his head lower.

Arno chews his lip a little and stares at him, as if they're suddenly not such a long distance apart again—separated by all the unsaid words. No man's words. But Arno tests the ground. "Do you believe them?"

Horst looks up at him, his face giving nothing away. "What can you believe in this place?"

Arno thinks for a moment to stretches out a hand and touch Horst's hand. "Whatever you want, it seems," says Arno.

Horst looks at him and frowns. "Little Arno is growing up," he says.

Now Arno frowns. Tries to copy Horst's heavy glare. He would like to cross over the centre of the cell and sit on Horst's bunk beside him. Like two comrades might. "What will happen to the Wolf Pack now they're leaderless?" asks Arno. "Has Lieutenant Wolff taken over?"

Horst coughs and lies down. "Nothing has changed," he says. "Von Krupp was not the leader." Then he rolls over to the wall, to let Arno know that the conversation is over. That he might as well be alone in the cell after all.

Private Strap walks slowly around the inner wall of the prison, as per his new orders, with his rifle held out before him, looking for any sign of movement in the dark. He makes his way carefully forward, pausing every few steps to lean against the cold stone walls and listen.

He closes his eyes like the Sergeant has taught him, so that his hearing will improve. He listens for every sound. There is a faint scuffling sound from one of the guards in the watchtower behind him, moving about. There is the soft growl of the ocean. And there is a low whisper of voices.

He opens his eyes and moves ahead a little. Listening carefully. Making sure that the footsteps he hears are his own. He keeps his mouth open just a little, so as to lessen the sound of his own breathing and heartbeat. He pauses to peer around behind him every ten steps. Just like the Sergeant has taught him. Scans the ground front and back carefully, looking for movement. But there is nothing there.

He turns his attention to the voices again. He moves on until he is under the windows of the cellblock. The voices are coming from within. He relaxes and leans up against the stone wall to listens to the muttered sounds from within. The harsh guttural tones of their language, and he wonders what they are saying? You could imagine those words meant anything—could imagine they were saying anything you wanted.

The nightmares are so numerous that night that Arno can barely keep track of them. A multitude of dark stirrings filling the prison, coming into their world to wreak havoc. He sees dark forms emerge from the shadows and wander down the corridors of the prison, like beasts stalking their prey. And he sees children lost in forests. And he sees half-naked women in soft cushions calling him to come to their embrace. And he sees sharp teeth. And soft breasts. And darkness. And he sees convicts of the old century brutalising one another. He sees fellow internees beating or buggering each other. He sees old men smashing the skulls of their guards. He sees guards shooting the internees down with machine guns. He sees a sudden shell-burst in the darkness and sees a line of soldiers advancing on him. Some with sharp fangs. Some with bosoms bared. Some more afraid than fearful. Some wanting to run. Some wanting to kill. He sees them merge and mingle and grow into a giant dark beast that solidifies into something menacing. Sees it drag its feet across the courtyard. Sees the way it has to push the door to the corridor open, rather than move through it. Sees it make its way towards his cell. Searching for him. And as it reaches his door he recognises it.

He wakes up with a start and looks to the empty doorway, understanding it is his own fear that he had seen coming for him. Which means it must be the men's own fears that are rising from the darkness to kill them. And how is he ever to protect the men from those?

10
Another Day

The gates are open early the next morning, before the first light has appeared in the sky. Arno is sitting up on his bed pondering everything he has come to understand, when he hears the heavy clang of the gates and the clatter of many booted soles running into the prison. He hears the soldiers running into the cells and sees all the lights come on. Hears the shouting as the soldiers run down the corridors, striking the cell doors with batons. Shouting for the men to rise and assemble in the corridors. Rifle bolts click as men look about themselves in fear, suddenly dragged back three years, to the nights they were roughly turned out of their homes and interred. The men stagger to their feet, quickly clutching some clothes about them, as the soldiers appear in their cells as if they have emerged from the stone walls somehow.

Arno moves out into the corridor with all the other men, where they listen to the soldiers going through their belongings. They hear their rough shouts as they move from cell to cell, tipping over boxes and tins, upsetting furniture and upsetting people's lives.

Arno looks up and can see the first light of the new day beginning to tint the dark sky outside the windows, from an angle he's never witnessed before, and he understands that no day will ever be like any other day again.

The guards search for over an hour and unearth one small still. They parade the two cellmates who own it up and down the corridor several times, while Sergeant Gore shouts out how they will not tolerate such blatant disregard to the regulations. Shouts out that they are being given better treatment than any internees anywhere in the Commonwealth. Shouts out that they should be grateful for the treatment they are receiving. Shouts out that such transgressions will be severely punished. Then, ignoring the two culprits, and holding the still before them, the soldiers turn and march out of the cells.

Arno wanders down the corridor and sees men picking through the rubble left by the guards, trying to rebuild some order. The men look around, shell-shocked. "What did they find?" he asks one man.

The man looks at him. As if it might be a trick question. Arno is about to ask him again, when he says, "Nothing."

"Just Heinrich's still," says another man.

"Was that what they were looking for?" asks Arno.

"Of course not!"

"Then what?"

"If you have to ask, then you don't need to know," the internee tells him, as if he is addressing a very young boy.

Breakfast is a quiet affair. A guard stands at the door to the hall where no guard has ever stood before. Rumours weave a slow path from table to table. The German raider has been seen on the horizon. A guard killed von Krupp. The *Emden* sailors are in contact with the ship. Wolff killed von Krupp. The townspeople at South West Rocks are preparing to march on the prison. The war is going bad for the British. The *Emden* sailors are attempting to take over the Wolf Pack. The Allied front is near collapse. There is going to be a rebellion in the camp. The Commandant has told the guards they can shoot internees on sight if they suspect trouble. Regular troops are being brought in to guard them. Herr Dubotzki still has a few photos of Pandora he is willing to sell.

It is mid-morning when the word is passed around that the Commandant has decided to restore some privileges, including limited times outside the prison, and Arno Friedrich follow a band of men outside and stares at the bright ocean. He breathes in that calming scent of the Australian beach and bush. The land of his birth that is denied to him. He feels a sense of calm filling him that is not possible inside the prison. He looks carefully for any sign of a ship out there. He puts his hands up to screen his eyes and turns his head slowly, but he cannot see anything.

He watches the workers make their way up the hill, under close guard, to continue work on the monument. Then he turns and makes his way down to the beach. He sits on the sand there and watches some of the elder men walking in the shallows. He watches them walk along the sand, turn and walk back. And then again. The same gait with which they pace up and down the cell corridors.

Arno makes his way down across the sand. He slowly undresses, laying his watch on his clothes and then limps into the water. It is very cold today. He keeps moving until he is thigh-deep, then drops into the icy water with a gasp. He swims fast, to get the blood moving, not stopping until he is level with the end of the breakwater. Treading water there he looks back at prison, feeling that strong pull of the current trying to drag him away. He is regretful about what Doctor Hertz had told him that morning at the infirmary, that Nurse Rosa will not be permitted to come to the prison for some time, but that Intern Meyer could perform his massage therapy for him.

And he thinks, this new world is not one he can survive in.

The burial ceremony for Herr von Krupp is held on the hilltop in the afternoon. His body has already been wrapped in a white sheet, sealed in a wooden coffin and lowered into one of the trenches by the monument, accompanied by the mocking warbles of currawongs and the shrill laugh of kookaburras. Over 400 internees, dressed in the remains of old suits and ties, the uniform of funerals, have made their way up the thin bush path to assemble by the half-built monument. They stand amongst the broken rocks and the piles of earthworks and stare solemnly at the small plinth as if it is his tombstone, cold sullenness in their eyes.

Across the trenches and rock works the Commandant stands with a small troop of guards. He is aware that his back is to the ocean, and is aware that his position is not a good one tactically. But he is also aware that his men have a bullet in the breach of their rifles. He says in a loud voice, "We are gathered together today in memory of Mister von Krupp." He waits for the internees to bow their heads a little, or to hold their hands together in prayer. But they stare at him fixedly, unknowable emotions in their eyes. Then he says, "I have granted permission for this service out of respect to the memory of Mister von Krupp, and I hope you will also respect his memory by appropriate behaviour here." He licks his lips a little. "He was a gentleman and will be remembered by us as one." Then, surprisingly, in his first role as a minister, he finds he has nothing else to say and so he beckons for Doctor Hertz to come forward.

Doctor Hertz steps across the broken ground and turns to face the internees. His first words are in English, "Thank you for the words you have spoken." Like many of the internees, even when he is talking English, he is thinking in German and it governs his syntax. But the words then turn to German. The Commandant and guards listen carefully, as if concentrating might help them understand the foreign sounds and help them to pick up what the doctor is saying. They hear the word *"Gott,"* mentioned several times—but can identify very little else. And not for the first time the Commandant wonders if he should begin a course in the German language. He suspects that while it might be good for his position, it would also be recorded on a file in Sydney somewhere and one day be dug up like an old skeleton and rattled in front him.

Those there who understand the doctor's words, hear him say, "The loss of one from amongst us is always a tragedy. But we can use that loss to bind us closer together. We can use it to remind us of who we are. We are imprisoned and far removed from our loved ones. But we should not succumb to despair. We should think of the suffering of our countrymen who are in the trenches. We should think of the suffering of our countrymen who are in other prison camps, far harsher than ours. We should think of the suffering of our countrymen far across the sea."

And all the men look up and stare towards the horizon with such a deep longing that the guards can't help sliding their fingers just that little bit closer to their rifle triggers. One snaps the bolt of his rifle loudly, and the internees stare at the guards and at the Commandant. A sudden shiver of fear ripples through them, like the chill of a cloud covering the winter sun. The internees take a few small steps backwards, and Herr Schwarz is jostled at the grave's edge—where he slips and falls heavily onto the wooden coffin. He lies there a moment as if unsure what has happened.

The Commandant has a sudden foreboding of tragedy and wants to shout out to his men, to restore some order. But again words have deserted him. Nobody knows quite what to do next, until a head rises from the grave and everyone turns to look at Herr Schwarz. He blinks as if has been caught out at something shameful and he slowly raises his hands in surrender.

The Commandant sees all the men relax their grips on their weapons and he thinks: how will we ever live in peace time after all this?

The Dark Knights are again gathered in the small stone building outside the prison walls, pressing close around a single candle. Listening to the Sergeant. Looking at each other. Trying to make sense out of what he is telling them. Certain it is another test.

"They will come in the dark," he says. "We will wake up and the first we will know of it is the sound of men disembarking in the bay. When first light arrives it will show large dark ships out there. Full of men. Then the shelling will start. They'll hurl round after round at us to try and cover the men splashing ashore. But we'll be all around the watchtowers with machine guns. We'll pin them down and anyone who raises a head, we'll blow it off. We'll shoot them down in the water and on the sand and it will run red with their blood. But they'll keep coming. Hundreds of them. Crawling their slow way up the cliffs. Digging in every few metres. Keeping their heads down. Moving slower. Getting cleverer. And we'll keep shooting at them. Watching the corpses float out on the tide. And we'll put an extra round into 'em just for good measure. But the survivors will dig in deeper. We'll be up there on the walls sniping down at them and they'll be down there sniping at us, see. And it will go on and on and on. Day after day, in the heat and the dust and flies and lice and the stink of blood and shit and we'll never give up until we've finally driven them back into the sea."

He looks around at the faces of the young men around him, all pressing so close they are almost touching.

"Don't you see?" he says. "Years from now they'll come here and erect a bloody great statue to you all—whether you live or die—and they'll say this was the greatest bloody battle ever fought on Australian soil—and in the major cities they'll march in our honour. They'll say, never forget the boys who fell at Trial Bay. That's what they'll say."

Arno cannot sleep. He tosses to the left. Then to the right. He places his head outside his blanket, then tucks it under again. He turns and looks over at Horst, who seems to be sobbing quietly again, his blanket jerking slowly under his clenched fists.

Arno closes his eyes tighter and tries to conjure up a memory of Western Australia before the war began. Tries to remember what he might have dreamed of there. He knows he should see images of dry landscapes and sun and wheat maybe—but he can only clearly remember that night they came to take him, when they threw him into the old truck and drove him away into the darkness.

He had made his way around the walls again earlier that evening, carefully avoiding the guards. But instead of searching inside the stone he found he was searching for traces of violence within the prison itself, and followed the stirrings to the base of the southwest watchtower. He waited there and listened until he was sure there was nobody up there again and then he cautiously made his way up the steps, into the guard tower and saw the empty bottles on the floor. Scattered like old bones, he thought. He saw a coil of rope in the corner, and the basket tied to it. He stood by the parapet and looked out over the bay. He witnessed the light and colour fade from the whole world, as he had never seen happen before at the prison. Saw just how much darkness there was in the world here.

Then he leaned out over the edge and looked at the distance down to the ground. He measured it in his mind, then made his way back down from the watchtower and returned to his cell. There was so much to write down now. So many things.

And sitting there, listening to Horst's soft sobs, he finds he is turning over memories like pages in a book. He remembers the long journey from the West to Sydney. Remembers arriving at the hot dusty camp at Holsworthy. There was a mass of men squeezed into the wire compounds there. Sixteen to a tent. Some were lucky enough to have unfurnished huts, sharing one pan to cook their meals and eating off the floor. There were Austrians and Turks and Germans all crammed in together—and even some Australians whom the military had deemed German, so as to intern them. Socialists mostly.

Holsworthy was hot and dry and dusty in the summer, and cold and muddy in the winter. They had to queue for hours for food and water, and had to dig their own latrine pits. Filthy stinking trenches with no cover nor privacy. Thousands of men squeezed into a small stinking barbed-wire pen. The strong victimised the weak. Stole from them. Bullied them. And the guards were just as brutal. Pricking them with bayonets if they disobeyed commands to work, or were too slow. Occasionally getting drunk and firing randomly into the tents at night.

It was like deliverance the day Arno and the other men were assembled and told they would be removed to another camp. Told they were specially selected. Then they were aboard trucks being ferried like cattle. Taken to the shores of that wide blue ocean—the Pacific. Just the size of it spoke of freedom to them. Then they were on the sea. And Arno Friedrich found he was not a natural sailor. The small vessel that carried them north from Sydney was flat bottomed and pitched terribly on the ocean. He was sick at the rails for most of the journey. Until they reached the calmer waters of Trial Bay. And when they finally arrived here, on an overcast afternoon, they could see the old castle sitting on the headland before them, like some Rhine castle from their legends.

The vessel carried them around into the bay and landed near the town of South West Rocks. The internees were off-loaded by armed guards, who cautiously pointed their rifles at them. These were the first Germans most of the local soldiers had ever seen, and they were not sure how to regard them without the pointed helmets and sharp-fanged teeth they'd seen in posters. They stood around looking more like lost travellers whose train had not appeared, wearing casual suits and holding suitcases. The guards coaxed them into columns and set them marching. People came from miles around to watch, as if it was some parade.

Small children jeered and threw rocks at them—which their parents only made half an effort to control. Probably wishing to join in, thought Arno, as he limped along on his crutches, trying to keep up with the column of men, having no desire to fall behind into the hands of the crowd.

Arno can remember it clearly as if he has often seen a photograph of the scene. A grainy shot of a long line of internees walking down a long dusty road carrying their suitcases and a few boxes—more like holiday makers than internees—flanked by the jeering locals, who stood there, shocked at the arrival of the Germans amongst them. Shocked at just how much like themselves they looked.

They made the final leg of the journey on foot—particularly hard for Arno. It was not until they got closer that they saw the castle for what it was—an old stone prison. Their new home.

Arno now puts his hands behind his head, and lies on his back, wondering if Nurse Rosa had been in the crowd on that day. He wonders what she thought as she watched the men dragging their old suitcases up the road? Wonders if she had seen him there amongst them?

Wonders if he ever asked her, would she tell him the truth?

And then, despite not wishing to, he is asleep. Arno dreams that night and it takes him a moment to realise that it is not one of the other prisoner's dreams that he is sharing—it is a dream of his own. He is floating above the prison, as if he was lying on a cloud holding him aloft, and he is looking down and can see right across time and place at the same instant.

He sees the peninsula forming from the landscape at the same time that he sees the convicts of the old century toiling away to build the prison and the breakwater at the same time that he sees the German internees arrive to occupy it at the same time he sees the strong currents of the bay pulling away the breakwater and then the peninsula and then the prison. Dragging them all far out to sea.

And he sees the indigenous people of the area, the Dainggatti, long dispossessed, living in the abandoned prison, as he sees people with cameras crawling all over the ruins as he sees the prison crumble apart as he sees it being rebuilt, as he sees the internees come marching in, in a long column, as he sees them marching out again. And he sees the many people who have died there, and suffered there, and felt anger and pain and despair and imprisonment there, their lives draining out of them and seeping into the stone of the prison. And their spirits or thoughts or pain mix into a potent force of ill-feeling that then fights to emerge again. Fights to take form and do violence to those who are still feeding it. Those who are most afraid, most angry, most despairing.

And now he sees himself in the prison, as the creatures in the walls are close to finally escaping together to wreak havoc as despondency inside the cells rises to its peak. And he is searching for Nurse Rosa. He has to find her and save her. If he can protect her from the things that arise from the walls to kill people he will gain the power to protect everyone from them.

He runs into the infirmary, but she's not there. He sees torn strips of her uniform on the floor, with bloodstains on them. He must find her quickly. He runs out into the yard and calls her name. He turns his head this way and that. Sees blood marks on the grass. Tries to run and follow them, but with each step he gets lighter and lifts a little higher into the air. He stops and tries to sink back down to the prison. He has to reach her and save her. But he is too high now. The winds grab him and pull at him, dragging him back towards the land. Towards the dry centre of this vast country. Towards the distant land to the west where he grew up.

And his last view of the prison is of it falling apart as the nightmare beings split the stone walls to emerge. Arno knows he has failed to save Rosa, and will never hear her hidden stories. Will never discover her past. So he fights against the current of the dream and refuses to let it pull him away. He struggles back closer to the prison on the headland and see Nurse Rosa standing on the beach. Waving out to sea. Waving at a dark shape gliding in the water. A shark, he thinks. But as it comes closer it forms into the shape of a German raider. Bristling with soldiers. Tall ogre-like men in spiked German infantry helmets.

He is then standing on the beach beside her and is shouting at her to run. But his crutches sink into the sand. He struggles to get away but cannot move. Then the boat is beaching on the sand. Dark and flecked with blood. Soldiers leap off and grab them. Nurse Rosa and he are as small as children in their hands. They throw his crutches to the ground and two of the soldiers drag him back to the boat and hurl them in. Then the boat lurches and is back on the water. Speeding off towards the horizon. One of the soldiers presses a helmet and uniform to him. Flicks a jacket to him on a short stick. Orders him to dress. He struggles with the buttons and trousers. The soldiers look away. Turn their gaze far off to the north. Towards the Great War.

And Arno is struggling to hide his erection. To hide the dreams that have brought it. Of Nurse Rosa and he. Together on the infirmary bed. The sound of battle outside. But she is calm and smiling. His erect cock in her hands. She massages it. Pressing it against her starched white uniform. Squeezing it firmly in her fingers. Her breasts lifting as she breathes faster. Smiling to him. The sound of battle getting closer. The feeling building within him. Starting in his feet. Travelling up his legs. His whole body goes rigid. Nurse Rosa's breasts and lips and uniform lying atop of him. His legs quivering. Like he's running. But not getting anywhere. The battle is upon him. She is upon him. And then he explodes.

11
Another Day

The explosion shakes the whole prison, startling everyone awake. Then guards are running through the corridors with rifles ready, ordering everybody to remain in the cells. Internees stand dazed in their doorways asking each other, "What was the noise?" "What is happening?"

The guard in the eastern watchtower, the only one to have seen the flash on the hill, recovers slowly and calls out that they are under attack. Other guards race to the other watchtowers. Looking out to sea. Looking into the bay. Looking for the shape of a ship there. Some guards at the guardhouse form a defensive formation in their pyjamas. Some face towards the prison. Some face out to sea. Waiting to be told what is happening.

The prisoners stand in their cells, looking at the nervous guards with rifles pointing at them, also waiting to be told what is happening. Everybody stands as still and as silent as the stone walls of the old prison, while light and colour slowly fill the world.

And finally the expectant guards can see there is no raider in the bay. No ships at sea. No holes in the prison wall. It's another perfect day. Except for a faint wisp of smoke up on the hill on the headland.

Eventually the Sergeant leads a small squad up the hill. He sees the damage and reports back to the Commandant. The internee's memorial has been destroyed. Blown up with explosives.

The Commandant, sitting squarely at his desk, considers this news, then asks the Sergeant if any of the guards have been responsible. The Sergeant quickly replies that he believes it to have been the work of men from South West Rocks. He says that he's heard talk that they believe the monument is being constructed as a signal to German vessels and felt they needed to act if the Army would not.

The Commandant frowns. "We'd better tell the internees," he says. "They will not be happy to hear this."

"It ain't their lot to be happy," says the Sergeant. "They are internees."

"They still deserve some right to preserve their memories," says the Captain. The Sergeant is about to challenge him when there is a knock on the door and both men turn to see a young lad in uniform standing there. He is holding out an official envelope. "Top secret dispatch," he says. "It came with the early train."

Arno looks at his watch. 8.47am. He leans against the wall and looks at the men assembled around the walls of the prison. The Commandant is working his way slowly down the list in front of him.

"Weiss, Dieter."

"Hier."

"Wien, Ernst."

"Hier."

"Wurtz, Rudolph."

"Hier."

Over 400 men present and accounted for. Then the Commandant lowers his clipboard and looks out over the rows of faces. "I have an announcement to make," he calls loudly.

The men shuffle a little. They already know what has happened. But they want to hear the official version of it. That it was an accident. That there will be no accusations until there has been an inquiry. That none of the guards could possibly have been involved.

But he says, "I have been notified this morning, by special courier, that the camp here is to be closed and you will be returned to Holsworthy before the end of this week."

The Commandant carefully watches the effect of the words on the men. He sees some whisper the words in German to those standing around them. Sees one old man drop his head into his hands. Sees another fall to his knees. Sees the look of sudden pain he has caused them. He is familiar with the feeling, for he felt it himself when he received the orders.

There are worse commands he could be giving though, for he knows that at the end of the war the Government plans to assemble all these men again and deport them back to Germany. Some officer will have to break the news to them and watch their faces as they try and understand that. Perhaps some of them will think it a good thing and imagine that they will be able to find those Alpine cafés and fine operas of their memories—not realising that was a different world. Their country will be in ruins, having given up everything—its factories and farms and professionals and labourers, from the oldest citizen to the young child—to war.

The Captain takes a deep breath, so that his voice will not betray him, and says, "You will only be able to take what you can carry in your hands. You will have three days to be ready and packed. This is a direct order of the Department of Defence. That is all."

He turns and walks back to his office and closes the door. Sits there as still as stone.

When Arno returns to his cell, he finds that Horst has discovered the rope he'd hidden under his bunk. He has thrown it up to the cell bars. Arno watches him for a few moments before understanding. One end is knotted into a noose. He swings forward quickly on his crutches and grabs the rope from Horst's fingers. But Horst hangs onto it, as if it is a lifeline to something better than internment. Arno pulls and tries to jerk it out of his grasp as Horst tries to get the rope over his neck. He kicks at Arno to keep him back. Knocks one crutch away and Arno falls to the ground. But he is still holding onto the rope. Horst tries to lift the noose to his neck once more, but he has to lift Arno's weight with it. Arno rises a little and grabs him by the arms.

"You don't know what you are doing," Horst protests.

"I am saving you," Arno says. His purpose in this life.

"Saving me from what?" Horst spits and struggles more violently for a moment and just when Arno feels he is about to be shaken free, Horst stops and collapses to the floor crying. Arno falls on top of him. Lies there a moment and then drags himself clear. He gathers his crutches and stands up. "What are you trying to do?" Arno asks him.

But Horst does not reply. He stands to his feet and slumps onto his bunk. Crawls in under the blankets, like he is tunnelling to somewhere safer. Arno sits opposite him and says, "They say we will have our own compound at Holsworthy. Away from the others."

Horst wriggles his head out a little and looks across at Arno. Shakes his head. "What does it matter?"

Arno shrugs. "Maybe it'd be different somehow."

Horst pulls his head back under the blanket. "I don't fear Holsworthy. Prison is prison."

"Then what do you fear?" asks Arno.

Horst says nothing for a long time, then he emerges slowly with his book in his hand. "Look," he says, holding open a page. Arno can see the letters and photos are pressed between the pages. He nods.

"Look," says Horst again. Arno takes the book and looks at it. There are two small black and white photos. Badly taken. Strong shadows across the faces. They show a woman and three small children.

"Who are they?" asks Arno.

"I don't know any more," says Horst. "They used to be my wife and children. But I don't know them anymore. I look at the photos and I read the letters, but it is like I can't understand who they are. The faces are different in my mind. And they have grown so much older since I have been gone. They will come and see me in Sydney and will be ashamed of me. And I will look at them and will not know them." He closes his eyes and turns his face to the cold stone wall.

Arno picks up the photographs and looks at the faces of the children and Horst's wife. He tries to see their features, but they are not clear enough. Then he looks at the spidery Gothic script of Horst's writing in the book. He reads a paragraph and sees it is a love letter. But not to Horst's wife. It is addressed to Pandora.

Arno closes the book and lays it on Horst's bunk.

Sergeant Gore is standing by the cold stone wall of the prison feeling the chill of rock enter his body. He closes his eyes just a moment and thinks he feels something else there. Something stirring. But of course it's just his imaginings. An idle distraction from having to do what he has to now do. It is just rock after all.

He takes a small step away from the wall. He sees the man he has been waiting for. The Sergeant beckons him over. It is Private Cutts-Smith, who wears the large scar across his face. He sees the Sergeant and gives him that familiar nod that veterans give each other. The one that says I know what you know. I've seen what you've seen.

But the Sergeant does not return the nod. He waits until the Private is standing before him and he says, "I know."

"Know what?" ask the other man.

"I know it's you."

The Private makes no protestation of innocence. Makes no denial of knowing what the Sergeant is talking about. He just smiles. That twisted sort of smile you might see on the face of a soldier who has been in the trenches too long and has started to think there is some sense in the killing. Some redemption in it.

"It has to stop," the Sergeant says. "You keep it up in Holsworthy and the MPs will hang you."

The Private just shrugs. As if that is the whole point of it. To get caught and executed. To end it all.

The Sergeant shakes his head a little. "Just leave it all here," he says. "When we're gone no one will remember what happened within these walls. It's another world."

The Private says nothing, but tilts his head back and looks up at the sky, as if watching the slow-moving clouds up there.

"Tell me it's going to stop," says the Sergeant. "If there's any more killings I'll have to shoot you myself."

"Fair enough then," says the Private at last. Then adds, before turning and walking away, "But I didn't do that last one."

Arno makes his way over the infirmary, hoping Doctor Hertz will be there. He must tell him about Horst. Must ask him to come and see him. At least to listen to his lungs and hears his cough. And perhaps to see what else is dark and disturbing inside him.

The yard is empty of men. They have all retreated to the dining hall— or to their cells—to absorb the news. So many of them have prayed for the day they would leave this prison, but now it is upon them they want to wish it away. Arno stands in the infirmary door and looks around. The room is empty. But he sees some movement in the room to the side. He moves across the floor and calls out, "Hello."

Nurse Rosa is there. Arno is surprised. He had not thought to see her again. She spins away from him quickly. She is getting changed. And Arno sees everything at once. Too fast to comprehend. The startled look on Meyer's face. The way he places the red cap quickly on his head. Tucks the wig in. Puts on that Nurse Rosa face. Sees Meyer become Rosa like it is an essential part of him. His escape from all this. Turns to look at Arno. That calm familiar look.

And Arno grips his crutches tightly, knowing they are stopping him from falling to the ground, because the whole world has just tipped on its side a little.

"Arno?" the nurse says. "Can I help you?"

But Arno shakes his head. He turns and flees across the yard. He staggers as if he has been wounded. Gasps for breath. Feels a sudden pain inside him. Is unable to stop it filling his body. He wants to go to his cell and tunnel under his blankets and hide from it. Wants to press up against the cold stone wall and let its chill enter him. Turn him to granite inside. Cold and unfeeling. Unable to be hurt like this.

Instead Arno finds his way to Herr Herausgeber's small office. Not sure where else to go. Not sure who else he can turn to. Herr Herausgeber is sitting there at his workbench staring despairingly at the newspaper copy in front of him. He turns and sees Arno. Smiles a wan smile, like the June afternoon sunshine. "There will be no more issues," he says. "No more records now."

He has started taking the photographs down off the office wall already, and it is starting to look much like the cell it always in truth was. "You could print it at Holsworthy," says Arno.

"No," says the editor. "It won't be the same. Holsworthy is too much like..." he searches for a word. Can't find it. Then says, *Die Welt."*—the world.

Arno watches him running his fingers over the columns of type before him. Herr Herausgeber takes the sheets of paper in front of him, gathers them together, and then places them in a folder. He then pulls more photographs down off the walls and places them in the folder too. "For the historians," he says.

Arno swallows what he was going to say, watching Herr Herausgeber dismantling the past. He reaches up and pulls one photograph down himself. Holds it in his hands. Feels the smooth chill texture of the paper under his fingers. Feels the smooth chill texture of the faces of the people in it. And he stops suddenly. He reaches up and pulls down two other photos. Touches the faces of both, as if suddenly possessed of a new way of seeing things. As if scales have suddenly fallen from his eyes. He touches the face of Herr Dubotzki. Touches the face of Pandora. Knows they are the same. He's not just captured her image—he's created it.

He looks up at Herr Herausgeber. Wonders if he knows it? Wonders if he would care anymore?

"Do you know about tomorrow's photograph yet?" Herr Herausgeber asks Arno.

"What photograph?"

"Tomorrow morning. There is to be a group photograph of all the internees. One last time. We will assemble around the inside walls of the prison and be photographed. Captured forever, huh?"

Arno doesn't even nod. He is looking again at the first photograph he took down from the wall. It shows a long line of men assembled in the prison yard. Bent and misshapen and blurred. At some points the photo is so indistinct the men have merged into the rock wall. He can't pick out any of the men and then he realises that once again he has not seen clearly what was right before him. It is the photo of the convicts from the old century.

Lieutenant Wolff is waiting for Arno in the yard and blocks his path. "Okay kid," he says. Voice low. "No more waiting. It's time to tell me about the escape plans now." There is no friendliness in his voice.

"Why are you so insistent that there is an escape plan?"

Wolff shows his teeth and pushes Arno roughly into the wall. He says, "Because if there isn't one, the only reason I can think of to explain your lousy German is that you are a spy for the Australians. Is that what you want me to believe? Want all the men here to believe?"

Arno can feel the jaws closing on him. He counts his breaths, like counting the stones blocks in his cell wall. One to twelve and back to one again. Then he says, "I could only take one other. What about your comrades?"

And the Lieutenant says, "Think of me as a lone wolf."

"Alright," Arno says, after considering that for a few moments. "I'm going to escape tonight."

"Tonight," says the Lieutenant. "Good. Good. We have to get out of here before they send us back to Holsworthy. There is nothing good for us there. The Black Hand gang will have a reception committee ready for us. I thought we'd live like kings here—take over and rule the place—but it was short-lived." He realises he's talking too much and stops.

"Meet me after dark under the southwest watchtower," says Arno "Near where we were the other night."

"But what about the guard in the watchtower?" asks Wolff.

"He won't be there," says Arno. "He is involved with some of the prisoners in an alcohol smuggling racket. You know about that, yes? He will not be there."

Wolff considers this. "And how do we get down from the wall?" he asks.

"I have a rope," says Arno. Wolff smiles. Yes, a rope.

"And then what?"

"We make our way around the bay," says Arno. "Through the dark woods to South West Rocks. We steal a fishing boat." The words come easy, as if he has already written them out several times.

"And where do we go?" asks Lieutenant Wolff. "They will follow us."

"You're a sailor," says Arno. "We will head out to sea."

"They will catch us," says Wolff, and he is remembering the *Emden* being shelled from afar. The explosions on the deck as comrades fell burned and bleeding around him. "They will send the navy after us."

"You're forgetting the German raider off the coast," says Arno.

"But that might as well be a dream," says Wolff. "What hope have we of ever finding it or reaching it?"

"We don't have to," says Arno. "We only have to make them believe we have reached it. We sail northwards across the bay. Towards Freedom Island there. It is uninhabited. We hide out there. They will think we've gone out to sea. They will send navy boats after us. But they won't find us. They will think we have rendezvoused with the German cruiser."

Wolff thinks about it carefully. Putting it together piece by piece. "Yes," he finally says. "You have been working this out for a long time, haven't you?"

Arno smiles.

"And you have experience at sea?" he asks Arno.

"Of course."

After lunch, the initial surge of packing slows and then stops. The internees cannot decide what to pack and what to leave behind. Almost everything they have accumulated in their rooms they have built themselves, turning the empty stone cells into living quarters. So the men return to their normal routines. Lessons and clubs and work parties. The kitchen staff are washing dishes and getting ready for dinner. The English class is meeting in the hall. The athletics club is organising a tennis tournament. But Arno only watches. And he is watched carefully by Lieutenant Wolff.

Once Arno turns to look at him and the Lieutenant gives him a long slow nod and the faintest of smiles. He knows that Wolff will kill him once they are outside the walls, as he knows so many things now. Arno has come to understand that the destructive monsters of our nightmares are not an aberration but always with us. And daily life in internment is not an escape from nightmares but a nightmare in itself—no less than the outside world at war was a larger nightmare.

So what escape was there? What protection?

Arno has some time to kill. Like every afternoon of internment. He sees that his watch has stopped. Probably when Lieutenant Wolff pushed him into the wall. But perhaps time has just stopped. The Commandant has restored afternoon access outside the prison, for two hours, and as Arno has no wish to spend any more time in his cell, he decides to spend time in the Germany he never knew. He makes his way down to the small village and sits on the outside veranda of the White Horse Inn. It has been mostly rebuilt. Just in time to be dismantled again. He counts out some sixpences and pennies from his pocket and orders a light snack. Beer and veal.

The cafe proprietor, Herr Schmidt, brings him the ale and mutton and tries to engage Arno in small talk. About the weather. About his health. About his life in Germany. About the idea of moving to Holsworthy. But Arno Friedrich says, "I have no clear memory of any other life than internment here." And so Herr Schmidt leaves him to his own company.

Arno does not wish to think about what the prison will look like in a week's time. The remains of furniture and bedding strewn about in the cells and corridors, and mementos and handcrafts left behind or broken. It would be like one of the towns in Europe where refugees have fled from the encroaching war.

Instead he stares around at the pictures on the walls about him. Internees in German cafes. Women smiling at the camera. All like a magician's illusion that you know the trick to, and can no longer see as anything but a trick. There is one large photo, hanging over the door behind him. It shows two men in sailor's uniforms, standing by an over-large life preserver. Their clothes are bright white. Behind them is a ship on the ocean, sailing towards them. Coming for them, Arno Friedrich thinks. Coming to take them to the war. He knows it is really the backdrop from some early play. Knows the German sailors don't wear clothes that white. Knows there is no life preserver large enough to save their lives when the time comes for the ship to take them away to Sydney.

He turns away from the photos and looks down towards the beach. He sees some men down there, standing quite still on the sands, like living photographs. And Arno has a sudden feeling that this war will never end for them. Even when the fighting one day stops they will be forever caught like this, reduced to colourless images of the people they actually are.

It is probably mid-afternoon when Arno leaves the café and makes his way down to the beach. He moves past the members of the athletics club, standing around on the sands as if unsure what to do with themselves, then past the ranks of middle-aged men wandering listlessly up and down. He stands and stares over the flat ocean, turned so he can see nothing of the prison behind him. Cannot see its chill stone walls. Cannot see the half-repaired Alpine cafes, restaurants and other fantasies. It seems such a truly perfect day today. Unlike any other day here.

Arno limps along the shore, letting his path wander in and out of the shallow clear water. He makes his way along the beach, heading towards the breakwater. They are meant to keep away from it, but he keeps going until he is standing beside it. Then he steps up onto the rough jumbled rocks. He feels the hardness beneath his bare foot. He places his crutches on the rock and climbs to the next block. It is much larger with jagged edges. There is a chill in the rocks despite the sun shining on them. He places his hands out for balance and then drags himself upwards.

He marvels at the toil and suffering of the men who built the breakwater. Some of the slabs of granite he stands on are large enough to fill his half of his cell. He tries to imagine what the look on Horst's face would be if he awoke one morning and found that Arno had turned into a giant slab of granite like this. Then he thinks how strong that current in the bay must be to carry away a large slab of the rock like the one under his feet.

He climbs on to the very top of the breakwater, standing on a large single slab of rock now, and he looks out to the open sea where he can see a distant squall approaching. A long thin grey line of clouds like a distant stone wall, is moving towards them.

He stands there, feeling how easily he could become one of those discarded rocks beneath his feet. Misshapen and broken. Cold and unfeeling with no sense of the past. Slowly being dragged out to sea. He sits down on the slab beneath him and feels for the pain and toil and suffering of those men of the last century. Lets it solidify his determination.

He looks up and sees the cloud front is approaching rapidly now. Other clouds have already obscured the afternoon sun and the prison walls are starting to lose their colour and fade already. Men are starting to leave the beach. He takes off his hat, shirt and shorts and places them carefully together on the rocks. When they find them it will be as if he had sunk into the rock, leaving them behind.

Then he takes his watch off. He doesn't need to know the time, whatever it is. For the time is now and he is ready. He steps down to the cold water's edge and wades out through the shallows. When he is up to his waist he begins swimming—strong slow strokes that carry him slowly out into the bay. He swims for some time until he feels the first pull of the ocean's current grasping at him. Then he turns and looks back towards the prison on the headland. Looks at those dark stone walls and tries to memorise them. Tries to imagine how they will look this evening. Dark and chill.

And then he imagines the last play they will perform within them. He writes the scene to himself as if he were writing it in his diary. He assigns characters to roles and decides how the final plot will be played out.

He sees Lieutenant Wolff enter the stage from the right. Moving his way slowly under the painted rock wall. Sticking closely to the shadows. Looking around for Arno. Unable to see him. He waits under the guard tower for some time, and then cautiously makes his way up the stairs. It is empty. Just as Arno had promised. There are empty grog bottles on the floor, but no rope. He looks out into the darkness and can't even see the ground on the far side of the wall. It is too far down. It makes him feel a little giddy. He looks away.

And as he waits there he sees the full moon start to rise over the sea. Like a bright spotlight skimming the top of the walls and the guard towers. He decides to return to the cell block. Decides he will be avenged on Arno for tricking him. But then he hears voices. Hears somebody coming up the steps of the watchtower. He presses back into the darkness and waits. The footsteps are a little awkward. There is more than one person. He crouches and tenses his muscles. Perhaps has a knife drawn. Like the one they will say he killed Herr von Krupp with. The one he had killed a guard with earlier that evening. Then they enter the tower. And he sees they are women.

He does not know what to do. He begins to rise to his feet. Then they see him. And he hears their surprise. Hears their voices. Understands that he has been mistaken. They are men dressed as women. Dressed expertly by Doctor Hertz, the leader of the Wolf Pack—the real director of the prisoners. The man who heals their bodies and their minds. Provides relief to the sick by creating the fantasies they use to camouflage their imprisonment. He is the one who controls the alcohol smuggling. He is the one who creates the women, and lets that longing for them rise up in some of the men so it subsumes them. And then he hires them out to the love-sick men and the guards.

He is everything Lieutenant Wolff should fear.

One of the internees now recognises Lieutenant Wolff and holds out a bottle to him. Tells him the first one is always free, but that he must pay for the next one. But Wolff does not take it. He looks into their faces. Sees one of the women is Nurse Rosa. But she talks to him in intern Meyer's voice. She asks him if he is there to rescue her. Asks if she should lower her long hair over the parapet for them both to climb down. Asks if he has come to run away with her and sail into the sunrise.

But Wolff says nothing. He feels desire and revulsion. Looks away.

The men are trying to whisper, but are too drunk. They then ask him where the guard is? They tell him the guard was meant to meet them there. They owe him, they say. They have to pay him that evening, they say. But Wolff is now backing towards the stairs. Needing to escape. He has gone half-way down when he meets the dark shape. It rises suddenly from the wall as if it had been a part of the shadows there. A part of the rock. A tall dark beast with large eyes and large teeth and dressed in khaki. And with a quick blow it drives a bayonet deeply into Lieutenant Wolff's chest. Into his heart. And Wolff, feeling the cold fingers of death inside himself, needs to know who his attacker is. He grabs for him. Pulls him a little closer. Sees the man he had attacked and thought he had killed earlier. Sees half a face distorted and scarred. Half a face calm and unravaged. But both eyes afire with the madness of war that keeps him going. A madness of the conflicting emotions of fear and hate and pain and forgetting that have sprung from deep within him and have overwhelmed him. A madness that has merged into the rock walls of the prison there, awaiting the moment to re-emerge.

Wolff calls out as he falls. A loud shriek like the sound of guns raining havoc down on his ship as it sunk in flames and smoke. A loud shriek that rouses the Sergeant. Brings him running with his pistol drawn. Knowing it is time to fight the one battle he has never prepared for, but has long feared. Having to confront one of his own men as the enemy. Having to shoot a madman and a murderer wearing the King's uniform.

But these are stories that will never be told. Will never be printed in Herr Herausgeber's newspaper. Never be photographed. Will never be recorded, and so will never have happened.

Arno can now feel the current pulling at him strongly. He has swum further out into the bay than he has ever swum before, and can feel the full grip of that current that pulls the breakwater away.

There will be an added pall of gloom over the prison after roll call the next day, he thinks. Perhaps the Doctor will announce it to the men.

"Arno Friedrich has been carried away by the sea," he will say. He will suggest they place his name on the monument if they can rebuild it before they leave. He will say it was a tragedy. He doubts he will use the word "dead".

So Arno Friedrich says it for him. *"Todt!"* He feels he could say whatever words he wants to out here. Could say anything at all. But he doesn't. He keeps his head down. Keeps swimming. Towards a dream. Strong slow strokes towards Freedom Island.

Trial Bay Memorial (Photo: Australian Heritage Restorations)

Trial Bay Gaol (Photo: Craig Cormick)

Author's Note

Over 500 Germans and Austrians were interned in the old prison at Trial Bay between 1915-1918.

Upon the outbreak of the First World War in 1914, all German subjects in Australia were made to report to authorities. In February 1915, over 6,700 were interned as enemy aliens. In NSW the single largest internment camp was constructed at Holsworthy near Sydney.

The internees sent to Trial Bay were specially selected and came from predominantly professional backgrounds: merchants, physicians, university lecturers and scientists.

The camp physician and theatre director was Dr Max Herz, a leading orthopaedic surgeon before his internment. Dr Herz also reported that the isolation and single-sex environment of the prison led to many cases of depression and self-abuse and perversity. Many of the other characters' names are taken from actual people too.

Internees constructed several beach huts, cafes and restaurants outside the walls of the prison and were allowed to wander freely on the headland for long hours during the day.

The Trial Bay theatre company began performances in August 1916, with an ensemble of forty men. Performances, supported by the 14-piece orchestra, centred on German farces and comedies, often featuring women roles—which always proved popular with the men.

The officers from the German ship *Emden,* sunk by the *HMS Sydney* off the Cocos Islands in 1914, were moved to Trial Bay as prisoners of war. The Commander of the *Emden* was Captain Karl von Müller.

In 1917 the German raider *Wolf* was sighted off the coast of NSW, causing concern that the inmates might somehow be in contact with it. This triggered the return of the inmates to Sydney in mid-1918.

Five inmates died at Trial Bay (or after being removed to Sydney for medical treatment) and a monument to them stands on a hill on the headland. It was later destroyed by locals who feared it was a signal to German ships, but has since been rebuilt.

The names on the monument are:
- Arno Friedrich (1888-1917) from Western Australia, died bathing on 25 June 1917 and was carried away by the sea.
- Horst W. Eckert (1887-1917) of Ceylon—buried in Sydney.
- Heinrich Albrecht (1864-1918) of Vegesach—buried in Sydney.
- Conrad Peter (1877-1917), former hotel director in Colombo.
- Herman Adam Merchant (1879-1916) of Hong Kong.

After the war many of the German internees were deported to Germany, despite having lived in Australia for many decades.